STARSHIP

"A book of epic proportions—the story of a tribe which has lost contact with its universe and lives on memories of its teachings. It is a static, hopeless life, but even in a society as deteriorated as this there are those who will not accept lack of hope. Such a one is Roy Complain, who leaves all that is known and goes to search out the mystery of his lost tribe. As he advances on his travels, the unknowns become greater instead of less, and what seemed to be a simple adventure story takes on moral and philosophical overtones. From the first page this combination of exciting conflicts both physical and mental provide the reader with a tense and moving experience."

Amazing Science Fiction

Avon Books by
Brian W. Aldiss

CRYPTOZOIC   02931 $.75

STARSHIP

BRIAN W. ALDISS

 AVON PUBLISHERS OF BARD, CAMELOT, DISCUS AND EQUINOX BOOKS

AVON BOOKS
A division of
The Hearst Corporation
959 Eighth Avenue
New York, New York 10019

ISBN: 0-380-00226-4

First Avon Printing, December, 1969
Fifth Printing

AVON TRADEMARK REG. U.S. PAT. OFF. AND
FOREIGN COUNTRIES, REGISTERED TRADEMARK—
MARCA REGISTRADA, HECHO EN CHICAGO, U.S.A.

Printed in the U.S.A.

For
who else but
TED CARNELL
Editor of *New Worlds* and *Science Fantasy*
and starter of *Non-Stop*

It is safer for a novelist to choose as his subject something he feels about than something he knows about.

L. P. HARTLEY

To travel hopefully is a better thing than to arrive . . .

R. L. STEVENSON

CONTENTS

A community which cannot or will not realize how insignificant a part of the universe it occupies is not truly civilized. That is to say, it contains a fatal ingredient which renders it, to whatever extent, unbalanced. This is the story of one such community.

An idea, which is man-conceived, unlike most of the myriad effects which comprise our universe, is seldom perfectly balanced. Inevitably, it bears the imprint of man's own frailty; it may fluctuate from the meager to the grandiose. This is the story of a grandiose idea.

To the community it was more than an idea: it became existence itself. For the idea, as ideas will, had gone wrong and gobbled up their real lives.

Part I

QUARTERS

I

Like a radar echo bounding from a distant object and returning to its source, the sound of Roy Complain's beating heart seemed to him to fill the clearing. He stood with one hand on the threshold of his compartment, listening to the rage hammering through his arteries.

"Well, go on out then if you're going! You said you were going!"

The shrill sarcasm of the voice behind him, Gwenny's voice, propelled him into the clearing. He slammed the door without looking back, a low growl rasping the back of his throat, and then rubbed his hands together painfully in an attempt to regain control of himself. This was what living with Gwenny meant, the quarrels arising out of nothing and these insane bursts of anger tearing like illness through his being. Nor could it ever be clean anger; it was muddy stuff, and even at its full flood the knowledge was not hidden from him that he would soon be back again, apologizing to her, humiliating himself. Complain needed his woman.

This early in the waking period, several men were about; later, they would be dispersed about their business. A group of them sat on the deck, playing Travel-Up. Complain walked over to them, hands in pockets, and stared moodily down between their ragged heads. The board, painted on the deck, stretched twice as far as the span of a man's outstretched arms. It was scattered with counters and symbols. One of the players leaned forward and moved a pair of his blocks.

"An outflank on Five," he said, with grim triumph, looking up and winking at Complain conspiratorially.

Complain turned away indifferently. For long periods of his life, this game had exerted an almost uncanny attraction on him. He had played it till his adolescent limbs cracked from squatting and his eyes could hardly focus on the silver tokens. On others too, on nearly all the Greene tribe, Travel-Up cast its spell; it gave them a sense of spaciousness and power lacking in their lives. Now Complain was free of the spell, and missed its touch. To be absorbed in anything again would be good.

He ambled moodily down the clearing, hardly noticing the doors on either hand. Instead, he darted his eyes about among the passers-by, as if seeking a signal. He saw Wantage hurrying along to the barricades, instinctively keeping the deformed left side of his face away from others' eyes. Wantage never played at the long board: he could not tolerate people on both sides of him. Why had the council spared him as a child? Many deformities were born in the Greene tribe, and only the knife awaited them. As boys, they had called Wantage "Slotface", and tormented him; but he had grown up strong and ferocious, which had decided them to adopt a more tolerant attitude towards him: their jibes now were veiled.

Hardly realizing the change from aimlessness to intent, Complain also headed in the direction of the barricades, following Wantage. The best of the compartments, naturally appropriated for council use, were down here. One of the doors was flung open and Lieutenant Greene himself came out, followed by two of his officers. Although Greene was now an old man, he was still an irritable one, and his jerky gait held something yet of the impetuous stride of his youth. His officers, Patcht and Zilliac, walked haughtily beside him, dazers prominent in their belts.

To Complain's great pleasure, Wantage was panicked by their sudden appearance into saluting his chief. It was a shameful gesture, almost a bringing of the head to the hand rather than the reverse, which was acknowledged by

12

a ghastly grin from Zilliac. Subservience was the general lot, although pride did not admit the fact.

When Complain's turn came to pass the trio he did it in the customary manner, turning his head away and scowling. Nobody should think *he*, a hunter, was not the equal of any other man. It was in the Teaching: "No man is inferior until he feels the need to show respect for another."

His spirits now restored, he caught up with Wantage, clapping his hand on the latter's left shoulder. Spinning in the other direction, Wantage presented a short fencing stick to Complain's stomach. He had an economical way of moving, like a man closely surrounded by naked blades. His point lodged neatly against Complain's navel.

"Easy now, my pretty one. Is that how you always greet a friend?" Complain asked, turning the point of the stick away.

"I thought—Expansion, hunter. Why are you not out after meat?" Wantage asked, sliding his eyes away from Complain.

"Because I am walking down to the barricades with you. Besides, my pot is full and my dues paid: I have no need of meat."

They walked in silence, Complain attempting to get on the other's left side, the other eluding his efforts. Complain was careful not to try him too far, in case Wantage fell on him. Violence and death were pandemic in Quarters, forming a natural balance to the high birth rate, but nobody cheerfully dies for the sake of symmetry.

Near the barricades, the corridor was crowded; Wantage, muttering that he had cleaning work to do, slipped away. He walked close to the wall, narrowly upright, with a sort of bitter dignity in his step.

The leading barricade was a wooden partition with a gate in it which entirely blocked the corridor. Two Guards were posted there continually. There, Quarters ended and the mazes of ponic tangle began. But the barrier was a temporary structure, for the position itself was subject to change.

The Greene tribe was semi-nomadic, forced by its inability to maintain adequate crops or live food to move along on to new ground frequently. This was accomplished by thrusting forward the leading barricade and moving up the rear ones, at the other end of Quarters, a corresponding distance. Such a move was now in progress. The ponic tangle, attacked and demolished ahead, would be allowed to spring up again behind them: the tribe slowly worked its way through the endless corridors like a maggot through a mushy apple.

Beyond the barricade, men worked vigorously, hacking down the tall ponic stalks, the edible sap, miltex, spurting out above their blades. As they were felled, the stalks were inverted to preserve as much sap as possible. This would be drained off and the hollow poles dried, cut to standard lengths and used eventually for a multitude of purposes. Almost on top of the busy blades, other sections of the plants were also being harvested: the leaves for medicinal use, the young shoots for table delicacies, the seed for various uses, as food, as buttons, as loose ballast in the Quarters' version of tambourines, as counters for the Travel-Up boards, as toys for babies (into whose all-sampling mouths they were too large to cram).

The hardest job in the task of clearing ponics was breaking up the interlacing root structure, which lay like a steel mesh under the grit, its lower tendrils biting deep into the deck. As it was chopped out, other men with spades cleared the humus into sacks; here the humus was particularly deep, almost two feet of it covering the deck: evidence that these were unexplored parts, across which no other tribe had ever worked. The filled sacks were carted back to Quarters, where they would be emptied to provide new fields in new rooms.

Another body of men were also at work before the barricade, and these Complain watched with special interest. They were of a more exalted rank than the others present; they were Guards, recruited only from the hunters, and the possibility existed that one day, through fortune or favor, Complain might rise to that enviable class.

As the almost solid wall of tangle was bitten back, doors were revealed, presenting black faces to the onlookers. The rooms behind these doors would yield mysteries: a thousand strange articles, useful, useless or meaningless, which had once been the property of the vanished race of Giants. The duty of the Guards was to break open these ancient tombs and appropriate whatever lay within for the good of the tribe, meaning themselves. In due time the loot would be distributed or destroyed, depending on the whim of the council. Much that emerged into the light of Quarters in this fashion was declared by the Lieutenancy to be dangerous, and was burned.

The business of opening these doors was not without its hazards, imaginary if not real. Rumor had it in Quarters that other small tribes, also struggling for existence in the tangle warrens, had silently vanished away after opening such doors.

Complain by now was not the only one caught by the perennial fascination of watching people work. Several women, each with an ample quota of children, stood by the barricade, getting in the way of the procession of humus and ponic bearers. To the constant small whine of flies, from which Quarters was never free, was added the chatter of small tongues: and to this chorus the Guards broke down the next door. A moment's silence fell, in which even the workers paused to stare half in fear at the opening.

The new room was a disappointment. It did not even contain the skeleton of a Giant to horrify and fascinate. It was a small store merely, lined with shelves loaded with little bags. The little bags were full of variously colored powders. A bright yellow and a scarlet one fell and broke, forming two fans on the deck, and in the air two intermingling clouds. Shouts of delight from the children, who rarely saw much color, caused the Guards to bark orders brusquely and begin to carry their discoveries away, forming a living chain to a truck behind the barricade.

Aware of a vague sense of anti-climax, Complain drifted away. Perhaps, after all, he would go hunting.

"But why is there light in the tangles when nobody is there to need it?"

The question came to Complain above the general bustle. He turned and saw the questioner was one of several small boys who clustered around a big man squatting in their midst. One or two mothers stood by, smiling indulgently, their hands idly fanning away the flies.

"There has to be light for the ponics to grow, just as

you could not live in the dark," came the answer to the boy. Complain saw the man who spoke was Bob Fermour, a slow fellow fit only for laboring in the fieldrooms. He was genial—rather more so than the Teaching entirely countenanced—and consequently popular with the children. Complain recalled that Fermour was reputed to be a storyteller, and felt suddenly eager to be diverted. Without his anger he was empty.

"What was there before the ponics were there?" a little girl demanded. In their unpracticed way, the children were trying to start Fermour on a story.

"Tell 'em the tale about the world, Bob!" one of the mothers advised.

Fermour glanced quizzically up at Complain.

"Don't mind me," Complain said. "Theories are less than flies to me." The powers of the tribe discouraged theorizing, or any sort of thought not on severely practical lines; hence Fermour's hesitation.

"Well, this is all guesswork, because we don't have any records of what happened in the world before the Greene tribe began," Fermour said. "Or if we do find records, they don't make much sense." He glanced sharply at the adults in his audience before adding quickly, "Because there are more important things to do than puzzle over old legends."

"What is the tale about the world, Bob? Is it exciting?" a boy asked impatiently.

Fermour smoothed the boy's fringe back from his eyes and said earnestly, "It is the most exciting tale that could possibly be, because it concerns all of us, and how we live. Now the world is a wonderful place. It is constructed of layers and layers of deck, like this one, and these layers do not end, because they eventually turn a circle on to themselves. So you could walk on and on for ever and never reach the end of the world. And all those layers are filled with mysterious places, some good, some evil; and all those corridors are blocked with ponics."

"What about the Forwards people?" the boy asked. "Do they have green faces?"

"We are coming to them," Fermour said, lowering his voice so that the youthful audience crowded nearer. "I have told you what happens if you keep to the lateral corridors of the world. But if you can get on to the main corridor you get on to a highway that takes you straight to distant parts of the world. And then you may arrive in the territory of Forwards."

"Have they really all got two heads?" a little girl asked.

"Of course not," Fermour said. "They are more civilized than our small tribe"—again the scanning of his adult listeners—"but we know little about them because there are many obstacles between their lands and ours. It must be the duty of all of you, as you grow up, to try and find out more about our world. Remember there is much we do not know, and that outside our world may be other worlds of which we cannot at present guess."

The children seemed impressed, but one of the women laughed and said, "Fat lot of good it'll do them, guessing about something nobody knows exists."

Mentally, Complain agreed with her as he walked away. There were a lot of these theories circulating now, all differing, all unsettling, none encouraged by authority. He wondered if it would improve his standing to denounce Fermour; but unfortunately everybody ignored Fermour: he was too slow. Only last wake, he had been publicly stroked for sloth in the fieldrooms.

Complain's more immediate problem was, should he go hunting? A memory of how often recently he had walked restlessly like this, to the barricade and back, caught him unawares. He clenched his fists. Time passing, opportunities lacking, and always something missing, missing. Again —as he had done since a child—Complain whirled furiously round his brain, searching for a factor which promised to be there and was not, ever. Dimly, he felt he was preparing himself—but quite involuntarily—for a crisis. It was like a fever brewing, but this would be worse than a fever.

He broke into a run. His hair, long and richly black, flopped over his wide eyes. His expression became disturbed. Usually his young face showed strong and agreeable lines under a slight plumpness. The line of jaw was true, the mouth in repose heroic. Yet over the countenance as a whole worked a wasting bitterness; and this desolation was a look common to almost the whole tribe. It was a wise part of the Teaching which said that one man's eyes should not meet another's directly.

Complain ran almost blindly, sweat bursting out on his forehead. Sleep or wake, it was perpetually warm in Quarters, and sweat started easily. Nobody he passed regarded him with interest: much senseless running took place in the tribe, many men fled from inner phantoms. Complain only knew he had to get back to Gwenny. Women held the magic salve of forgetfulness.

She was standing motionless, a cup of tea in her hand, when he broke into their compartment. She pretended not to notice him, but her whole attitude changed, the narrow planes of her face going tense. She was sturdily built, her stocky body contrasting with the thinness of her face. This firmness seemed to emphasize itself now, as though she braced herself against a physical attack.

"Don't look like that, Gwenny. I'm not your mortal enemy." It was not what he had meant to say, nor was its tone placating enough, but the sight of her brought some of his anger heading back.

"Yes, you are my mortal enemy!" she said distinctly, still looking away. "No one I hate like you."

"Give me a sip of your tea then, and we'll both hope it poisons me."

"I wish it would," she said venomously, passing over the cup.

He knew her well enough. Her rages were not like his; his had to subside slowly; hers were there, then gone: she would make love to him within a moment of slapping his face. And then she made love best.

"Cheer up," he said. "You know we were quarreling over nothing, as usual."

"Nothing! Is Lidya nothing? Just because she died at birth . . . our only little babe, and you call her nothing."

"Better to call her nothing than use her as a weapon between us, eh?" As Gwenny took the cup back, he slid his hand up her bare arm and slipped his fingers adroitly into the top of her blouse.

"Stop it!" she screamed, struggling. "Don't be so foul! Is that all you can think of, even when I'm talking to you? Let me go, you nasty beast."

But he did not. Instead, he put his other arm round her waist and pulled her closer. She tried to kick. He neatly butted her behind the knee with his knee, and they fell to

18

the floor. When he brought his face close, she tried to bite his nose.

"Take your hands away!" she gasped.

"Gwenny . . . Gwenny, come on, sweet," he coaxed.

Her manner changed abruptly. The haggard watchfulness of her face was submerged in dreaminess.

"Will you take me hunting with you after?"

"Yes," he said. "Anything you say."

What Gwenny said or did not say, however, had small effect on the irresistible roll of events. Two girls, Ansa and Daise, remote relations by marriage of Gwenny's, arrived breathless to say that her father, Ozbert Bergass, had taken a turn for the worse and was asking for her. He had fallen ill with the trailing rot a sleep-wake ago, and Gwenny had already been once to his distant apartment to see him. It was thought he would not last long: people who fell ill in Quarters seldom lasted long.

"I must go to him," Gwenny said. The independence children had to maintain of their parents was relaxed at these times of ultimate crisis; the law permitted visiting of sick beds.

"He was a great man in the tribe," Complain said solemnly. Ozbert Bergass had been senior guide for many sleep-wakes, and his loss would be felt. All the same, Complain did not offer to go and see his father-in-law; sentiment was one of the weaknesses the Greene tribe strove to eradicate. Instead, when Gwenny had gone, he went down to the market to see Ern Roffery the Valuer, to enquire the current price of meat.

On his way, he passed the pens. They were fuller of animals than ever before, domesticated animals fitter and more tender than the wild ones the hunters caught. Roy Complain was no thinker, and there seemed to him a paradox here he could not explain to himself. Never before had the tribe been so prosperous or its farms so thriving; the lowest laborer tasted meat once in a cycle of four sleep-wakes. Yet Complain himself was less prosperous than formerly. He hunted more, but found less and received less for it. Several of the other hunters, experiencing the same thing, had already thrown up the hunt and turned to other work.

This deteriorating state of affairs Complain simply at-

19

tributed to a grudge Roffery the Valuer held against the hunter clan, being unable to integrate the lower prices Roffery allowed for wild meat with the abundance of domestic fare.

Consequently, he pushed through the market crowd and greeted the valuer in surly fashion.

" 'spansion to your ego," he said grudgingly.

"Your expense," the Valuer replied genially, looking up from an immense list he was painfully compiling. "Running meat's down today, hunter. It'll take a good sized carcass to earn six loaves."

"Hem's guts! And you told me wheat was down the last time I saw you, you twisting rogue."

"Keep a civil turn of phrase, Complain: your own carcass isn't worth a crust to me. So I did tell you wheat was down. It *is* down—but running meat's down more."

The Valuer preened his great moustaches and burst out laughing. Several other men idling nearby laughed too. One of them, a burly, stinking fellow called Cheap, bore a pile of round cans he was hoping to exchange in the market. With a savage kick, Complain sent the cans flying. Roaring with rage, Cheap scrambled to retrieve them, fighting to get them back from others already snatching them up. At this Roffery laughed the louder, but the tide of his humor had changed, and was no longer against Complain.

"You'd be worse off living in Forwards," he said consolingly. "They are a people of miracles there. Create beasts for eating from their breath, catching them in the air, they do. They don't need hunters at all." He slammed violently at a fly settling on his neck. "And they have vanquished the curse of flying insects."

"Rubbish!" said an old man standing nearby.

"Don't contradict me, Eff," the Valuer said. "Not if you value your dotage higher than droppings."

"So it is rubbish," Complain said. "Who would be fool enough to imagine a place without flies?"

"I can imagine a place without Complains," roared Cheap, who had now recovered his cans and stood ferociously by Complain's shoulder. They faced each other now, poised for trouble.

20

"Go to, larrup him," the Valuer called to Cheap. "Show him I want no hunters interrupting my business."

"Since when was a scavenger of tins of more merit in Quarters than a hunter?" the old man called Eff asked generally. "I warn you, a bad time's coming to this tribe. I'm only thankful I shan't be here to see it."

Growls of derision for the old man and dislike for his sentiments arose on all sides. Suddenly tired of the company, Complain edged away and made off. He found the old man following and nodded cautiously to him.

"I can see it all," Eff said, evidently anxious to continue his tidings of gloom. "We're growing soft. Soon nobody will bother to leave Quarters or clear the ponics. There won't be any incentives. No brave men will be left—only eaters and players. Disease and death and attacks by other tribes will come; I see it as sure as I see you. Soon only tangles will exist where the Greene tribe was."

"I have heard that Forwards folk are good," Complain said, cutting into this tirade. "That they have sense and not magic."

"You've been listening to that fellow Fermour then," Eff replied grumpily, "or one of his ilk. Some men are trying to blind us to who are our real enemies. I call them men but they aren't men, they're—Outsiders. That's what they are, hunter, Outsiders: supernatural entities. I'd have 'em killed if I had my way. I'd have a witch-hunt. Yes, I would. But we don't have witch-hunts here any more. When I was a kid we always used to be having them. I tell you, the whole tribe's going soft, soft. If I had my way. . . ."

His breathless voice broke off, drying up perhaps before some old megalomaniac vision of massacre. Complain moved away from him almost unnoticed: he saw Gwenny approaching across the clearing.

"Your father?" he enquired.

She made a faint gesture with one hand, indicative of nothing.

"You know the trailing rot," she said tonelessly. "He will be making the Long Journey before another sleep-wake is spent."

"In the midst of life we are in death," he said solemnly: Bergass was a man of honor.

"And the Long Journey has always begun," she replied, finishing the quotation from the Litany for him. "There is no more to be done. Meanwhile, I have my father's heart and your promise of a hunting. Let us go now, Roy. Take me into the ponics with you—please."

"Running meat's down to six loaves a carcass," he told her. "It's not worth going, Gwenny."

"You can buy a lot with a loaf. A pot for my father's skull, for instance."

"That's the duty of your step-mother."

"I want to come with you hunting."

He knew that note in her voice. Turning angrily on his heel, he made for the leading barricade without another word. Gwenny followed demurely.

II

Hunting had become Gwenny's great passion. It gave her freedom from Quarters, for no woman was allowed to leave the tribal area alone, and it gave her excitement. She took no part in the killing, but she crept like Complain's shadow after the beasts who inhabited the tangles.

Despite its growing stock of domesticated animals and the consequent slump in the value of wild stock, Quarters had not enough meat for its increasing needs. The tribe was always in a state of unbalance; it had only been formed two generations ago, by Grandfather Greene, and would not be entirely self-sufficient for some while. Indeed, a serious accident or set-back might still shatter it, sending its component families to seek what reception they could find with other tribes.

Complain and Gwenny followed a tangle trail for some way beyond the leading Quarters barricade and then branched into the thicket. The one or two hunters and catchers they had been passing gave way to solitude, the crackling solitude of the tangles. Complain led them up a small companionway, pushing through the crowded stalks rather than cutting them, so that their trail should be less obvious. At the top he halted, Gwenny peering eagerly, anxiously over his shoulder.

The individual ponics pressed up toward the light in bursts of short-lived energy, clustering overhead. The general illumination was consequently of a sickly kind, rather better for imagining things in than actually seeing them. Added to this were the flies and clouds of tiny midges that drifted among the foliage like smoke: vision was limited and hallucinatory. But there was no doubt a man stood watching them, a man with beady eyes and chalk-white forehead.

He was three paces ahead of them. He stood alertly. His great torso was bare and he wore only shorts. He seemed to be looking at a point a little to their left. Yet so uncertain was the light that the harder one peered the harder it was to be sure of anything, except that the man was there. And then he was not there.

"Was it a ghost?" Gwenny hissed.

Slipping his dazer into his hand, Complain pressed forward. He could almost persuade himself he had been tricked by a pattern of shadow, so silently had the watcher vanished. Now there remained no sign of him but trampled seedlings where he had stood.

"Don't let's go on," Gwenny whispered nervously. "Suppose it was a Forwards man—or an Outsider."

"Don't be silly," he said. "You know there are wild men who have run amok and live solitary in the tangles. He will not harm us. If he had wanted to shoot us, he would have done so then."

All the same, his skin crawled uneasily to think that even now this stray might be drawing a bead on them, or otherwise planning their deaths as surely and invisibly as if he had been a disease.

"But his face was so white," Gwenny protested.

He took her arm firmly, and led her forward. The sooner they were away from the spot, the better.

They moved fairly swiftly, once crossing a pig run, and passed into a side corridor. Here Complain squatted with his back to the wall and made Gwenny do the same.

"Listen, and see if we are being followed," he said.

The ponics slithered and rustled, and countless small insects gnawed into the silence. Together, they formed a din which seemed to Complain to grow until it would split his head. And in the middle of the din was a note which should not be there.

Gwenny had heard it too.

"We are getting near another tribe," she whispered. "There's one down this alley."

The sound they could hear was the inevitable one of babies crying and calling, which announced a tribe long before its barricades were reached, even before it could be smelled. Only a few wakes ago, this area had been pig territory, which meant that a tribe had come up from another level and was slowly approaching the Greene hunting preserves.

"We'll report this when we get back," Complain said, and led her the other way.

He worked easily along, counting the turns as they went, so as not to get lost. When a low archway appeared to their left, they moved through it, picking up a pig trail. This was the area known as Sternstairs, where a great hill led down to lower levels. A crashing sounded from over the brink of the slope, followed by an unmistakable squealing. Pig!

Motioning Gwenny to stay where she was at the top of the hill, Complain, dexterously sliding his bow from his shoulder and fitting an arrow to it, commenced the descent. His hunter's blood was up, all worries forgotten, and he moved like a wraith. Gwenny's eye sped him an unnoticed message of encouragement.

With room for once to reach something like their full stature, the ponics on the lower level had grown up into thin trees, arching overhead. Complain slipped to the brink of the drop, peering down through the tall ponics. An animal moved down there, rooting contentedly; he could see no litter, although the squealing had sounded like the cries of small creatures.

As he worked cautiously down the slope, also overwhelmed with the ubiquitous tangle, he felt a momentary pang for the life he was about to take. A pig's life! He squashed the pang at once; the Teaching did not approve of "softness".

There were three piglets beside the sow. Two were black and one brown: shaggy, long-legged creatures like wolves, with prehensile noses and scoop jaws. The sow obligingly turned a broadflank for the readying arrow. She raised her head suspiciously and probed with her little eye through the poles round her.

"Roy! Roy! Help—"

The cry came piercingly from above: Gwenny's voice, raised to the striking pitch of fear.

The pig family took fright instantly, breaking through the stalks at speed, the young determinedly keeping up their mother's pace. Their noise did not quite cover the sounds of a scuffle above the hunter's head.

25

Complain did not hesitate. At the startlement of Gwenny's first cry, he had dropped his arrow. Without attempting to pick it up, he whipped the bow over his shoulder, pulled out his dazer and dashed back up the slope of Sternstairs. But a stretch of uphill tangle is not good running ground. When he got to the top, Gwenny was gone.

A crashing sounded to his left and he ran that way. He ran doubled up, making himself as small a target as possible, and was rewarded by the sight of two bearded men bearing Gwenny off. She was not struggling; they must have knocked her unconscious.

It was the third man Complain did not see who nearly settled him. This man had dropped behind his two companions, stepping back into the stalks to cover their retreat. Now he set an arrow whipping back along the corridor. It twanged past Complain's ear. He dropped instantly, avoiding a second arrow, and groveled quickly back along the trail. Being dead helped nobody.

Silence now, the usual crumbling noise of insane plant growth. Being *alive* helped nobody either. The facts hit him one by one and then altogether. He had lost the pigs; he had lost Gwenny; he would have to face the council and explain why they were now a woman short. Shock for a moment obscured the salient fact: he had lost Gwenny. Complain did not love her, often he hated her; but she was his, necessary.

Comfortingly, anger oiled up in his mind, drowning the other emotions. Anger! This was the salve the Teaching taught. Wrenching up handfuls of root-bound soil, he pelted them from him, distorting his face, working up the anger, creaming it up like batter in a bowl. Mad, mad, mad ... he flung himself flat, beating the ground, cursing and writhing. But always quietly.

At last the fit worked itself off, and he was left empty. For a long time he just sat there, head in hand, his brain washed as bare as tidal mud. Now there was nothing for it but to get up and go back to Quarters. He had to report. In his head his weary thoughts ran.

I could sit here forever. The breeze so slight, never changing its temperature, the light only seldom dark. The

*ponics rearing up and failing, decaying around me. I should
come to no harm but death. . . .*

*Only if I stay alive can I find the something missed, the
big something. Something I promised myself as a kid.
Perhaps now I'll never find it, or Gwenny could have
found it for me—no she couldn't: she was a substitute
for it, admit it. Perhaps it does not exist. But when
something so big has non-existence, that in itself is existence. A hole. A wall. As the priest says, there's been a
calamity.*

*I can almost imagine something. It's big. Big as . . . you
couldn't have anything bigger than the world or it would
be the world. World, ship, earth, planet . . . other people's
theories, no concern of mine: theories solve nothing.
Mere unhappy muddles, more unhappy muddles, middles,
mutters.*

Get up, you weak fool.

He got himself up. If there was no reason for returning
to Quarters, there was equally no reason for sitting here.
Possibly what most delayed his return was the foreknowledge of all the practiced indifference there: the guarded
look away, the smirk at Gwenny's probable fate, the
punishment for her loss. He headed slowly back through
the tangle.

Complain whistled before coming into view of the
clearing in front of the barricade, was identified, and
entered Quarters. During the short period of his absence a
startling change had taken place; even in his dull state, he
did not fail to notice it.

That clothing was a problem in the Greene tribe the
great variety of dress clearly demonstrated. No two people
dressed alike, from necessity rather than choice, individu-
ality not being a trait fostered among them. The function
of dress in the tribe was less to warm the body than to
serve, Janus-faced, as guard of modesty and agent of
display; and to be a rough and ready guide to social
standing. Only the *élite*, the Guards, the hunters and
people like the valuer, could usually manage something
like a uniform. The rest muddled by with a variety of
fabrics and skins.

But now the drab and the old in costume were as bright

27

as the newest. The lowliest blockhead of a laborer sported flaring green rags!

"What the devil's happening here, Butch?" Complain asked a passing man.

"Expansion to your ego, friend. The guards found a cache of dye earlier. Get yourself a soak! There's going to be a honey of a celebration."

Further on, a crowd was gathered, chattering excitedly. A series of stoves were ranged along the deck; over them, like so many witches' cauldrons, boiled the largest utensils available. Yellow, scarlet, pink, mauve, black, navy blue, skyblue, green and copper, the separate liquids boiled, bubbled and steamed, and around them churned the people, dipping one garment here, another there. Through the thick steam their unusual animation sounded shrilly.

This was not the only use to which the dye was being put. Once it had been decreed that the dye was no use to the council, the Guards had thrown the bags out for anyone to have. Many bags had been slit open and their contents thrown against walls or floor. Now the whole village was decorated with round bursts or slashes or fans of bright color.

Dancing had started. In still wet clothes, trailing rainbows which merged into brown puddles, women and men joined hands and began to whirl about the open spaces. A hunter jumped onto a box, beginning to sing. A woman in a yellow robe leaped up with him, clapping her hands. Another rattled a tambourine. More and more joined in the throng, singing, stamping round the cauldrons, up the deck, turning about, breathlessly but gladly. They were drunk on color: most of them had hardly known it before.

Now the artificers and some of the Guards, aloof at first, joined in too, unable to resist the excitement in the humid air. The men were pouring in from the fieldrooms, sneaking back from the various barricades, eager for their share of pleasure.

Complain eyed it all dourly, turned on his heel and went to report to the Lieutenancy.

An officer heard his story in silence and curtly ordered him before Lieutenant Greene himself.

Losing a woman could be a serious matter. The Greene

28

tribe comprised some nine hundred souls, of which nearly half were under age and only about one hundred and thirty were women. Mating duels were the commonest form of trouble in Quarters.

He was marched in front of the Lieutenant. Guard-flanked, the old man sat at an ancient desk, eyes carefully guarded under grizzled eyebrows. Without a movement or sign he conveyed displeasure.

"Expansion to your ego, sir," Complain offered humbly.

"At your expense," came the stock response. And then, growled, "How did you manage to lose your woman, Hunter Roy Complain?"

Haltingly, he explained how she had been seized at the top of Sternstairs. "It may have been the work of Forwards," he suggested.

"Don't raise that bogey here," Zilliac, one of Greene's attendants barked. "We've heard those tales of super-races before, and don't believe them. The Greene tribe is master of everything this side of Deadways."

As Complain gave his story, the Lieutenant grew gradually more angry. His limbs began to shake; his eyes filled with tears; his mouth distorted till his chin was glistening with saliva; his nostrils filled with mucus. The desk commenced to rock in unison with his fury. As he rocked, he growled, and under the shaggy white hair his skin turned a pale maroon. Through his fear Complain had to admit it was a brilliant, daunting performance.

Its climax came when the Lieutenant, vibrating like a top with the wrath pouring from him, fell suddenly to the ground and lay still. At once Zilliac and his fellow, Patcht, stood over the body, dazers at the ready, faces twitching with reciprocal anger.

Slowly, very slowly and tremblingly, the Lieutenant climbed back on to his chair, exhausted by the necessary ritual. "He'll kill himself one day, doing that," Complain told himself. The thought warmed him a little.

"Now to decide your punishments under the law," the old man said, in a husk of a voice. He glanced around the room in a helpless fashion.

"Gwenny was not a good woman for the tribe, despite her brilliant father," Complain said, moistening his lips. "She couldn't produce any children, sir. We did have one, a girl, who died before weaning. She could not have any more, sir—Marapper the priest said so."

"Marapper's a fool!" Zilliac exclaimed.

"Your Gwenny was a well-figured girl," Patcht said. "Nicely set up. Quite a beddable girl."

"You know what the laws say, young man," the Lieutenant said. "My grandfather formed them when he formed the tribe. They are next to the Teaching in importance in our . . . in our lives. What is all that row outside? Yes, he was a great man, my grandfather. I remember on the day he died he sent for me. . . ."

Fear glands were still working copiously in Complain, but in a sudden moment of detachment he saw the four of them, each pursuing an elusive thread in his own being, conscious of the others only as interpretations or manifestations of his own fears. They were isolated, and every man's hand was against his neighbor.

"What shall the sentence be?" Zilliac growled, cutting into the Lieutenant's reminiscences.

"Oh, ah, let me see. You are already punished by losing your woman, Complain. There is no other available woman for you at present. What is all that noise outside?"

"He must be punished or it may be thought you are losing your grip," Patcht suggested craftily.

"Oh, quite, quite; I *was* going to punish him. Your suggestion was unnecessary, Patcht. Hunter—er, huh, Complain, for the next six sleep-wakes you will suffer six strokes, to be adminstered by the Guard captain before each sleep, starting now. Good. You can go. And, Zilliac, for hem sake go and see what all that row is outside."

So Complain found himself outside again. A wall of noise and color met him. Everyone seemed to be here, dancing senselessly in an orgy of enjoyment. Normally he would have flung himself in too, being as eager as anyone to throw off the oppressive routines of life; but in his present mood he merely slunk round the outside of the crowd, avoiding their eyes.

Nevertheless, he delayed the return to his compartment. (He would be turned out of there now: single men did not have their own rooms.) He loitered sheepishly on the fringes of the merriment, his stomach heavy with expectation of the coming punishment, while the bright dance whirled by. Several groups, divided from the main one in biparous fashion, jigged rapturously to the sound of stringed instruments. The noise was incessant, and in the frenetic movements of the dancers—heads jerking, fingers twitching—an onlooker might have found cause for alarm. But there were few non-participants. The tall, saturnine doctor, Lindsey, was one; Fermour was another, too slow for this whirl; Wantage was another, pressing his maimed face away from the throng; the Public Stroker was another. The latter had his appointments to keep, and at the proper time appeared before Complain with a guard escort. Roughly, the clothes were stripped from his back and the first installment of his punishment was administered.

A crowd of eyes usually watched these events. For once there was something better happening: Complain suffered almost privately. Tomorrow he might expect more attention.

Pulling his shirt down over his wounds, he went sickly back to his compartment. He entered, and found Marapper the priest awaiting him.

III

Henry Marapper the priest was a bulky man. He squatted patiently on his haunches, his big belly dangling. The posture was not an unconventional one for him, but his time of calling was. Stiffly, Complain stood before the crouching figure, awaiting greeting or explanation; neither came and he was forced to say something first. Pride stifled everything but a grunt. At this Marapper raised a grubby paw.

"Expansion to your ego, son."

"At your expense, father."

"And turmoil in my id," capped the priest piously, making the customary genuflection of rage without troubling to rise.

"I have been stroked, father," Complain said heavily, taking a mug of yellowish water from a pitcher; he drank some and used some to smooth down his hair.

"So I heard, Roy, so I heard. I trust your mind is eased by the degradation?"

"At considerable cost to my spine, yes."

He began to haul his shirt over his shoulders, taking his time, flinching a little. The pain, as the fibers of the garment tugged out of the wounds, was almost pleasant. It would be worse next sleep-wake. Finally he flung the bloody garment on to the floor and spat at it. Irritation moved in him to see how indifferently the priest had watched his struggle.

"Not dancing, Marapper?" he asked tartly.

"My duties are with the mind, not the senses," the other said piously. "Besides, I know better ways to oblivion."

"Such as being snatched away into the tangles, I suppose?"

"It pleases me to hear you taking your own part so

sharply, my friend; that is how the Teaching would have it. I feared to find you in the doldrums: but happily it seems my comfort is not needed."

Complain looked down at the face of the priest, avoiding the bland eyes. It was not a handsome face. Indeed, at this moment it hardly seemed a face at all, but a totem roughly molded in lard, a monument perhaps to the virtues by which man survived: cunning, greed, self-seeking. Unable to help himself, Complain warmed to the man; here was someone he knew and could consequently deal with.

"May my neuroses not offend, father," he said. "You know I have lost my woman, and my life feels considerably down at heel. Whatever I have laid claim to—and that's little enough—has gone from me, or what remains will be forcibly taken. The guards will come, the guards who have already whipped and will whip me again tomorrow, and turn me out of here to live with the single men and boys. No rewards for my hunting, or comfort for my distress! The laws of this tribe are too harsh, priest—the Teaching itself is cruel cant—the whole stifling world nothing but a seed of suffering. Why should it be so? Why should there not be a chance of happiness? Ah, I will run amok as my brother did before me; I'll tear through that fool crowd outside and cut the memory of my discontent into every one of them!"

"Spare me more," the priest cut in. "I have a large parish to get around; your confessions I will hear, but your rages must be kept to entertain yourself." He rose to his feet, stretching, and adjusted the greasy cloak around his shoulders.

"But what do we get out of life here?" Complain asked, fighting down an impulse to clamp his hands around that fat neck. "Why are we here? What is the *object* of the world? You're a priest—tell me straightforwardly."

Marapper sighed windily, and raised his palms in a gesture of rejection. "My children, your ignorance staggers me: what determination it has! 'The world', you say, meaning this petty, uncomfortable tribe. The world is more than that. We—everything: ponics, Deadways, the Forwards people, the whole shoot—are in a sort of container called a Ship, moving from one bit of the world to

33

another. I've told you this time and time again, but you won't grasp it."

"That theory again!" Complain said sullenly. "What if the world *is* called Ship, or Ship the world, it makes no difference to us."

For some reason, the ship theory, well known although generally disregarded in Quarters, upset and frightened him. He tightened his mouth and said, "I wish to sleep now, father. Sleep at least brings comfort. You bring only riddles. Sometimes I see you in my sleep, you know; you are always telling me something I ought to understand, but somehow I never hear a word."

"And not only in your dreams," said the priest pleasantly, turning away. "I had something important to ask you, but it must wait. I shall return tomorrow, and hope to find you less at the mercy of your adrenalin," he added, and with that was gone.

For a long while Complain stared at the closed door, not hearing the sounds of revelry outside. Then, wearily, he climbed up on to the empty bed.

Sleep did not come. His mind ran over the endless quarrels he and Gwenny had suffered in this room—the search for a more cruel and crushing remark, the futility of their armistices. It had gone on for so long and now it was finished: Gwenny was sleeping with someone else from now on. Complain felt regret and pleasure mixed.

Suddenly, tracing over the events which led to Gwenny's abduction, he recalled the ghostly figure that had faded into the ponics at their approach. He sat up in bed, uneasy at something more than the uncanny expertise with which the figure had vanished. Outside his door, all was now quiet. The race of his thoughts must have gone on for longer than he had imagined; the dance was done, the dancers overcome by sleep. Only he with his consciousness pierced the tomb-like veil that hung over the corridors of Quarters. If he opened his door now, he might hear the distant, never-ending rustle of ponic growth.

But nervousness made the thought of opening his door dreadful to him. Complain recalled in a rush the legends of strange beings which were frequently told in Quarters.

There were, firstly, the mysterious peoples of Forwards. Forwards was a distant area; the men there had alien

34

ways and weapons, and powers unknown. They were slowly advancing through the tangle and would eventually wipe out all the small tribes: or so the legends ran. But however formidable they might be, it was acknowledged they were at least human.

The mutants were sub-human. They lived as hermits, or in small bands amid the tangles, driven there from the tribes. They had too many teeth, or too many arms, or too few brains. They could sometimes only hobble or creep or scuttle, owing to a deformity in the joints. They were shy; and because of this a number of weird attributes had been wished on them.

And then there were the Outsiders. The Outsiders were inhuman. Dreams of old men like Eff were troubled perpetually by the Outsiders. They had been created supernaturally out of the hot muck of the tangles. Where nobody penetrated, *they* had stirred into being. They had no hearts nor lungs, but externally resembled other men, so that they could live undetected among mortals, gathering power, and syphoning off the powers of men, like vampires drawing blood. Periodically among the tribes witch-hunts were held; but the suspects, when carved up for examination, always had hearts and lungs. The Outsiders invariably escaped detection—but everyone knew they were there: the very fact that witch-hunts took place proved it.

They might be gathering outside the door now, as menacingly as that silent figure had faded into the ponics.

This was the simple mythology of the Greene tribe, and it did not vary radically from the hierarchy of hobgoblins sustained by the other tribes moving slowly through that region known as Deadways. Part of it, yet entirely a separate species, were the Giants. The Forwarders, the mutants and the Outsiders were all known to exist; occasionally a mutant would be dragged in living from the tangles and made to dance before the people until, tiring of him, they despatched him on the Long Journey; and many warriors would swear they had fought solitary duels with Forwarders and Outsiders; but there was in these three orders of beings an elusive quality. During wakes, in company, it was easy to discount them.

The Giants could not be discounted. They were real.

Once everything had belonged to them, the world had been theirs, some even claimed that men were descended from them. Their trophies lay everywhere and their greatness was plain. If ever they returned, there would be no resisting.

Dimly, behind all these phantasmal figures, lived another: less a figure than a symbol. His name was God and he was nothing to be scared of: but nobody ever spoke his name any more, and it was a curious thing to wonder how it was still handed on from generation to generation. It had some undefined connection with the phrase "for hem sake", which sounded emphatic without meaning anything precise. God had finished as a mild swear word.

What Complain had glimpsed that wake in the ponics was altogether more alarming than *that*.

In the midst of his anxiety, Complain recalled something else: the sound of crying he and Gwenny had heard. The two separate facts slipped smoothly together. The man—the approaching tribe. The man had not been an Outsider, or anything so mysterious. He had merely been a flesh and blood hunter from the other tribe. As simple, as obvious as that...

Complain lay back, relaxing. His stupidity had been gently nuzzled out of the way by a little deduction. Although slightly appalled to think how the obvious had eluded him, he was nevertheless proud to consider this new lucidity. He never *ratiocinated* enough. Everything he did was too automatic, governed by the local laws or the universal Teaching, or his own private moods; this should not be from now on. From now on, he would be more like—well, Marapper, for instance, *valuing* things—but immaterial things, as Roffrey valued the material ones.

Experimentally, he cast around for other facts to match up. Perhaps if you could collect enough facts, even the ship theory might be turned into sense.

He should have reported the approaching tribe to Lieutenant Greene. That was an error. If the tribes met, there would be hard fighting; the Greenes must be prepared. Well, that report must go in later.

Almost surreptitiously, he dropped asleep.

No aroma of cooking greeted Complain when he woke. He sat up stiffly, groaned, scratched his head and climbed out of bed. For a time he thought that nothing but wretchedness filled him; then he felt, underneath the wretchedness, a resilience stirring. He was going to act, was going to be driven to act: how, would resolve itself later. The big something was promising itself to him again.

Hauling on his slacks, he paddled over to the door and pulled it open. Outside, a strange silence beckoned. Complain followed it into the Clearing.

The revels were now over. The actors, not bothering to return to their apartments, lay where irresistible sleep had found them, among the bright ruins of their gaiety. On the hard deck they lay sleeping stupidly, or woke without troubling to move. Only children called as usual, prodding somnolent mothers into action. Quarters looked like a broad battlefield; but the slain had not bled, and suffering was not yet finished for them.

Complain walked quietly among the sleepers. In the Mess, patronized by single men, he might be able to get food. He stepped by a pair of lovers sprawled over the Travel-Up pitch. The man, Complain saw, was Cheap; he still had his arm around a plump girl, tucked inside her tunic; his face was in Orbit; their feet straggled across the Milky Way. Little flies crept up her leg and under her skirt.

A figure was approaching. Not without misgiving, Complain recognized his mother. The law in Quarters, not rigorously enforced, was that a child should cease to communicate with his brothers and sisters when he was hip high, and with his mother when he was waist high. But Myra was a garrulous woman; what her waist proscribed, her tongue discarded, and she talked firmly to her many children whenever possible.

"Greetings, Mother," Complain grunted. "Expansion to your ego."

"At your expense, Roy."

"May your womb likewise expand."

"I'm getting too old for that courtesy, as you well know," she said, irritated that he should choose to be so formal with her.

"I'm off to get a meal, Mother."

"Gwenny *is* dead then. I knew it! Bealie was there at

37

your stroking and heard the announcement. It'll finish her poor old father off, you see. I was sorry I couldn't get there for it—for the stroking I mean—I shan't miss the others if I can possibly help it—but I got the most glorious shade of green in the scrambles. I dyed everything. I dyed this smock I've got on now; do you like it? It really is the most exciting thing—"

"Look, Mother, my back hurts: I don't feel like talking."

"Of course it hurts, Roy; you mustn't expect it not to. What it'll be like when you've finished your punishment, I shudder to think. I've got some fat I'll rub on it for you, and that'll ease the pores. Doctor Lindsey ought to look at it later, if you've got a spare bit of game to exchange for his advice—and you ought to have now, with Gwenny gone. Never did really like her—"

"Look, Mother—"

"Oh, I'll come with you if you're going to Mess. I wasn't really going anywhere special. I did hear, quite on the quiet of course—from old Toomer Munday, although hem knows where she got it from—that the Guards found some tea and coffee in the dye store. You notice they didn't scrabble *that* around! The Giants grew better coffee than we can manage."

The flow of words wove round him, as abstractedly he ate. Later, she took him to her room and smoothed fat across the welts on his back. As she did so, she offered him advice he had heard from her before.

"Remember, Roy, things won't always be bad; you've just struck a bad patch. Don't let it get you down."

"Things are always bad, Mother, what's there to live for?"

"You shouldn't talk like that. I know the Teaching says about not hiding any bitterness within you, but you don't look at things the way I do. As I always say, life is a mystery. The mere fact of being alive—"

"Oh, I know all that. Life's a drug on the market, as far as I'm concerned."

Myra looked hard at his angry face, and the lines on hers rearranged themselves into an expression of softness.

"When I want to comfort myself," she said, "I think of a great stretch of blackness, sweeping off for ever in all directions. And in this blackness, a host of little lanterns begin to burn. Those lanterns are our lives, burning bravely. They show us our surroundings. But what the surroundings mean, who lit the lamps, *why* they were lit. . . ." She sighed. "When we make the Long Journey, when our lamp goes out, perhaps we shall know more."

"And you say that *comforts* you?" Roy asked scornfully. It was a long while since he had heard the lantern parable from his mother, and soothing to hear it again now, but he could not allow her to see this.

"Yes. Yes, it comforts me. You see, our lanterns are burning together *here*." She touched a spot on the table between them with a small finger. "I'm thankful mine isn't burning alone *here*, out in the unknown." She indicated a spot an arm's length away.

Shaking his head, Complain stood up.

"I don't see it," he confessed. "It might very well be better out over there."

"Oh, yes, it might. But it would be different. That's what I'm afraid of. It would all be different: everything would be different."

"I expect you're probably right. I just wish it was different here. By the way, Mother, my brother Gregg who left the tribe and went alone into the tangles—"

"You still think of him?" the old lady asked eagerly. "Gregg was a good one, Roy; he'd have made a Guard if he had stayed."

"Do you think he might still be alive?"

She shook her head decisively. "In the tangles? You may be certain the Outsiders got him. Pity, a great pity— Gregg would have made a good Guard. I've always said so."

Complain was about to go when she said sharply, "Old Ozbert Bergass still breathes. They tell me he calls for his daughter Gwenny. It is your duty to go to him."

She spoke, for once, undeniable truth. And for once duty was colored with pleasure: Bergass was a tribal hero.

One-armed Olwell, carrying a brace of dead duck over the crook of his good arm, gave Complain a surly greeting; otherwise, he did not meet a moving soul. The rooms in which Bergass had his household were now far in the rear of Quarters. Once, these rooms had been at the leading barricade. As the tribe inched its way forward, they had gradually slipped back; when they had been in the midst of the tribe, Ozbert Bergass had been at the height of his power. Now, in his old age, his rooms lay far to the rear of anyone else's. The last barrier, the barricade between humanity and Deadways, stood just beyond his doors. Indeed, several empty rooms separated him from his nearest neighbors: his former neighbors, weaklings, had evacuated some while since, moving back to the center of things; he, stubborn old man, stayed where he was, stretching lines of communication and living in glorious squalor with an inordinate number of women.

Down here had been no revelry. In contrast with the temporary cheerfulness of the rest of Quarters, Bergass's passage looked sinister and chill. Long ago, probably in the time of the Giants, some sort of an explosion had taken place. The walls were blackened for some distance, and in the deck overhead a hole bigger than a man's length gaped. Here, outside the old guide's doors, no lights burned.

The continued advance of the tribe had added to this neglect, for a few ponics, seeding themselves determinedly across the rear barrier, grew in shaggy, stunted procession along the dirty deck, thigh high only.

Uncomfortably, Complain banged on Bergass's door. It opened, and a babel of sound and steam emerged, wreathing like a cloud of insects round Complain's face.

"Your ego, mother," Complain said politely to the old witch who peered out at him.

"Your expense, warrior. Oh, it's you, Roy Complain, is it? What do you want? I thought every fool young man was drunk. You'd better come in. Don't make a noise."

It was a large room, absolutely cluttered with dried ponic poles. They lined all the walls, making of the room a dead forest. Bergass had had an obsession that the very fabric of their world, walls and deck, might be demolished, and the tribe live in the ponic tangles in rooms built of these poles. He had tried this experiment himself in a broad part of Deadways and survived; but nobody else had taken up his idea.

A smell of broth filled the place, emanating from a great steaming cauldron in one corner. A young girl stirred this stew. Other women, Complain saw through the steam, stood about the room. Ozbert Bergass himself, surprisingly enough, sat on a rug in the middle of the room. He was delivering a speech which nobody heeded, all being busy talking to each other. Complain wondered how his knock had ever been heard.

He knelt down beside the old man. The trailing rot was far advanced. Starting, as always, from his stomach, it was working its short way up to the heart. Soft brown rods as long as a man's hand trailed out of his flesh, giving the withered body the aspect of a corpse pierced by decaying sticks.

". . . and so the ship was lost and man was lost and the very losing was lost," the old man said huskily, fixing blank eyes on Complain. "And I have climbed all among the wreckage and I know, and I say that the longer time goes on the less chance we have of finding ourselves again. Yon fool women do not understand, you do not care, but I've told Greene many a time he does wrong by his tribe. 'You're doing wrong', I've told him, 'destroying everything you come across just because it is not necessary to you. These books you burn, these rolls of film', I said, 'you destroy them because you think someone might use them against you. But they hold secrets we ought to know', I said, 'and you're a fool; we ought to be piecing things together, not destroying them. I tell you I've traveled more decks than you know exist', I said. . . . What do you want, sir?"

Since this interruption in the monologue seemed to be addressed to him, Complain answered that he came to be of service if possible.

"Service?" Bergass asked. "I've always fended for myself. And my father before me. My father was the greatest guide of them all. Do you know what has made us the tribe we are? I'll tell you. My father was out searching with me when I was a youngster and he found what the Giants used to call an armory. Yes, chambers full of dazers—full of 'em! But for that discovery the Greenes would not be what we are; we should have died out by now. Yes, I could take you to the armory now, if you dare to come. Away beyond the center of Deadways,

41

where feet turn into hands and the floor moves away from you and you swim in the air like an insect. . . ."

"He's babbling now," Complain thought. Pointless to tell him about Gwenny while he was jabbering about feet turning into hands. But the old guide stopped suddenly and said, "How did you get here, Roy Complain? Give me some more broth, my stomach's dry as wood."

Beckoning to one of the women for a bowl, Complain said, "I came to see how you were faring. You are a great man: I am sorry to find you like this."

"A great man," the other muttered stupidly, then, with a burst of fire, "Where's my broth? By hem's bladders, what are those whores doing? Washing their —s in it?"

A young woman hastily passed over a bowl of broth, winking mischievously at Complain as she did so. Bergass was too feeble to help himself, and Complain spooned the fatty stuff into his mouth. The guide's eyes, Complain observed, were seeking his, as if with a secret to impart; it was said that the dying always tried to look into someone else's eyes, but habit made Complain reluctant to meet that bright gaze. Turning away, he was suddenly conscious of the filth everywhere. There was enough dirt on the deck for ponics to seed in; even the dead ponic poles were caked in greasy condensation.

"Why is not the Lieutenant here? Where is Lindsey the doctor? Should not Marapper the priest be attending you?" he burst out angrily. "You should have better attendance here."

"Steady with that spoon, laddie. Just a minute while I make water . . . ah, my damned belly. Tight. Very tight. . . . The doctor—I had my women send the doctor away. Old Greene, he won't come, he's afraid of the rot. Besides, he's getting as old as I am; Zilliac'll knock him off one of these fine sleepwakes and take control himself. . . . Now there's a man—"

Seeing Bergass was wandering again, Complain said desperately, "Can I get you the priest?"

"The priest? Who, Henry Marapper? Come nearer, and I'll tell you something, just between us two. A secret. Never told anyone else. Easy. . . . Henry Marapper's a son of mine. Yes! I don't believe in his bag of lies any more than I believe—"

He interrupted himself with a fit of croaking which for a moment Complain took for gasps of pain; then he realized it was laughter, punctuated by the words, "My son!" There was no point in staying. With a curt word to one of the women, he got up, suddenly disgusted, leaving Bergass shaking so violently that his stomach growths clapped together. The other women stood about disinterestedly, hands on hips or making the perpetual fanning gesture against the flies. Snatches of their talk beat unheeded against Complain's ears as he left.

" . . . and where's he get all those clothes from, I'd like to know. He's only a common farm hand. I tell you he's an informer. . . ."

"You're too free with your kisses, young Wenda. Believe me, when you get to my age—"

" . . . nicest dish of brains I've *ever* had."

" . . . that Ma Cullindram has just had a little of seven. All still-born but one poor little tyke. It was quins last time, if you remember. I told her straight, I said 'You want to be firm with your man—' "

" . . . gambling away his earnings—"

" . . . lying. . . ."

" . . . never laughed so much. . . ."

Back in the dark corridor, he leaned for a time against a wall, sighing with relief. He had done nothing, had not even broken the news of Gwenny's death that he had come to tell Bergass, yet something had happened inside him. It was as if a great weight were rolling forward in his brain; it brought pain, but it enabled him to see more clearly. From it, he instinctively knew, some sort of climax would crystalize.

It had been overpoweringly hot in Bergass's room; Complain was dripping sweat. From the corridor, now he listened, he could still hear the rumble of women's voices. Suddenly a vision of Quarters as it really was came into his mind. It was a great cavern, filled exhaustingly with the twitter of many voices. Nowhere any real action, only the voices, dying voices.

IV

The wake wore slowly on and, as the sleep period drew nearer, Complain's stomach, in anticipation of the next dose of his punishment, grew more uneasy. One sleep-wake in four, in Quarters and in all the known territories round about, was dark. Not an absolute dark, for here and there in the corridors square pilot lights burned like moons; in the apartments it was entirely dark and moonless. This was an accepted law of nature. There were old people to say that their parents recalled how in their youth the darks had not lasted so long; but old people notoriously remember wrongly, spinning out strange tales from the stuff of their vanished childhoods.

In the darks, the ponics crumpled up like sacking. Their slender rods cracked, and all but the lustiest shoots turned black. This was their brief winter. When the light returned, fresh shoots and seedlings climbed energetically up, sweeping away the sacking in a new wave of green. And they in turn would be nipped in four more sleep-wakes. Only the toughest or most favored survived this cycle.

Throughout this wake, most of the few hundred Quarters remained inert, the greater part supine. Their barbaric outbreaks of festivity were always succeeded by this mass quiescence. They were expended but, more than that, they were unable to plunge once more into the rigors of routine. Inertia overcame the whole tribe. Despondence lay over them like sheets, and outside the barricades the ponic tangle made inroads on the clearings. Only hunger would get them to their feet again.

"You could murder the lot without a hand being raised against you," Wantage said, something like inspiration showing on the right side of his face.

"Why don't you then?" Complain said jeeringly. "It's in the Litany, you know: an evil desire suppressed multiplies itself and devours the mind it feeds in. Go to, Slotface!"

Instantly, he was seized by the wrist and a sharp blade whisked horizontally to within an inch of his throat. Glaring into his face was a terrible visage, one half creased in fury, the other creased permanently into a meaningless smile; a large grey eye stared detachedly beyond them, absorbed in its own private vision.

"Don't dare call me that again, you filthy meat," Wantage snarled. Then he twitched his face away, dropping his knife hand, turning his back, anger fading to mortification as he recalled his deformity.

"I'm sorry." Complain regretted the remark as he uttered it, but the other did not turn around again.

Slowly, Complain also moved on, nerves jangled by the encounter. He had run into Wantage on his return from the tangles, where he had been investigating the approaching tribe. If they made contact with the Greene tribe, which was by no means certain, it would not be for some while; the first trouble would be clashes between rival hunters. That might mean death; certainly it would mean release from monotony. Meanwhile, he would keep the knowledge to himself. Let someone with a fondness for authority break the news to the Lieutenant.

On his way to the Guards' quarters for punishment he encountered nobody but Wantage. Inertia still ruled; even the Public Stroker refused to be drawn forth to perform.

"There'll be other sleep-wakes," he said. "What are you in such a hurry for? Clear off and let me lie. Go and find a new woman."

So Complain went back to his compartment, stomach slowly unknotting. Somewhere in a narrow side corridor, someone played a stringed instrument; he caught the words, sung in a tenor voice:

> "... this continuum
> ... far too long
> ... Gloria."

An old song, poorly remembered; he shut it off sharply with his closing door. Once again Marapper waited for

45

him, greasy face cupped in his hands, rings glittering on his fat fingers.

Complain was suddenly undermined by the sensation that he knew what the priest was going to say; he seemed to have lived this scene over before. He tried to break through the web-like illusion, but could not.

"Expansion, son," said the priest, languidly making the rage sign. "You look bitter; are you?"

"Very bitter, father. Only killing could ease it." Through his words, try as he would to say something unexpected, Complain's sense of re-enacting a scene persisted.

"There are more things than killing. Things you do not dream of."

"Don't give me that crap, father. You'll be telling me next that life is a mystery and rambling on like my mother. I feel I *need* to kill someone."

"You shall, you shall," the priest soothed. "And it is good you should feel so. Never grow resigned, my son; that way is death for us all. We are being punished here for some wrong our forefathers committed. We are all maimed! We are all blind—we thrust out in wrong directions. . . ."

Complain had climbed wearily on to his bunk. The illusion of re-living the scene had gone; and directly it was gone, it was forgotten. Now he wanted only to sleep. Tomorrow he would be evicted from his single room and stroked; now he wanted only to sleep. But the priest had stopped talking. Complain glanced up and found Marapper leaning on his bunk, gazing at him. Their eyes met for a moment, before Complain pulled his hurriedly away.

One of the strongest taboos in their society was directed against one man's looking another straightly in the eyes; honest, well-intentioned men gave each other only side glances. Complain stuck out his lower lip truculently.

"What the hem do you want with me, Marapper?" he exploded. He was tempted to tell the priest that he had just learned of his bastardy.

"You didn't get your six strokes, Roy, boy, did you?"

"What's that to you, priest?"

"A priest knows no self-seeking. I ask for your good; besides, I have a personal interest in your answer."

"No, I wasn't beaten. They're all flat out, as you know—even the Public Stroker."

The priest's eyes were after his again. Complain heaved over uncomfortably and faced the wall; but the priest's next question brought him around again.

"Do you ever feel like running amok, Roy?"

Despite himself, Complain had a vision: he was running through Quarters with his dazer burning, everyone scattering, fearing him, respecting him, leaving him master of the situation. His heart beat uncomfortably. Several of the best and most savage men of the tribe—even Gregg, one of his own brothers—had run amok, bursting through the settlement, some escaping to live afterwards in unexplored areas of tangle, or joining other communities, afraid to return and face their punishment. He knew it was a manly, even an honorable thing to do; but it was not a priest's business to incite it. A doctor might recommend it if a man were mortally sick; a priest should unite, not disrupt his tribe, by bringing the frustration in human minds up to the surface, where it might flow freely without curdling into neurosis.

For the first time, he realized Marapper was wrestling with a crisis in his own life, and wondered momentarily if it had any connection with the fact of Bergass's illness.

"Look at me, Roy. Answer me."

"Why are you speaking to me like this?" He was sitting up now, almost forced there by the urgency in the priest's voice.

"I must know what you are made of."

"You know what the Litany tells us: we are the sons of cowards, our days are passed in fear."

"This you believe?" the priest asked.

"Naturally. It is the Teaching."

"I need your aid, Roy. Would you follow where I led you—even out of Quarters, into Deadways?"

All this was spoken low and fast. And low and fast beat the indecision in Complain's blood. He made no effort to come to a consciously debated decision; the nerves must be arbiter: mind was not trustworthy—it knew too much.

"That would require courage," he said at length.

The priest slapped his great thighs, yawning in nervous enthusiasm with a sound like a tiny shriek.

"No, Roy, you lie, true to the list of liars who begot you. If we went, we should be escaping, fleeing, evading the responsibilities of grown men in society. Ha, we shall slip away furtively. It will be the old back-to-nature act, boy, a fruitless attempt to return to the ancestral womb. Why, it would be the very depth and abysm of cowardice to leave here. Now, will you come with me?"

Some meaning beyond the words themselves hardened a decision in Complain. He would go! Always there had been that cloud just beyond his comprehension, from which he must escape. He slid off the bunk, trying to hide this decision from Marapper's wily eyes until he had learned more of the venture.

"What should we two do alone in the tangles of Dead-ways, priest?"

The priest thrust a great thumb searchingly up one nostril and spoke with his gaze steady over his fist. "We shall not go alone. Four others come with us, picked men. I have been preparing for this for some while, and all is now ready. You are discontented, your woman is taken: what have you to lose? I strongly advise you to come—for your own sake, of course—although it will suit me to have someone about with a weak will and a hunter's eye."

"Who are the four others, Marapper?"

"I will tell you *that* when you say you are coming. If I were betrayed to the Guards, they would slit all our throats—mine especially!—in twenty places."

"What are we going to do? Where are we going?"

Marapper rose slowly to his feet and stretched. With long fingers he raked through his hair, making at the same time the most hideous sneer he could devise, twisting the two great slabs of his cheeks, one up, one down, until his mouth coiled between them like knotted rope.

"Go by yourself, Roy, if you so distrust my leadership! Why, you're like a woman, all bellyache and questioning. I'll tell you no more, except that my scheme is something too grand for your comprehension. Domination of the ship! That's it! Nothing less! Complete domination of the ship—you don't even know what the phrase means."

Cowed by the priest's ferocious visage, Complain merely said, "I was not going to refuse to come."

"You mean you will come?"

"Yes."

Marapper gripped his arm fervently, without a word. His cheeks gleamed.

"*Now* tell me who the other four are who come with us," Complain said, alarmed the moment he had committed himself.

Marapper released his arm.

"You know the old saying, Roy: the truth never set anyone free. You will learn soon enough. It is better that I do not tell you now. I plan we shall start early next sleep. Now I shall leave you; I have work still to do. Not a word to anyone."

Half out of the door, he paused. Thrusting a hand into his tunic, he pulled something out and waved it triumphantly. Complain recognized it as a book, the collection of reading matter used by the extinct Giants.

"This is our key to power!" Marapper said dramatically, thrusting it back into its place of concealment. Then he closed the door behind him.

Idle as statuary, Complain stood in the center of the floor, only his head working. And in his head there was only a circle of thought, leading nowhere. But Marapper was the priest, Marapper had knowledge most others could not share, Marapper must lead. Belatedly, Complain went to the door, opened it and peered out.

The priest had already gone from sight. Nobody was near except Meller, the bearded artist. He was painting a bright fresco on the corridor wall outside his room, dabbing on with shrewdly engrossed face the various dyes he had collected the sleep-wake before. Beneath his hand, a great cat launched itself up the wall. He did not notice Complain.

It was growing late. Complain went to eat in the almost deserted Mess. He fed in a trance. He returned, and Meller was still painting in a trance. He shut his door and prepared slowly for bed. Gwenny's grey dress still hung on a hook by the bed; he snatched it down suddenly and flung it out of sight behind a cupboard. Then he lay down and let silence prolong itself.

Suddenly into the room burst Marapper, bulbously, monumentally out of breath. He slammed the door behind him, gasping and tugging the corner of his cloak which had caught in the jamb.

"Hide me, Roy—quick! Quickly, don't stare, you fool. Get up, get your knife out. The Guards'll be here, Zilliac'll be here. They're after me. They'd massacre poor old priests as soon as look at them."

As he spoke, he ran to Complain's bunk, swung it out from the wall and began to crouch behind it.

"What have you done?" Complain demanded. "Why are they after you? Why hide here? Why drag me into it?"

"It's no compliment. You just happened to be near and my legs were never constructed for running. My life's in danger."

While he was talking, Marapper stared wildly about, as if for a better hiding place, and then evidently decided to stay where he was. By adjusting a blanket over the far side of the bed he was screened from the doorway.

"They must have seen me come in here," he said. "It's not that I care for my own skin, but I've got plans. I let one of the Guards in on this scheme of ours and he went straight in and told it to Zilliac."

"Why should I—" Complain began hotly. A scuffle outside gave them the briefest warning and then the door was hurled open, rebounding on its hinges. It missed Complain by inches only, for he stood half behind it.

The crisis powered his inspiration. Flinging both hands over his face, he bent forward, groaning loudly and staggering, making believe the edge of the door had struck him. Through his fingers he saw Zilliac, the Lieutenant's right-hand man, next in line for the lieutenancy, burst into the room and kick the door shut behind him. He glared contemptuously at Complain.

"Hold your filthy row, man," Zilliac shouted. "Where's the priest? I saw him come in here."

As he turned, dazer ready, to survey the room, Complain whipped up Gwenny's wooden stool by one leg and brought it down at the base of Zilliac's skull, square across the tense neck. A delightful splintering sound of wood and bone, and Zilliac toppled full length. He had barely hit the deck before Marapper stood up. With a heave, all teeth showing, he tipped the heavy bunk over sideways, sending it falling across the fallen man.

50

"I've got him!" the priest exclaimed. "Hem's guts, I've got him!" He gathered up Zilliac's dazer, moving with agility for a heavy man, and faced the door.

"Open up, Roy! There'll doubtless be others outside, and it's now or never if we're getting out of this with breathable throats."

But the door swung open at that moment without Complain's aid. Meller the artist stood there, sheathing a knife, his face pale as boiled fowl.

"Here's an offering for you, priest," he said. "I'd better bring him in before someone comes along."

He grabbed the ankles of a guard who lay crumpled in the corridor. Complain went to his aid, and together they dragged the limp body in and closed the door. Meller leaned against the wall mopping his forehead.

"I don't know what you're up to, priest," he said, "but when this fellow heard the rumpus in here, he was off to fetch his friends. I thought it looked most convenient to despatch him before you had a party."

"May he make the Long Journey in peace," Marapper said weakly. "It was well done, Meller. Indeed, we've all done well for amateurs."

"I have a throwing blade," Meller explained. "Fortunately—for I dislike hand-to-hand fighting. Mind if I sit down?"

Moving dazedly, Complain knelt between the bodies and felt for a heart beat. Directly action had started, the ordinary Complain had been shuffled away for another, an automatic man with defter movement and sure impulse. He it was who took over when the hunt was on. Now his hand searched Zilliac and the crumpled Guard and found there was no pulse between the two of them.

Death was as common as cockroaches in the small tribes. "Death is the longest part of a man", said a folk poem. This stretched-out spectacle, so frequently met with, was the subject of much of the Teaching: there had to be a formal way of dealing with it. It was fearful, and fear must not be allowed to lodge in a man. The automatic man in Complain, confronted with death now, fell straight into the first gesture of prostration, as he had been brought up to do.

Seeing their cue, Marapper and Meller instantly joined

51

him, Marapper crying softly aloud. Only when their intricate business was over and the last Long Journey said did they lapse back into something like normality.

Then they sat looking at each other, scared, sheepishly triumphant, across the quiet bodies. Outside, all was silence; only the prevailing indolence after the recent merry-making saved them from a crowd of sightseers and inevitable exposure. Slowly, Complain found himself able to think again.

"What about the Guard who passed on your scheme to Zilliac?" he asked. "We shall have trouble from him soon, Marapper, if we stay here."

"If we stayed here forever *he* would not trouble us," the priest said, "except to offend our nostrils. He lies here before us now." He pointed to the man Meller had dragged in, adding: "Which makes it look as if my plans have been passed on no further. So we are fortunate: we still have a little while before a search starts for Zilliac. He, I suspect, was nourishing some little scheme of his own on the quiet, otherwise he would have had an escort. So much the better for us. Come, Roy, we must move at once. Quarters is no longer healthy for us."

He stood up on legs unexpectedly shaky and promptly sat down again. He rose again with more care, saying defensively: "For a man of sensibility, I worked neatly with that bunk, eh?"

"I've yet to hear what they were after you for, priest," Meller said.

"The greater credit to the speed of your assistance," said Marapper smoothly, making toward the door. Meller put his arm across it and answered, "I want to hear what you are involved in. It seems to me I am now involved in it too."

When Marapper drew up but did not speak, Complain said impetuously, "Why not let him come with us, Marapper?"

"So . . ." the artist said reflectively. "You're both leaving Quarters! Good luck to you, friends—I hope you will find whatever you are going looking for. Myself, I'd rather stay here safely and paint, thanks for the invitation."

"Brushing aside the minor point that no invitation was

offered, I agree with all you say," Marapper said. "You showed up well just now, friend, but I need only real men of action with me: and at that I want a handful, not an army."

As Meller stepped aside and Marapper took hold of the door handle, the latter's attitude softened and he said, "Our lives are of microscopically small moment, but I believe that we now owe them to you, painter. Back to your dyes now with our thanks, and not a word to anyone."

He made off down the corridor, Complain hurrying to get by his side. Sleep had closed over the tribe. They passed a late sentry, going to one of the rear barricades; two young men and two girls in bright rags were attempting to recapture the spirit of the past revelry; otherwise, the place was deserted.

Turning sharply down a side corridor, Marapper led the way to his own quarters. Glancing about him furtively, he produced a magnetic key and opened the door, pushing Complain in ahead of him. It was a large room, but crowded with the acquisitions of a lifetime, a thousand articles bribed or begged, things meaningless since the extinction of the Giants, and now merely fascinating totems of a more varied and advanced civilization than theirs. Complain stared about him almost helplessly, regarding without recognizing a camera, electric fans, jigsaw puzzles, books, switches, condensers, a bed pan, a bird cage, vases, fire extinguishers, keys in bundles, two oil paintings, a scroll labeled "Map of the Moon (Devizes Sector)", a toy telephone and a crate full of bottles containing a thick sediment called "Shampoo". Loot, all loot, with little perhaps but curiosity value.

"Stay here while I get the other three rebels," Marapper said, making to go. "Then we'll be on the move."

"Supposing *they* betray you as the Guard did?"

"They won't—as you'll know when you see them," Marapper said shortly. "I only let the Guard in on it because he saw this going in here." He thumped the book inside his tunic.

After he had gone, Complain heard the magnetic lock click into place. If something did go awry with the priest's plans, he would be trapped here with much awkward explaining to do on his release, and would probably die for Zilliac's death. He waited tensely, picking nervously at an irritation in one hand. He glanced down at length, and saw a minute splinter embedded in the flesh of his palm. The legs of Gwenny's stool had always been rough.

Part II

DEADWAYS

I

In Quarters, a well-worn precept said "Leap before you look"; rashness was proverbially the path of wisdom, and the cunning acted always on the spur of the moment. Other courses of conduct could hardly be entertained when, with little reason for any action, a brooding state of inaction threatened to overwhelm every member of the tribe. Marapper, who was adept at twisting any counsels to his own advantage, used these arguments of expediency to rouse the last three members of his expedition.

They followed him grudgingly, snatching up packs, jackets and dazers, and moving sullenly behind him through the corridors of their village. Few saw them go, and those few were indifferent, for the recent festivities had provided a generous quota of hangovers. Marapper stopped before the door of his compartment and felt for his key.

"What are we halting here for? We'll be caught if we hang about here, and chopped into little pieces. Let's get into the ponics if we're going."

Marapper swung a surly slab of cheek toward the questioner. Then he turned it away again, not deigning to reply. Instead, he pushed open the door and called, "Come out, Roy, and meet your companions."

Wary, a good hunter avoiding a possible trap, Complain appeared with his dazer in his hand. Quietly, he surveyed

55

the three who stood by Marapper; he knew them all well: Bob Fermour, elbows resting placidly on the two bulging pouches strapped to his belt, grinning non-committally; Wantage, rotating his fencing stick endlessly in his hands; and Ern Roffery, the valuer, face challenging and upleasant. For long seconds, Complain stared at them as they stood waiting.

"I'm not leaving Quarters with that lot, Marapper," he said definitely. "If they are the best you can find, count me out. I thought this was going to be an expedition, not a Punch and Judy show."

The Priest clucked impatiently like a dyspeptic hen, and started toward him, but Roffery brushed him away and confronted Complain with one hand on the butt of his dazer. His moustache vibrated within six inches of Complain's chin.

"So, my running meat specialist," he said. "That's how you feel. Don't recognize your superiors when you see them, eh? If you think. . . ."

"It is how I feel," Complain said. "And you can stop picking at that toy in your holster or I'll fry your fingers off. The priest told me this was going to be an expedition, not a rake-out of the red light rooms."

"So it is an expedition," the priest roared, butting himself in between them and shaking his face from one to the other, spitting in his rage. "It is an expedition, and by hem you'll all come into Deadways with me if I have to carry your corpses there one by one. You fools, barking here like dogs at each other's stupid faces, you contemptible fools, do you reckon that either of you is worth a credit's worth of the other's attention, let alone mine? Get your stuff together and move, or I'll call the Guards on to you."

This threat was so palpably foolish that Roffrey burst into scoffing laughter.

"I joined you to get away from sallow countenances like Complain's, priest," he said. "Still, on your head be it! Lead on, you're chief!"

"If you feel like that about it, why waste time making a stupid scene?" Wantage snapped.

"Because I'm second in command here and I make what scenes I like," Roffery answered.

56

"You aren't second in command, Ern," Marapper said, explaining in kindly fashion. "There's just me in command and you lot following, equal in the sight of the law."

At this Wantage laughed jeeringly and Fermour said, "So if the pack of you have stopped bitching, perhaps we can move out of here before someone discovers us and settles all our troubles for good."

"Not so fast," Complain said. "I still want to know what that valuer is doing here. Why doesn't he go back to his valuing? He had a soft job; why did he leave it? It doesn't make sense to me: I shouldn't have left it, in his place."

"But you don't happen to have the guts of a frog," Roffery growled, straining against the priest's outflung arm. "We've all got our own reasons for coming on this mad jaunt, and my reason's none of your business."

"What are you making such a fuss about anyway, Complain?" Wantage shouted. "Why are you coming? I'm dead sure I don't want your company!"

The priest's short sword was suddenly between them. They could see his knuckles white from his grip on the handle.

"As I am a holy man," he growled, "I swear by every drop of rancid blood in Quarters I'll Long Journey the next man that speaks."

They stood there stiff with hostility, not speaking.

"Sweet, peace-making blade," Marapper whispered, and then, in ordinary tones, unhitching a pack from his shoulder, "Strap this harness on your back, Roy, and pull yourself together. Ern, leave your dazer alone—you're like a girl with a dolly. Soften up, the lot of you, and start walking with me. Keep in a bunch. We've got to get through one of the barriers to get into Deadways, so take your lead from me. It won't be easy."

He locked the door of his compartment, glanced thoughtfully at the key and then slipped it into a pocket. Without another sign to the others, he started to walk down the corridor. They hesitated only momentarily, and then fell obediently in beside him. Marapper's iron stare remained firmly fixed ahead, relegating them all to another, inferior universe.

At the next corridor junction, he turned left and, at the

next but one, left again. This led them into a short cul-de-sac with a mesh gate filling all the far end; a Guard stood before it, for this was one of the side barriers.

The Guard was relaxed but alert. He sat on a box, resting his chin on his hand, but directly the five came in view around the corner he jumped up and leveled a dazer at them.

"I should be happy to shoot," he cried, giving the standard challenge. Eyes hard, legs braced, he made it sound more than a cliché.

"And I to die," responded Marapper amiably. "Tuck your weapon away, Twemmers; we are no Outsiders. You sound a little nervy, methinks."

"Stop or I fire!" the Guard, Twemmers, called. "What do you want? Halt, all five of you!"

Marapper never paused in his stride, and the others came slowly on with him. For Complain, there was a certain fascination about it that he could not explain.

"You are getting too short-sighted for that job, my friend," the priest called. "I'll see Zilliac and get you taken off it. It is I, Marapper your priest, the agent of your doubtful sanity, with some well-wishers. No blood for you tonight, man."

"I'd shoot anybody," Twemmers threatened ferociously, waving his weapon, but backing toward the mesh gate beinhd him.

"Well, save it for a better target—although you'll never have a bigger," said the priest. "I have something important here for you."

During this interchange, Marapper's advance had not faltered. They were now almost on the Guard. The wretched man hesitated uncertainly; other Guards were within hail, but a false alarm could mean lashes for him, and he was anxious to preserve his present state of misery intact. Those few seconds' indecision were fatal. The priest was up to him.

Drawing the short sword swiftly from under his cloak, Marapper with a grunt dug it deep into the Guard's stomach, twisted it, and caught the body neatly over his shoulder as it doubled forward. He hoisted it until Twemmer's limp hands knocked against the small of his back, and then grunted again, with satisfaction.

"That was neatly done, father," Wantage said, impressed. "Couldn't have improved on it myself!"

"Masterly!" Roffery exclaimed, respect in his voice. It was good to see a priest who so ably practised what he preached.

"Pleasure," grunted Marapper, "but keep your voices low or the hounds will have us. Fermour, take this, will you?"

The body was transferred to Bob Fermour's shoulder; he, being five foot eight, and nearly a head taller than the others, could manage it most easily. Marapper wiped his blade daintily on Complain's jacket, holstered it, and turned his attention to the mesh gate.

From one of his voluminous pockets, he produced a pair of wire cutters, and with these snicked a connection on the gate. He tugged at the handle; it gave about an inch and then stuck. He heaved and growled, but it moved no further.

"Let me," Complain said.

He set his weight against the gate and tugged. It flew suddenly open with a piercing squeal, running on rusted bearings. A well was now revealed, a black, gaping hole, seemingly bottomless. They shrank back from it in some dismay.

"That noise should attract most of the Guards in Quarters," Fermour said, inspecting with interest a notice, "RING FOR ELEVATOR", by the side of the shaft. "Now what, priest?"

"Pitch the Guard down there, for a start," Marapper said. "Look lively!"

The body was hurled into the blackness, and in a moment they had the satisfaction of hearing a heavy thud.

"Sickening!" exclaimed Wantage with relish.

"Still warm," Marapper whispered. "No need for death rites—just as well if we are to continue to claim our life rights. Now then, don't be afraid, children, this dark place is man-made; once, I believe, a sort of carriage ran up and down it. We've got to follow Twemmer's example, although less speedily."

Cables hung in the middle of the opening. The priest leaned forward and seized them, then lowered himself gingerly hand over fist down fifteen feet to the next level.

The lift shaft yawning below him, he swung himself on to the narrow ledge, clung to the mesh with one hand and applied his cutters with the other. Tugging carefully, levering with his foot against an upright, he worked the gate open wide enough to squeeze through.

One at a time, the others followed. Complain was the last to leave the upper level. He climbed down the cable, silently bidding Quarters an uncordial farewell, and emerged with the others. The five of them stood silently in rustling twilight, peering about them.

They were on strange territory, but one stretch of ponic warren is much like another.

Marapper shut the gate neatly behind them and then faced forward, squaring his shoulders and adjusting his cloak.

"That's quite enough action for one wake, for an old priest like me," he said, "unless any of you care to resume our dispute about leadership?"

"That was never under dispute," Complain said, looking challengingly past Roffery's ear.

"Don't try and provoke me," the latter warned. "I follow our father, but I'll chop anyone who starts trouble."

"There'll be enough trouble here to satisfy the most swinishly stupid appetite," Wantage prophesied, swinging the bad side of his face toward the walls of growth about them. "It would make most sense if we stopped yapping and saved our swords for someone else's stomachs."

Reluctantly, they agreed with him.

Marapper brushed at his short cloak, scowling thoughtfully; it was bloodied at the hem.

"We shall sleep now," he said. "We will break into the first convenient room and use that for camp. This must be our routine every sleep: we cannot remain in the corridors —the position is too exposed. In a compartment we can post guards and sleep safe."

"Would we not be better advised to move further from Quarters before we sleep?" Complain asked.

"Whatever I advise *is* the best advice," Marapper said. "Do you think any one of those supine mothers' sons back there is going to risk his scabby neck by entering an unknown stretch of ponics, with all its possibilities for ambush? Just to save my breath answering these inane suggestions, you'd better all get one thing perfectly clear—you are doing what I tell you to do. That's what being united means, and if we aren't united we aren't anything. Hold firm to that idea and we'll survive. Clear enough? Roy? Ern? Wantage? Fermour?"

The priest looked into their set faces as if he were holding an identification parade. They hooded their eyes from his gaze, like a quartet of drowsy vultures.

"We've agreed to all that once already," Fermour said impatiently. "What more do you want us to do, kiss your boots?"

Although all were in some measure in agreement with him, the other three growled angrily at Fermour, he being a somewhat safer target for growls than the priest.

"You can kiss my boots only when you've earned that privilege," Marapper said. "But there is something else I want you to do. I want you to obey me implicitly, but I also require you to swear you will not turn on one another. I'm not asking you to trust each other, or anything stupid like that. I'm not asking for any breaches of the canons of the Teaching—if we're to make the Long Journey, we're making it Orthodox. But we cannot afford constant quareling and fighting; your easy times in Quarters are over.

"Some of the dangers we may meet, we know about—mutants, outsiders, other tribes, and finally the terrible people of Forwards themselves. But have no doubt that there will also be dangers of which we know nothing. When you feel spite for one of your fellows, nurse that bright spark for the unknown: it will be needed."

He looked searchingly at them again.

"Swear to it," he commanded.

"That's all very well," Wantage grumbled. "Of course I agree, but it obviously means sacrificing—well, our own characters. If we do that, it's up to you to do the same sort of thing, Marapper, and give up all these speeches. Just tell us what you want us to do and we'll do it without holding an oration over it."

"Fair enough," said Fermour quickly, before fresh argument could break out. "For hem sake let's swear and then get some sleep."

They agreed to forego the privilege of private quarrels, and pressed slowly into the ponic fringes, the priest leading, fishing out an enormous bundle of magnetic keys. Some yards on, they came to the first door. They halted, and the priest began to try his keys one by one on to the shallow impression of the lock.

Complain, meanwhile, pushed on a little further and called back to them after a minute.

"There's a door here which has been broken into," he said. "Another tribe has evidently passed this way at some time. It would save us trouble if we went in here."

They moved up to him, pressing back the rattling canes. The door stood open only a finger's breadth, and they eyed it with some apprehension. Every door presented a challenge, an entry to the unknown; all knew of tales of death leaping from behind these silent doors, and the fear had been ingrained in them since childhood.

Drawing his dazer, Roffery lifted his foot and kicked out. The door swung open. Within, the briefest of scuttles was heard, and then dead silence. The room was evidently large, but dark, its sources of illumination having been broken—how long ago? Had there been light within, the ponics would have forced the door in their own remorseless way, satisfying their unending thirst for light, but they had even less use than man for the corners of darkness.

"Only rats in there," Complain said, a little breathlessly. "Go on in, Roffery. What are you waiting for?"

For answer, Roffery took a torch from his pack and shone it ahead. He moved forward, the others crowding after him.

It was a big room as rooms went, eight paces by five; it was empty. The nervous eye of Roffery's torch flicked sharply over the usual grille in the ceiling, blank walls and a floor piled with wreckage. Chairs, and desks, their drawers flung aside, their paraphernalia scattered, had been savagely attacked with a hatchet. Light-weight steel cabinets were dented, and lay face down in the dust. The five men stood suspiciously on the threshold, wondering dimly how long ago the havoc had been wrought, feeling perhaps a memory of that savagery still in the air, for savagery—unlike virtue—endures long after its originators have perished.

"We can sleep here," Marapper said shortly. "Roy, have a look through that door over there."

The door at the far side of the room was half open. Skirting a broken desk, Complain pushed at the jamb; a small lavatory was revealed, the china bowl broken, piping torn away. A path of ancient rust ran down the wall, but the water had long ceased to flow. As Complain looked, a shaggy white rat sped from the wreckage past him with a drop-sided scamper; Fermour kicked at it and missed, and it vanished into the ponic tangle of the corridor.

"This will do," Marapper repeated. "We will eat and then you will draw lots for guard duty."

They ate frugally from the supplies in their packs, wrangling over the meal as to whether or not a guard was necessary. Since Complain and Fermour held it was necessary and Roffery and Wantage held it was not, the sides were equally balanced, and the priest did not find himself bound to join the disagreement. He ate in silence, wiped his hands delicately on a rag, and then said, from a still full mouth, "Roffery, you will guard first, then Wantage, so that you two will have the earliest opportunity of proving yourselves right. Next sleep, Fermour and Complain will guard."

"You said we should draw lots," Wantage said angrily.

"I changed my mind."

He said it so bluntly that Roffery instinctively abandoned that line of attack and remarked, "You, I suppose, father, never guard?"

Marapper spread his hands and edged a look of child-like innocence on to his face. "My dear friends, your priest guards you all the time, awake or asleep."

Rapidly, he pulled a round object from under his cloak and continued, changing the subject, "With this instrument, which I had the forethought to relieve Zilliac of, we can scientifically regulate our spells of guard so that no man does more than another. You see that it has on this side a circle of numbers and three hands or pointers. It is called a watch, so called after a period of guard, which is—as you know—also a watch. The Giants made it for this purpose, which shows that they too had Outsiders and madmen to deal with."

Complain, Fermour and Wantage inspected the watch with interest; Roffery, who had handled such things in his job as valuer, sat back superciliously. The priest retrieved his possession and began to turn a small stud on its side.

"I do this to make it work," he explained grandly. "Of the three pointers, the little one goes very rapidly; that we can disregard. The two big ones go at different speeds, but we need only bother with the slower one. You see it is now touching the figure eight. Ern, you will stay awake until it touches the figure nine; then you will rouse Wantage. Wantage, when the pointer points to ten, you will rouse us all, and we will begin our journey. Clear?"

"Where are we going?" Wantage inquired sullenly.

"We will go into all that when we have slept," Marapper said, in a tone of finality. "Sleep comes first. Wake me if you hear anybody moving outside—and don't wake me for false alarms. I am apt to be irritable if my dreams are disturbed."

He rolled over into a corner, kicked a shattered office stool away and composed himself for sleep. Without much hesitation, the others did likewise, except Roffery, who watched them unlovingly.

They were all lying on the floor when Wantage spoke hesitantly. "Father, Father Marapper," he called, with a note of pleading in his voice. "Will you not give us a prayer for the safety of our skins?"

"I'm too tired to intercede for anyone's skin," Marapper replied.

"A short prayer, father."

"As you wish. Children, expansion to our egos, let us pray." He commenced to pray as he lay hunched on the dirty floor, his words coming indifferently at first, and then gaining power as he drew interest from his train of thought.

"O Consciousness, we gathered here are doubly unworthy to be thy vessels, for we know we have imperfections and do not seek to purge them as we ought to do. We are a poor lot, in a poor way of life; yet as we contain thee there is hope for us. O Consciousness, direct particularly these five of the poor vessels here, for there is more hope for us than for those we left behind, and therefore there is more room for thee in us. We know that when thou art not here there is only the adversary, Subconscious, in us; make our thoughts to swim solely in thee. Make our hands quicker, our arms stronger, our eyes sharper, and our tempers fiercer: that we may overcome and kill all who oppose us. May we smite and sunder them! May we scatter their entrails through the length of the ship! So that we come in the end to a position of power, in full possession of thee, and in thy full possession. And may thy spark breathe in us until that last dread moment when the adversary claims us, and we too take the Long Journey."

As he had intoned, the priest had risen to his knees and stretched his hands above his head. Now he, with all the others copying the movement, drew his outstretched right index finger symbolically, ritualistically, across his throat.

"Now shut up, the lot of you," he said, in his normal tone, and settled again in his corner.

Complain lay with his back to a wall and his head on his pack; he slept usually like an animal, lightly, and with no dozing stages between sleep and waking. But in these strange surroundings he lay for some while with his eyes half-shut, trying to think. He thought only in generalized pictures: Gwenny's empty bunk; Marapper standing triumphant over Zilliac; Meller, with the jumping animal growing under his fingers; a greasy broth bubbling out Ozbert Bergass's life; the tensed muscles on Wantage's neck, ready to twitch his head away from prying eyes; the Guard, Twemmer, tumbling tiredly into Marapper's arms. And behind the pictures lay the significant fact that they concerned only what had passed, and that for what was to come he could find no pictures, for he was following into unknown realms: he was moving into the other darkness his mother had spoken of and feared.

He drew no conclusions, wasted no time in worry; indeed, he felt a kind of hope, for, as a village saying had it, the devil you don't know may conquer the one you do.

He could see, before he slept, the desolate room lit by the light percolating from the corridor and, through the outer door, a section of the everlasting tangle. In the changeless, draughtless heat, the ponics rustled ceaselessly;

65

occasionally, a click sounded near at hand as a seed was flicked into the room. The plants grew so rapidly that, when Complain woke, the younger ones would be inches taller and the older ones wilting against the restriction of the bulkheads; then, choking and choked would alike be nipped by the next dark. But he failed to see in this ceaseless jostling a parallel with the human lives about him.

II

"You snore, priest," Roffery said pleasantly, as they ate together at the beginning of the next wake.

The relationship between them had subtly changed, as if some occult power had been active during the sleep. The feeling that they were five rivals snatched almost casually from Quarters had vanished; they were still rivals, in the sense that all men were rivals, but now there was a mute acknowledgement of union against the forces about them. The period of watch had undoubtedly been good for Roffery's soul, and he seemed almost submissive. Of the five of them, Wantage alone appeared to be in no way altered. His character had been eroded by constant loneliness and mortification, as the flow of water wears away a wooden post, and he no longer had anything in him amenable to change; he could only be broken or killed.

"We must move as far as possible this wake," Marapper said. "The coming sleep-wake is a dark, as you know, and it may not be advisable to travel then, when our torches will give us away to any watchers. Before we go, however, I will condescend to tell you something of our plans; and for that it is necessary to say something about the ship."

He looked around at them, grinning and eating extravagantly as he spoke.

"And the first point is, that we are in a ship. All agreed there?"

His gaze forced some sort of a reply from each of them; an "Of course" from Fermour; an impatient grunt from Wantage, as if he found the question irrelevant; an airy wave of the hand, meaningless, from Roffery; and from Complain "No".

To the latter, Marapper immediately turned his full attention.

"Then you'd better understand quickly, Roy," he said. "Firstly, the proofs. Listen hard—I feel strongly on this question, and a show of determined stupidity might make me regrettably angry."

He walked around the shattered furniture as he spoke, very emphatic and solid, his face heavy with seriousness.

"Now, Roy—the great thing is, that not being in a ship is vastly different from being in it. You know—we all know—only what being in one is like; it is that which makes us think there is only ship. But there are many places which are *not* ship—huge places, many of them. . . . This I know because I have seen records left by the Giants. The ship was made by the Giants, for their own purposes which are—as yet—hidden from us."

"I've heard this argument in Quarters," Complain said unhappily. "Suppose I believe all you say, Marapper. What then? Ship or world, what's the difference?"

"You don't see. Look!" Savagely, the priest leaned forward and snatched a handful of ponic leaves, waving them before Complain's face.

"These are *natural*, something grown," he said.

He burst into the rear room, giving the broken china bowl a resounding kick.

"That is *made*, artificial," he said. "Now do you see? The ship is an artificial thing. The world is natural. We are natural beings, and our rightful home is not here. The whole ship is made by the Giants."

"But even if it is so—" Complain began.

"It *is* so! It *is* so! The proof is around you all the time—corridors, walls, rooms, all artificial—but you are so used to it, you can't see it is proof."

"Never mind if he can't see it," Fermour told the priest. "What does it matter?"

"I can see it," Complain said angrily. "I just can't accept it."

"Well, sit there and be quiet and chew it over, and meanwhile we'll go on," Marapper said. "I have read books, and I know the truth. The Giants built the ship for a purpose; somewhere, that purpose has been lost, and the Giants themselves have died. Only the ship is left."

He stopped pacing and leaned against a wall, resting his forehead against it. When he spoke again, it was almost to himself.

"Only the ship is left. Only the ship and, trapped in it, all the tribes of man. There was a catastrophe: something went terribly awry somewhere, and we have been left to a terrible fate. It is a judgment passed on us for some awful, unguessable sin committed by our forefathers."

"To the hull with all this chatter," Wantage said angrily. "Why don't you try and forget you're a priest, Marapper? Let's hear how this has any bearing on what we are going to do."

"It has every bearing," Marapper said, sticking his hands sulkily into his pockets, and then withdrawing one to pick at a tooth. "Of course, I'm only really interested in the theological aspects of the question. But the point as far as you are concerned is that the ship, by definition, has come *from* somewhere and is going *to* somewhere. These somewheres are more important than the ship; they are where we should be. They are natural places.

"All that is no mystery, except to fools; the mystery is, why is there this conspiracy to keep us from knowing where we are? What is going on here behind our backs?"

"Something's gone wrong somewhere," Wantage answered eagerly. "It's what I've always said: something's gone wrong."

"Well, cease to say it in my presence," the priest snapped. It seemed to him that his position of authority was weakened by allowing others to agree with him. "There is a conspiracy. We have been plotted against. The driver or captain of this ship is concealed somewhere, and we are forging on under his direction, knowing neither the journey nor the destination. He is a madman who keeps himself shut away while we are all punished for this sin our forefathers committed."

This sounded to Complain both horrifying and unlikely, although no more unlikely than the whole idea of being in a moving vessel. Presumably accepting one premise meant accepting the other, so he said nothing. A vast feeling of insecurity engulfed him. Looking around unobtrusively at the others present, he detected no particular signs that they agreed enthusiastically with the priest: Fermour was

69

smiling rather derisively, Wantage's face presented its usual meaningless glare of disagreement, and Roffery was tugging impatiently at his moustache.

"Now here is my plan," said the priest, "and unfortunately I need your co-operation to help carry it out. We are going to find this captain, hunt him down wherever he may be hiding. He is well concealed, but no locked doors shall save him from us. When we reach him, we kill him—and we shall be in control of the ship!"

"And what do we do with it when we've got it?" Fermour asked, in a tone carefully designed to counteract Marapper's runaway enthusiasm.

The priest looked blank only for a moment.

"We will find a destination for it," he said. "You leave that sort of detail to me."

"Where exactly do we discover this captain fellow?" Roffery inquired.

For answer, the priest flung back his cloak and felt inside his tunic; with a flourish, he produced the book Complain had already seen. He waved the title under their eyes, but this meant little except to Roffery, the only fluent reader among them. To the others, the syllables were intelligible, but they were unable to master unfamiliar words without long effort. Pulling the book out of their reach again, Marapper explained condescendingly that it was called "Manual of Electrical Circuits of Starship". He also explained—for this explanation gave him an opportunity for boasting—how the book had come into his possession. It had been lying in the store in which Zilliac's Guards had found the cache of dyes, and had been confiscated and added to a pile of goods awaiting inspection in the Lieutenancy. There Marapper had seen it and, recognizing its value instantly, had pocketed it for his own use. Unfortunately, one of the Guards had caught him, and the silence of this loyal man could only be bought by the promise that he should go with Marapper and find power for himself.

"That being the Guard, presumably, which Meller despatched outside my room?" Complain asked.

"The same," said the priest, automatically making the token of mourning. "When he had thought over the

70

scheme he very likely decided he could get most profit from it by revealing it all to Zilliac."

"Who knows he was wrong about that?" Roffery commented sardonically.

Ignoring this thrust, the priest spread his book open and thumped a diagram.

"Here is the whole key to my campaign," he said impressively. "This is a plan of the entire ship."

To his annoyance, he had to interrupt his speech at once to explain what a plan was, the concept being entirely new to them. This was Complain's turn to be superior to Wantage, for while he quickly grasped the idea, the latter could not be made to comprehend the two-dimensional representation of a three-dimensional object as large as the ship; analogies with Meller's sub-life-size paintings did not help him, and eventually they had to leave the matter as assumed, just as Complain now had to "assume" they were in a ship without anything he could regard as rational evidence.

"Nobody has ever had a plan of the complete ship before," Marapper told them. "It was fortunate it fell into my hands. Ozbert Bergass knew as much about the layout as anyone, but he was only really familiar with the Stern-stairs region and a part of Deadways."

The plan showed the ship to be shaped like an egg, elongated so that the middle was cylindrical, both ends coming to a blunted point. The whole was composed o eighty-four decks, which showed a circular cross-section when the ship was opened through its width, each being proportioned like a coin. Most of the decks (all but a few at each end) consisted of three concentric levels, upper, middle and lower; these had corridors in them, connected by lifts and companion ways; around these corridors were ranged the apartments. Sometimes the apartments were just a nest of offices, sometimes they were so big they filled a whole level. All decks were connected together by one large corridor running right through the longitudinal axis of the ship: the Main Corridor. But there were also subsidiary connections between the circular corridors of one deck and those of the decks on either side.

One end of the ship was clearly labeled "Stern". At the

71

other end was a small blister labeled "Control"; Marapper planted his finger on it.

"This is where we shall find the captain," he said. "Whoever is here has power over the ship. We are going there."

"This plan makes it as easy as signing off a log," Roffery declared, rubbing his hands. "All we've got to do is strike along the Main Corridor. Perhaps we weren't such fools to join you after all."

"It won't be as easy as that," Complain said. "You've spent all your wakes comfortably in Quarters, you don't know what conditions are like. Main Corridor is fairly well known to hunters, but it does not go anywhere, as a proper corridor should."

"Despite your naïve way of putting things, you are correct, Roy," the priest agreed. "But I have found in this book the reason why it does not go anywhere. All along the Main Corridor, between each deck, were emergency doors. Each circle of deck was built to be more or less self-sufficient, so that in time of crisis it could be cut off on its own and its inhabitants still survive."

He flipped through pages of complex diagrams.

"Even I cannot pretend to understand all this, but it is clear that there was an emergency, a fire or something, and the doors of the Main Corridor have remained closed ever since."

"That's why—ponics apart—it's so difficult to get anywhere," Fermour added. "All you can do is go round in circles. What we have to do is find the subsidiary connections which are still open, and advance through them. It means constant detouring instead of just moving straightforwardly."

"I'll give you the instructions, thanks," said the priest, shortly. "Since you all seem to be so clever, we'll be on our way without further ado. Get that pack on your back, Fermour, and get moving!"

They shuffled obediently to their feet. Outside the compartment, Deadways waited; it was not inviting.

"We'll have to go through Forwards area to reach control," Complain said.

"Frightened?" Wantage sneered.

"Yes, Slotface, I am."

Wantage turned away, resentful but too preoccupied to quarrel, even over the use of his nickname.

They moved through the tangles in silence. Progress was slow and exhausting. A solitary hunter on his own ground might creep among ponics without cutting them, by keeping close to the wall. Moving in file, they found this method less attractive, since branches were apt to whip back and catch the man behind. This could be avoided by spacing themselves out, but by common consent they were keeping as close together as possible, it being uncomfortable on the nerves to be exposed either at the front or the rear of the little party. There was, too, another objection to walking by the walls: here the chitinous ponic seeds lay thickest, where they had dropped after being shot against this barrier, and they crunched noisily as they were trodden on. To Complain's experienced hunter's eye, their plenitude was a sign that there were few wild animals in the area, the seeds being delicacies to dog and pig alike.

No diminution in the plague of flies was noticeable. They whined endlessly about the traveler's ears. As Roffery in the lead swung his hatchet at the ponics, he wielded it frequently around his head, in a dangerous attempt to rid himself of this irritation.

When they came to the first subsidiary connection between decks, it was clearly enough marked. It stood in a short side corridor and consisted of two single metal doors a yard apart, each capable of closing off the corridor, although now blocked open with the ubiquitous green growth. Before one, the words "Deck 61" were stencilled and, after the other, "Deck 60". Marapper grunted in satisfaction at this, but was too hot to make further comment. Complain on his hunting had come across such connections before, and seen similar inscriptions, but they had meant nothing; now he tried to integrate the previous knowledge into the conception of a moving ship: but as yet the idea was too new to be acceptable.

On Deck 60 they met other men.

Fermour was now in the lead, hacking his way stoically ahead, when they came level with an open door. Open doors always signified danger, but since they had to pass the thresholds, they grouped together and passed *en bloc.*

73

So far, these distractions had been uneventful. This time, they were confronted by an old woman.

She lay naked on the floor, a tethered sheep sleeping by her side. She was looking away from them, so that they had an excellent view of her left ear. This, by the humor of some strange disease, had swollen up like a sponge, standing out from her skull and pushing back a mat of rancid gray hair. The tissue of this abnormality was a startling pink, in contrast to the pallor of her face.

Slowly she swung her head around, fixing them with two owl eyes. Without changing her expression, she began to scream hollowly. Even as she did so, Complain noticed that her right ear was normal.

The sheep woke and ran away to the end of its rope, blaring and coughing in alarm.

Before the party of five could move away, the noise had summoned two men from a rear compartment. They came and stood defensively behind the screaming woman.

"They'll do us no harm!" said Fermour with relief.

That was immediately obvious. Both men were old. One bent almost double with the promise of the Long Journey he would shortly take, the other painfully thin and lacking an arm, which had evidently been parted from him in some ancient knife fight.

"We ought to kill them," Wantage said, one half of his face suddenly agleam. "Especially that monstrosity of a hag there."

At these words, the woman stopped screaming and said rapidly, "Expansion to your separate egos, plague on your eyes, touch us and the curse that is on us will be on you."

"Expansion to your ear, madam," said Marapper sulkily. "Come on, heroes, we don't need to linger here. Let's move before somebody rougher comes to investigate her crazy screaming."

They turned back into the tangles. The three in the room watched them go without stirring. They might have been the last remnants of a Deadways tribe; more likely, they were fugitives, eking out a slender existence in the wilds.

From then on, the travellers found signs of other mutants and hermits. The ponics were frequently trampled, progress being consequently easier; but the mental strain of keeping watch on all sides was greater, although they were never actually challenged.

The next subsidiary connection between decks that they came to was closed, and the steel door, fitting closely into its sockets, resisted their united attempt at opening it.

"There must obviously *be* a way to open it," Roffery said angrily.

"Tell the priest to look it up in his damned book," Wantage replied. "For me, I'm sitting down here and having something to eat."

Marapper was all for pressing on, but the others agreed with Wantage, and they made a meal in silence.

"What happens if we come on a deck where all the doors are like that?" Complain wanted to know.

"That won't happen," Marapper said firmly. "Otherwise we should never have heard of Forwards at all. There obviously is a route—probably more than one—left open to those parts. We just have to move to another level and try there."

Finally they found their way into Deck 59 and then, with encouraging rapidity, into 58. By that time, it was growing late: a dark sleep-wake was almost upon them. Again they grew uneasy.

"Have any of you noticed anything?" Complain asked abruptly. He was now leading the procession again, and liberally splashed with sweat and miltex. "The ponics are changing type."

It was true. The springy stems grew more fleshy and less resilient. The leafage seemed reduced, and there were more of the waxy green flowers in evidence. Under foot there was a change too. Generally, the grit was firm, intersected by a highly organized root system which drained every available drop of moisture. Now the walking was softer, the soil dark and moist.

The further they went, the more pronounced these tendencies became. Soon, they were splashing through mud. They passed a tomato plant, and another fruit-bearer they could not identify, and several other types of growth straggling among the evidently weakened ponics. This change, being unfamiliar, worried them. All the same, Marapper called a halt, since if they did not shortly find a place to rest they would be overtaken by darkness.

They pushed into a side room which someone had already broken into. It was piled high with rolls of heavy material, which seemed to be covered by an intricate pattern. The probing beam of Fermour's torch dislodged a swarm of moths. With a thick, buttery sound, they rose from the fabric, leaving it patternless, but sagging with deep-chewed holes. About the room they whirled, or past the men into the corridor. It was like walking into a dust storm.

Complain dodged as a large moth bore toward his face. For the softest moment he had an odd sensation that he was to recall later: although the moth flew by his ear, he had an hallucinatory idea it had plunged straight on into his head; he seemed to feel it big in his very mind; then it was gone.

"We shouldn't get much sleep here," he said distastefully, and led on down the marshy corridor.

Through the next door that opened to them, they found an ideal place to pitch camp. This was a machine shop of some kind, a large chamber filled with benches and lathes and other gadgets in which they had no interest. A tap supplied them with an unsteady flow of water which, once turned on, they could not turn off; it trickled steadily down the sink, to the vast reclamation processes functioning somewhere below the deck on which they stood. Wearily, they washed and drank and ate some of their provisions. As they were finsihing, the dark came on, the natural dark which arrived one sleep-wake in four.

No prayers were requested, and the priest volunteered none. He was tired and, too, he was occupied with a thought which dogged the others. They had travelled only three decks: a long spell of walking lay between them and Control. For the first time, Marapper was realizing that, whatever assistance his chart gave them, it did not show the true magnitude of the ship.

The precious watch was handed to Complain, who would wake Fermour when the large hand had made its full circuit. Enviously, the hunter watched the others sprawl under benches and drift to sleep. He remained doggedly standing for some while, but eventually fatigue forced him to sit. His mind ranged actively over a hundred questions and then it, too, grew weary. He sat propped with his back to a bench, staring at the closed door; through a circle of frosted glass inset in the door, a dim pilot light glowed in the corridor outside. This circle apparently grew larger and larger before him, swimming, rotating, and Complain closed his eyes to it.

He woke again with a start, full of apprehension. The door now stood wide open. In the corridor, the ponics, most of their light source gone, were dying rapidly. Their tops had buckled, and they huddled against each other like a file of broken-backed old men kneeling beneath a blanket. Ern Roffery was not in the room.

Pulling out his dazer, Complain got up and went to listen at the doorway. It seemed highly unlikely that anything could have abducted Roffery: there would have been a scuffle which would have aroused the others. Therefore he had gone voluntarily. But why? Had he heard something in the corridor?

Certainly there was a distant sound, as throaty as the noise of running water. The longer Complain listened, the louder it seemed. With a glance back at his three sleeping companions, Complain slipped out to trace the sound. This alarming course seemed to him slightly preferable to having to wake the priest and explain that he had dozed.

Once in the corridor, he cautiously flashed a torch and picked up Roffery's footprints in the sludge, pointing toward the unexplored end of this level. Walking was easier now that the tangle was sagging in the center, away from the walls. Complain moved slowly, not showing a light and keeping his dazer ready for action.

At a corridor junction he paused, pressing on again with the liquid sound to guide him. The ponics petered out and were replaced by deck, washed bare of soil by a stream of water. Complain allowed it to flow against his boots, walking carefully so as not to splash. This was new in his experience. A light burned ahead. As he neared it, he saw it was shinning in a vast chamber beyond two plate-glass doors. When he got to the doors, he stopped; on them was painted a notice, "Swimming Pool", which he pronounced to himself without understanding. Peering through the doors, he saw a shallow flight of steps going up, with pillars at the top of them; behind one pillar stood the shadowy figure of a man.

77

Complain ducked instantly away. When the man did not move, Complain concluded he had not been seen and looked again, to observe that the figure was staring away from him. It looked like Roffery. Cautiously, Complain opened one of the glass doors; a wave washed against his legs. Water was pouring down the steps, converting them into a waterfall.

"Roffery!" Complain called, keeping his dazer on the figure. The three syllables he uttered were seized and blown to to an enormous booming, which moaned several times around the cavern of darkness before dying. They washed away with them everything but a hollow stillness, which now sounded loud in its own right.

"Who's there?" challenged the figure, in a whisper.

Through his fright, Complain managed to whisper his name back. The man beckoned him. Complain stood motionless where he was and then, at another summons, slowly climbed the steps. As he came level with the other he saw with certainty that it was the valuer.

Roffery grabbed his arm.

"You were sleeping, you fool!" he hissed in Complain's ear.

Complain nodded mutely, afraid to rouse the echoes again.

Roffery dismissed that subject. Without speaking, he pointed ahead. Complain looked where he was bid, puzzled by the expression on the other's face.

Neither of them had ever been in such a large space. Lit only by one bulb which burned to their left, it seemed to stretch for ever into the darkness. The floor was a sheet of water on which ripples slid slowly outwards. Under the light, the water shone like metal. Breaking this smooth expanse at the far end, was an erection of tubes which suspended planks over the water at various heights, and to either side were rows of huts, barely distinguishable for shadow.

"It's beautiful!" Roffery breathed. "Isn't it beautiful?"

Complain stared at him in astonishment. The word "beautiful" had an erotic meaning, and was applied only to particularly desirable women. Yet he saw that there was a sight here which needed a special choice of vocabulary. His eyes switched back to the water: it was entirely outside their experience. Previously, water had meant only a dribble from a tap, a spurt from a hose, or the puddle at the bottom of a utensil. He wondered vaguely what this amount could be for. Sinister, uncanny, the view had another quality also, and it was this Roffery was trying to describe.

"I know what it is," Roffery murmured. He was staring at the water as if hypnotized, the lines of his face so relaxed that his appearance was changed. "I've read about this in old books brought me for valuing, dreamy rubbish with no meaning till now." He paused, and then quoted, " 'Then dead men rise up never, and even the longest river winds somewhere safe to sea.' This is the sea, Complain, and we've stumbled on the sea. I've often read about it. For me, it proves Marapper's wrong about our being in a ship; we're in an underground city."

This meant little to Complain; he was not interested in labels of things. What struck him was to perceive something he had worried over till now: why Roffery had left his sinecure to come on the priest's hazardous expedition. He saw now that the other had a reason akin to Complain's own: a longing for what he had never known and could put no name to. Instead of feeling any bond with Roffery about this, Complain decided he must more than ever beware of the man, for if they had similar objectives, they were the more likely to clash.

"Why did you come up here?" he asked, still keeping his voice low to avoid the greedy echoes.

"While you were snoring, I woke and heard voices in the corridor," Roffery said. "Through the frosted glass I saw two men pass—only they were too big for men. They were Giants!"

"Giants! The Giants are dead, Roffery."

"These were Giants, I tell you, fully seven feet high. I saw their heads go by the window." In his eyes, Complain read the uneasy fascinated memory of them.

"And you followed them?" Complain asked.

"Yes. I followed them into here."

At this Complain scanned the shadows anew.

"Are you trying to frighten me?" he asked.

"I didn't ask you to come after me. Why be afraid of

the Giants? Dazers'll dispatch a man however long he measures."

"We'd better be getting back, Roffery. There's no point in standing here; besides, I'm meant to be on watch."

"You might have thought of that before," Roffery said. "We'll bring Marapper here later to see what he makes of the sea. Before we go, I'm just going to look at something over there. That was where the Giants disappeared to."

He indicated a point hear at hand, beside the huts, where a square of curb was raised some four inches above the waterline. The solitary light which overhung it looked almost as if it had been temporarily erected by the Giants to cast a glow there.

"There's a trapdoor inside that curb," Roffery whispered. "The Giants went down there and closed it after them. Come on, we'll go and look."

This seemed to Complain foolhardy in the extreme, but not venturing to criticize he merely said, "Well, keep to the shadows in case anyone else comes in here."

"The sea's only ankle deep," Roffery said. "Don't be afraid of getting your feet wet."

He seemed strangely excited, like a child, with a child's innocent disregard of danger. Nevertheless, he obeyed Complain's injunction and kept to the cover of the walls. They paddled one behind the other on the fringes of the sea, weapons ready, and so came to the trapdoor, dry behind its protecting curb.

Pulling a face at his companion, Roffery stooped down and slowly lifted the hatch. Gentle light flowed out from the opening. They saw an iron ladder leading down into a pit full of piping. Two overalled figures were working silently at the bottom of the pit, doing something with a stopcock. As soon as the hatch was opened, they must have heard the magnified hiss of running water in the chamber above them, for they looked up and fixed Roffery and Complain with an astonished gaze. Undoubtedly they were Giants: they were monstrously tall and thick, and their faces were dark.

Roffery's nerve deserted him at once. He dropped the hatch down with a slam, and turned and ran. Complain splashed close behind. Next second, Roffery disappeared, swallowed by the water. Complain stopped abruptly. He could see at his feet, below the surface of the sea, the lip of a dark well. Roffery bobbed up again, a yard from him, in the well, striking the water and hollering. In the darkness, his face was apoplectic. Complain stretched out a hand to him, leaning forward as far as he dared. The other struggled to grasp it, floundered, and sank again in a welter of bubbles. The hubbub in the vast cavern was deafening.

When he appeared again, Roffery had found a footing, and stood chest-deep in the water. Panting and cursing, he pushed forward to seize Complain's hand. At the same time, the trapdoor was flung open. The Giants were coming out. As Complain whirled around, he was aware of Roffery pausing to grab at his dazer, which would not be affected by damp, and of a pattern of crazy light rippling on the ceiling high above them. Without aiming, he fired his own dazer at a head emerging from the vault. The daze went wide. The Giant launched himself at them, and Complain dropped his weapon in panic. As he bent to scrabble for it in the shallow water, Roffery fired over his stooped back. His aim was better than Complain's.

The Giant staggered and fell with a splash which roused the echoes. As far as Complain could remember afterwards, the monster had been unarmed.

The second Giant was armed. Seeing the fate of his companion, he crouched on the ladder, shielded by the curb, and fired twice. The first shot got Roffery in the face. Without a sound, he slipped beneath the water.

Complain dived flat, kicking up spray, but he was an easy target for the marksman. His temple stopped the second shot. Limply, he slumped into the water, face down.

III

A t the center of the human mechanism is the will to live. So delicate is this mechanism that some untoward experience early in life can implant within it the opposite impulse, the will to die. The two drives lie quietly side by side, and a man may pass his days unaware of their existence; then some violent crisis faces him and, stripped momentarily of his superficial characteristics, his fatal duality is bare before him; and he must stop to wrestle with the flaw within before he can fight the external foe.

It was so with Complain. After oblivion, came only the frantic desire to retreat back into unconsciousness. But unconsciousness had rejected him, and the prompting soon came that he must struggle to escape from whatever predicament he was in. Then again, he felt no urge to escape, only the desire to submit and fade back into nothing. Insistently, however, life returned.

He opened his eyes for a moment. He was lying on his back in semi-darkness. A grey roof of some kind was only a few inches above his head. It was flowing backwards, or he was moving forwards: he could not tell which, and closed his eyes again. A steady increase in bodily sensation told him his ankles and wrists were lashed together.

His head ached, and a foul smell pervaded his lungs, making breathing an agony. He realized the Giant had shot him with some kind of gas pellet, instantly effective but ultimately, perhaps, innocuous.

Again he opened his eyes. The roof still seemed to be traveling backwards, but he felt a steady tremor through his body, telling him he was on some kind of moving vehicle. Even as he looked, the movement stopped. He saw a Giant loom beside him, presumably the one who had shot and captured him. Through half-closed eyes,

Complain saw the immense creature was on hands and knees in this low place. Feeling on the roof, he now knuckled some kind of switch, and a section of the roof swung upwards.

From above came light and the sound of deep voices. Complain was later to recognize this slow, heavy tone as the typical manner of speech of the Giants. Before he had time to prepare for it, he was seized and dragged off the conveyance and passed effortlessly up through the opening. Large hands took hold of him and dumped him not ungently against the wall of the room.

"He's coming around," a voice commented, in a curious accent Complain hardly understood.

This observation worried him a great deal; partly because he thought he had given no indication he was recovering, partly because the remark suggested they might now gas him again.

Another body was handed up through the opening, the original Giant climbing up after it. A muttered conversation took place. From the little Complain could hear, he gathered that the body was that of the Giant Roffery had killed. The other Giant was explaining what had happened. It soon became apparent he was talking to two others, although Complain, from where he lay, could see only wall.

He slumped back into a mindless state, trying to breathe the dirty odor out of his lungs.

Another Giant entered from a side room and began talking in a peremptory tone suggestive of command. Complain's captor began to explain the situation over again, but was cut short.

"Did you deal with the flooding?" the newcomer asked.

"Yes, Mr. Curtis. We fitted a new stopcock in place of the rusted one and switched the water off. We also unblocked the drainage and fitted a length of new piping there. We were just finishing off when Sleepy Head here turned up. The pool should be empty by now."

"All right, Randall," the peremptory voice addressed as Curtis said. "Now tell me why you started chasing these two dizzies."

There was a pause, then the other said apologetically, "We didn't know how many of them there were. For all

83

we knew, we might have been ambushed in the inspection pit. We had to get out and see. I suppose that if we had realized to begin with that there were only two of them, we should have let them go without interfering."

The Giants spoke so sluggishly that Complain had no difficulty in understanding most of this, despite the strange accent. Of its general intention he could make nothing. He was almost beginning to lose interest when he became the topic of conversation, and his interest abruptly revived.

"You realize you are in trouble, Randall," the stern voice said. "You know the rules: it means a court martial. You will have difficulty in proving self-defense, to my mind. Especially as the other dizzy was drowned."

"He wasn't drowned. I fished him out of the water and put him on the closed inspection hatch to recover in his own time." Randall sounded surly.

"Leaving that question aside—what do you propose doing with this specimen you've brought here?" Curtis demanded.

"He'd have drowned if I had left him there."

"Why bring him here?"

"Couldn't we just knock him off and have done with it, Mr. Curtis?" One of the Giants spoke for the first time since Curtis had come in.

"Out of the question. Criminal breach of the rules. Besides, could you kill a man in cold blood?"

"He's only a dizzy, Mr. Curtis," spoken defensively.

"Could he go for rehabilitation?"Randall suggested, in the tone of one dazzled by the brightness of his own idea.

"He's far too old, man! You know they only take children. What the deuce was the idea of bringing him here?"

"Well, as I say, I couldn't leave him there, and after I fished his pal out, I—well, it's pretty creepy there and—I thought I heard something. So I—nipped him to safety with me quickly."

"It's quite obvious you panicked, Randall," Curtis said. "We certainly don't want a spare dizzy here. You'll have to take him back, that's all." The voice was curt and decisive. Complain took heart from it; nothing would suit him better than to taken back. Not, he realized, that he had much fear of the Giants; now he was among them,

84

they seemed too slow and gentle for malice. Curtis's was not an attitude he understood, but it was certainly convenient.

There was some argument between the Giants as to how Complain's return should be effected. Randall's friends sided with him against the one in command, Curtis; the latter lost his temper.

"All right," he snapped, "come into the office, the lot of you, and we'll buzz through to Little Dog and get an authoritative ruling."

"Losing your nerve, Curtis?" one of the others asked, as they followed him through—with that crazy, slow-motion walk the Giants had—into the other room, slamming the door on Complain without a glance at him. Complain's immediate thought was that they were fools to leave him unguarded; he could now escape back through the hole in the floor by which he had come. This illusion burst the moment he tried to roll over. As soon as he attempted to move a muscle, it filled with a brittle ache, and the pervasive stench in his lungs seemed to turn solid. He groaned and lay back, his head against the curve of the wall.

Complain was alone only for a second after the Giants had gone. A grating noise sounded from the region of his knees. Craning his neck slightly, Complain saw a small section of the wall, a jagged patch roughly six inches square, slide out. From this hole, nightmare figures emerged.

There were five of them, bursting out at an immense rate, circling Complain, jumping him, and then reporting back like lightning to the hole. They evidently carried some sort of reassurance, for three more figures promptly whisked into view, beckoning the others behind them. They were all rats.

The five scouts wore spiked collars round their necks; they were small and lean of body; one had lost an eye, in the vacant socket of which gristle twitched sympathetically with the glances of the surviving pupil. Of the next three to appear, one was jet black and obviously the leader. He stood upright, pawing the air with little mauve hands. He wore no collar, but the upper half of his body was accoutered with an assembly of bits of metal—a ring, a button, a thimble, nails—evidently intended for armor; around his waist was a buckler with an instrument like a small sword attached. He squeaked furiously and the five scouts circuited Complain again, flashing along his leg, grinning momentarily into his eye, scrapping over his neck, slithering down his blouse.

The rat-leader's two bodyguards waited nervously, ever glancing back, flicking their whiskers. They stood on all fours, and wore only shabby little patches like cloaks over their backs.

During this activity, Complain did an amount of involuntary flinching. He was used to rats, but there was an organized quality to these that disturbed him; also, he fancied that he could manage little by the way of defense should they decide it suited their cause to gnaw his eyes out.

But the rats were on something other than a delicacy hunt. The rearguard now appeared. Panting from a hole in the wall came four more buck rats. They dragged a small cage which, under the whistled orders of the rat-leader, was pulled rapidly to a position before Complain's face, where he had every opportunity of inspecting it and inhaling the odor from it.

The animal in the cage was larger than the rats. From the fur at the top of its oval skull sprouted two long ears; its tail was merely a white scut of fluff. Complain had not seen a creature of this species before, but he recognized it from the descriptions of old hunters back in Quarters. It was a rabbit, scarce because natural prey for the rat. He looked at it with interest, and it stared nervously back at him.

As the rabbit was drawn up, the five original scout rats spread out by the inner door, keeping watch for the Giants' return. The leader-rat whisked forward to the cage; the rabbit shrank away, but was tethered by all four legs to the bars of his prison. The leader-rat ducked his head at the sword in his buckler, standing erect again with a fierce little blade fitting over his two front teeth, a tiny scythe which he twitched avidly about in the direction of the rabbit's neck.

This display of menace over, he sheathed the blade again and darted vigorously between cage and Complain's

86

face, gesticulating. Obviously, the rabbit understood what was intended. Complain stared puzzledly at it. The pupils of its eyes appeared to swell, and he flinched in his mind from a feeling of tentative discomfort. The feel remained. It soaked about his brain with the cautious advance of a puddle around cobbles. He tried to shake his head, but the eerie sensation maintained itself and strengthened. It was seeking something, witlessly, like a dying man blundering around darkened rooms, feeling for the light switch. Complain broke into a sweat, grinding his teeth as he tried mentally to repel the beastly contact. Then it found its correct port of entry.

His mind blossomed into an immense shout of interrogation.

WHY ARE——

WHO IS——

WHAT DO——

HOW CAN——

DO YOU——

CAN YOU——

WILL YOU——

Complain screamed with anguish.

Instantly, the desolating gibberish ceased, the formless inquiry died. The scout rats leaped from their posts, and they and the four driver rats spun the imprisoned rabbit around and shot the cage back into the wall. Spurring them savagely, the rat-leader followed with his guard. Next moment, the square of wall banged down behind them—only just in time, for a Giant burst into the room to find what the screaming was about.

He rolled Complain over with his foot. The latter stared up hopelessly at him, trying to speak.

Reassured, the Giant lumbered back to the other room, this time leaving open the connecting door.

"The Dizzy's got a headache," he announced.

Complain could hear their voices. They sounded to be talking at some kind of machine. But he was almost totally absorbed by the ordeal with the rats. A madman had lived for a moment within his skull! The Teaching warned him that his mind was a foul place. The holy trinity, Froyd, Yung and Bassit, had gone alone through the terrible barriers of sleep, death's brother; there they found—not nothing, as man had formerly believed—but grottoes and subterranean labyrinths full of ghouls and evil treasure, leeches, and the lusts that burn like acid. Man stood revealed to himself: a creature of infinite complexity and horror. It was the aim of the Teaching to let as much of this miasmic stuff out to the surface as possible. But supposing the Teaching had never gone far enough?

It spoke, allegorically, of conscious and subconscious. Supposing there was a real Subconscious, a being capable of taking over the mind of a man? Had the trinity been down all the slimy corridors? Was this Subconscious the madman who screamed inside him?

Then he had the answer, simple yet unbelievable. The caged creature had brought its mind into contact with his. Reviewing that fizzing questionnaire, Complain knew it had come from the animal and not some dreadful creature inside his own head. The ordeal was at once made tolerable. One can shoot rabbits.

Ignoring the how of it with true Quarters' philosophy, Complain dismissed the matter.

He lay still, resting, trying to breathe the clinging smell from his lungs, and in a short while the Giants returned.

Complain's captor, Randall, picked him up without further ado and opened the trapdoor in the floor. Their argument had evidently been settled in Curtis's favor. Randall eased himself and his burden back into the low tunnel. He put Complain on to the conveyance and, by the sound of things, climbed on himself behind his captive's head.

With a quiet word to the Giants above, he started the motor. Again the gray roof flowed overhead, punctuated by crisscrossing pipe, wire and tube.

At length they stopped. Fumbling on the roof, the Giant pressed his fingers to it, and a square opened above them. Complain was hauled out of the hole, carried a few yards, bundled through a door, and dropped. He was back in Deadways; its smell to a hunter was unmistakable. The Giant hovered over him wordlessly, a shadow in shadows, and then vanished.

The darkness of the dim sleep-wake embraced Complain like a mother's arms. He was back home, among dangers he was trained to face. He slept.

Phantom legions of rats swarmed over him, pinning him down. The rabbit came; it climbed into his head and slithered down the long warrens of his brain.

Complain woke, groaning, humiliated by the beastliness of his dream. It was still dark. The rigidity in his limbs, induced by the gas pellet, had relaxed, his lungs were clear. Carefully, he stood up.

Shielding his torch till it gave the barest whisper of light, Complain moved to the door and looked out at blackness. As far as he could see, a gulf stretched infinitely before him. He slid out, feeling along to the right, and found a row of doors. Using the light again, he found damp, bare tile underfoot. Then he knew where he was; a hollowness in his ear reinforced the certainty. The Giant had brought him back to what Roffery had called the sea.

Getting his bearings, Complain flashed the light cautiously. The sea itself had gone. He walked to the edge of the pit into which Roffery had fallen. It was empty, all but dry. Roffery had gone. The walls of the pit glinted with festoons of rust, blood-colored; in the warm air, the floor of the pit was drying rapidly.

Complain turned and walked from the chamber, minding not to wake the haggard echoes. He headed back to Marapper's camp. The ground still squelched lightly underfoot, holding its moisture. He brushed gently by the sagging muck of last season's ponics, and came to the camp door. He whistled eagerly, wondering who would be on guard: Marapper? Wantage? Fermour? Almost lovingly, he thought of them, reversing the old Quarters' adage to whisper to himself: "Better the devils you know than the ones you don't."

His signal went unanswered. Holding himself tense, he pushed into the room. It was empty. They had moved on. Complain was alone in Deadways.

Self-control snapped then; he had gone through too much. Giants, rats, rabbits, he could bear—but not the scabrous solitudes of Deadways. He rioted around the room, flinging up the splintered wood, kicking, cursing, out into the corridor, roaring, swearing, tearing a way through the vegetable mash, howling, blaspheming.

A body cannoned into him from behind. Complain sprawled in the tangle, fighting insanely to turn and tackle his assailant. A hand clamped itself unshakeably over his mouth.

"Shut up, you drab-spawned he-hag!" a voice snarled in his ear.

He ceased struggling. A light was turned on to him and three figures hunched over him.

"I—I thought I'd lost you!" he said. Suddenly he began to cry. Reaction turned him into a child again. His shoulders heaved, the tears poured down his cheeks.

Marapper smacked him efficiently across the face.

IV

They traveled. Grimly, cutting, pushing, they worked through the ponics; circumspectly, they moved through dark regions where no lights burned and no ponics grew. They passed through badly plundered areas, whose doors were broken, whose corridors were piled high with wreckage. Such life as they met was timid, eluding them where possible; but few creatures lived here—a rogue goat, a crazed hermit, a pathetic band of sub-men who fled when Wantage clapped his hands. This was Deadways, and the emptiness held unrecorded eras of silence. Quarters was left far behind the travelers, and forgotten. Even their nebulous destination was forgotten, for the present, with its ceaseless call upon their physical reserves, required all their attention.

Finding the subsidiary connections between decks was not always easy, even with the help of Marapper's plan. Lift-shafts were often blocked, levels frequently proved dead ends. But they gradually moved forward; the fifties decks were passed, then the forties, and so they came, on the eighth wake after leaving Quarters, to Deck 29.

By now, Roy Complain had begun to believe in the Ship theory. The reorientation had been insensible but thorough. To this, the intelligent rats had greatly contributed. When Complain had told his companions of his capture by the Giants, he had omitted the rat incident; something fantastic about it, he knew instinctively, would have defied his powers of description and awoken Marapper's and Wantage's derision; but he now found his thoughts turning frequently to those fearsome creatures. He saw a parallel between the lives of the rats and the human lives emphasized in their man-like conduct of ill-treating a fellow creature, the rabbit. The rats survived where they could,

91

giving no thought to the nature of their surroundings; Complain could only say the same of himself until now.

Marapper had listened to the tale of the Giants intently, commenting little. Once he said, "Then do they know where the Captain is?"

He was particularly pressing for full details of what the Giants had said to each other. He repeated the names "Curtis" and "Randall" several times, as if muttering a spell.

"Who was this little dog they went to speak to?" he asked.

"I think it was a name," Complain said. "Not a real little dog."

"A name of *what*?"

"I don't know. I tell you I was half-conscious." Indeed the more he thought, the less clear he was as to what exactly had been said. Even at the time, the episode had been sufficiently outside his normal experience to render it half incredible to him.

"Was it another Giant's name, do you think, or a thing's name?" the priest pressed, tugging at the lobe of his ear, as if to extract the facts that way.

"I don't *know*, Marapper. I can't remember. They just said they were going to talk to 'little dog'—I think."

At Marapper's insistence, the party of four inspected the hall marked "Swimming Pool", where the sea had been. It had completely dried up now. There was no sign of Roffery, which was baffling, considering that one of the Giants had said that the valuer would recover from the gas pellet as Complain had done. They searched and called, but Roffery did not appear.

"His moustache will be hanging over a mutant's bunk by now," Wantage said. "Let's get a move on!"

They could find no hatch which might have led to the Giants' room. The steel lid covering the inspection pit where Complain and Roffery had first seen the two Giants was as secure as if it had never opened. The priest shot Complain a sceptical glance, and there the matter was left. Taking Wantage's advice, they moved on.

The whole incident lowered Complain's stock considerably. Wantage, quick to seize advantage, became undisputed second-in-command. He followed Marapper, and

Fermour and Complain followed him. At least it made for peace in the ranks, and outward accord.

If, during the periods of intent silence when they pushed along the everlasting rings of deck, Complain changed into someone more thoughtful and self-sufficient, the priest's nature also changed. His volubility had gone, and the vitality from which it sprang. At last he realized the true magnitude of the task he had set himself, and was forced to put his whole will to enduring.

"Been trouble here—old trouble," he said at one place in their trek, leaning against the wall and looking ahead into the middle level of Deck 29. The others paused with him. The tangles stretched for only a few yards in front of them, then began the darkness in which they could not grow. The cause of the light failure was obvious: ancient weapons, such as Quarters did not possess, had blasted holes in the roof and walls of the corridor. A heavy cabinet of some kind protruded through the roof, and the nearby doors had been buckled out of their sockets. For yards around, everywhere was curiously pock-marked and pitted from the force of the explosion.

"At least we'll be free of the cursed tangle for a space," Wantage remarked, drawing his torch. "Come on, Marapper."

The priest continued to lean where he was, pulling at his nose between first finger and thumb.

"We must be getting close to Forwards' territory," he said. "I'm afraid our torches may give us away."

"You walk in the dark if you feel like it," Wantage retorted. He moved forward, Fermour did the same. Without a word, pushing past Marapper, Complain followed suit. Grumbling, the priest tagged on; nobody suffered indignity with more dignity than he.

Getting near the edge of shadow, Wantage flicked his torch on, probing it ahead. Then the strangeness began to take them. The first thing that Complain, whose eyes were trained to notice such things, observed which went against natural law was the lie of the ponics. As always, they tailed off and grew stunted towards the lightless passage, but here they were peculiarly whispy, their stalks looking flaccid, as if unable to support their weight, and they ventured further from the overhead glow than usual.

Then his footsteps failed to bite on ground.

Already, Wantage was floundering ahead of him. Fermour had gone into an odd high-stepping walk. Complain felt strangely helpless; the intricate gears of his body had been thrown out of kilter—it was as if he was trying to march through water, yet he had an unaccountable sensation of lightness. His head swam. Blood roared in his ears. He heard Marapper exclaim in astonishment, and then the priest blundered into his back. Next moment, Complain was sailing on a long trajectory past Fermour's right shoulder. He doubled up as he went, striking the wall with his hip. The ground rose slowly to meet him and, spreading both arms, he landed on his chest and went sprawling. When he looked dizzily into the darkness, he saw Wantage, still gripping his torch, descending even more slowly.

On the other side of him, Marapper was floundering like a hippopotamus, his eyes bulging, his mouth speechlessly opening and shutting. Taking the priest's arm, Fermour spun him expertly around and pushed him back into the safe area. Then Fermour bunched his stocky form and dived out into the dark for Wantage, who was blaspheming quietly near the floor; glissading off the wall, Fermour seized him, braked himself with an out-thrust heel, and floated softly back on the rebound. He steadied Wantage, who staggered like a drunken man.

Thrilled by this display, Complain saw at once that here was an ideal way of travel. Whatever had happened in the corridor—he dimly supposed that the air had changed in some way, although it was 'still breathable—they could proceed quickly along it in a series of leaps. Getting cautiously to his feet and snapping on his torch, he took a tentative jump forward.

His cry of surprise echoed loudly down the empty corridor. Only by putting up his hand did Complain save himself a knock on the head. The gesture sent him into a spin, so that he eventually landed on his back. He was dizzy: everything had been the wrong way up. Nevertheless, he was ten yards down the corridor. The others, fixed in a drum of light with a green backcloth, looked distant. Complain recalled the rambling memories of Ozbert Bergass; what had he said, in the truth Complain had mistaken for delirium? "The place where hands turn into feet and you fly through the air like an insect." Then the old guide had roved this far! Complain marveled to think of the miles of festering tunnel that lay between them and Quarters.

He rose too hastily, sending himself spinning again. Unexpectedly, he vomited. It floated forward in the air, forming up into globelets, splashing around him as he made a clumsy retreat back to the others.

"The ship's gone crazy!" Marapper was saying.

"Why doesn't it show this on your map?" Wantage asked angrily. "I never did trust that thing."

"Obviously the weightlessness occurred *after* the map was made. Use your damned brains if you've got any," Fermour snapped. This unusual outburst was perhaps explained by the anxiety in his next remark. "I should think we've made enough racket to bring all Forwards on our trail; we'd better get back from here quickly."

"Back!" Complain exclaimed. "We can't go back! The way to the next deck lies up there. We'll have to get through one of these broken doors and work our way through the rooms, keeping parallel to the corridor."

"How in the hull do we do that?" Wantage asked. "Have you got something that bores through walls?"

"We can only try, and hope there will be connecting doors," Complain said. "Bob Fermour's right— it's madness to stay here. Come on!"

"Yes, but look here—" Marapper began.

"Oh, take a Journey!" Complain said angrily. He burst open the buckled nearest door and pushed his way in; Fermour followed close behind. With a glance at each other, Marapper and Wantage came too.

They were fortunate in that they had chosen a large room. The lights still functioned, and the place was stacked with growth; Complain chopped at it savagely, keeping near the wall next to the corridor. Again the lightness enveloped them as they advanced, but the effect was less serious here, and the ponics afforded them some stability.

They came level with a rent in the wall. Wantage peered past the ragged metal into the corridor. In the distance, a circular light winked out.

"Someone's following us," he said. They looked uneasily

into each other's faces, and with one accord pressed onward again.

A metal counter on which ponics now sprouted in profusion blocked their way. They were forced to skirt it, going toward the center of the room to do so. This—in the days of the Giants—had been some kind of mess hall; long tables flanked with tubular steel chairs had covered the length and breadth of it. Now, with slow, vegetable force, ponics had borne up the furniture, entangling themselves in it, hoisting it waist high, where it formed a barrier to progress. The further they went, the more they were impeded. It proved impossible to get back to the wall.

As if in a nightmare, they cut their way past chairs and tables, half-blinded by midges which rose like dust from the foliage and settled on their faces. The thicket grew worse. Whole clumps of ponic had collapsed under this self-imposed strain and were rotting in slimy clumps, on top of which more plants grew. A blight had settled in, a blue blight sticky to the touch, which soon made the party's knives difficult to handle.

Sweating and gasping, Complain glanced at Wantage, who labored beside him. The good side of the man's face was so swollen that his eye hardly showed. His nose ran, and he was muttering to himself. Catching Complain's eyes upon him, he began to curse monotonously.

Complain said nothing. He was too hot and worried.

They moved through a stippled wall of disease. The going was slow, but finally they broke through to the end of the room. Which end? They had lost all sense of direction. Marapper promptly sat down with his back to the smooth wall, settling heavily among the ponic seeds. He swabbed his brow exhaustedly.

"I've gone far enough," he gasped.

"Well, you can't go any further," Complain snapped.

"Don't forget I didn't suggest all this, Roy."

Complain drew a deep breath. The air was foul; he had the nasty illusion that his lungs were coated with midges.

"We've only got to work our way along the wall till we come to a door. It's easier going here," he said. Then, despite his determination, he sank down beside the priest.

Wantage began to sneeze.

Each onslaught bent him double. The ruined side of his face was as swollen as the good one; his present distress completely hid his deformity. On his seventh sneeze, all the lights went out.

Instantly, Complain was on his feet, flashing his torch into Wantage's face.

"Stop that sneezing!" he growled. "We must keep quiet."

"Turn your torch off!" Fermour snapped.

They stood in indecisive silence, their hearts choking them. Standing in that heat was like standing in a jelly.

"It could be just a coincidence," Marapper said uneasily. "I can remember sections of lights failing before."

"It's Forwards—they're after us!" Complain whispered.

"All we've got to do is work our way quietly along the wall to the nearest door," Fermour said, repeating Complain's earlier words almost verbatim.

"Quietly?" Complain sneered. "They'd hear us at once. Best to stand still. Keep your dazers ready—they're probably trying to creep up on us."

So they stood there, sweating. Night was a hot breath about them, sampled inside a whale's belly.

"Give us the Litany, Priest," Wantage begged. His voice was shaking.

"Not now, for gods ache," Fermour groaned.

"The Litany! Give us the Litany!" Wantage repeated.

They heard the priest flop down on to his knees. Wantage followed suit, wheezing in the thick gloom.

"Get down, you two bastards!" he hissed.

Marapper began monotonously on the General Belief. With an overpowering sense of futility, Complain thought, "Here we finish up in this dead end, and the priest prays; I don't know why I ever mistook him for a man of action." He nursed the dazer, cocking an ear into the night, half-heartedly joining in the responses. Their voices rose and fell; by the end of it they all felt slightly better.

". . . and by so discharging our morbid impulses we may be freed from inner conflict," the priest intoned.

"And live in psychosomatic purity," they repeated.

"So that this unnatural life may be delivered down to Journey's End."

"And sanity propagated," they replied.

"And the ship brought home." The priest had the last word.

He crept around to each of them in the grubby dark, his confidence restored by his own performance, shaking their hands, wishing expansion to their egos. Complain pushed him roughly away.

"Save that till we're out of this predicament," he said. "We've got to work our way out of here. If we go quietly, we can hear anyone who approaches us."

"It's no good, Roy," Marapper said. "We're stuck here and I'm tired."

"Remember the power you were after?"

"Let's sit it out here!" the priest begged. "The ponic's too thick."

"What do you say, Fermour?" Complain asked.

"Listen!"

They listened, ears strained. The ponics creaked, relaxing without light, preparing to die. Midges pinged about their heads. Although vibrant with tiny noises, the air was almost unbreathable; the wall of diseased plants cut off the oxygen released by the healthy ones beyond.

With frightening suddenness, Wantage went mad. He flung himself on to Fermour, who cried out as he was bowled over. They were rolling about in the muck, struggling desperately. Soundlessly, Complain threw himself on to them. He felt Wantage's wiry frame writhing on top of Fermour's thick body; the latter was fighting to shake off the hands around his throat.

Complain wrenched Wantage away by the shoulders. Wantage threw a wild punch, missed, grabbed for his dazer. He brought it up, but Complain had his wrist. Twisting savagely, he forced Wantage slowly back and then hit out at his jaw. In the dark, the blow missed its target, striking Wantage's chest instead. Wantage yelped and broke free, flailing his arms wildly about his body.

Again Complain had him. This time, his blow connected properly. Wantage went limp, tottered back into the ponics and fell heavily.

"Thanks," Fermour said; it was all he could manage to say.

They had all been shouting. Now they were silent, again listening. Only the creak of the ponics, the noise that went with them all their lives, and continued when they had made the Long Journey.

Complain put out his hand and touched Fermour; he was shaking violently.

"You should have used your dazer on the madman," Complain said.

"He knocked it out of my hand," Fermour replied. "Now I've lost the bloody thing in the muck."

He stooped down, feeling for it in a pulp of ponic stalks and miltex.

The priest was also stooping. He flashed a torch, which Complain at once knocked out of his hand. The priest found Wantage, who was groaning slightly, and got down on one knee beside him.

"I've seen a good many go like this," Marapper whispered. "But the division between sanity and insanity was always narrow with poor Wantage. This is a case of what we priests term hyper-claustrophobia; I suppose we all have it in some degree. It causes a lot of deaths in the Greene tribe, although they aren't all violent like this. Most of them just snap out like a torch." He clicked his fingers to demonstrate.

"Never mind the case history, priest," Fermour said. "What in the name of sweet reason are we going to do with him?"

"Leave him and clear out," Complain suggested.

"You don't see how interesting a case this is for me," said the priest reprovingly. "I've known Wantage since he was a small boy. Now he's going to die, here in the darkness. It's a wonderful, a humbling thing to look on a man's life as a whole: the work of art's completed, the composition's rounded off. A man takes the Long Journey, but he leaves his history behind in the minds of other men.

"When Wantage was born, his mother lived in the tangles of Deadways, an outcast from her own tribe. She had committed a double unfaith, and one of the men concerned went with her and hunted for her. She was a bad woman. He was killed hunting: she could not live in the tangle alone, so she sought refuge with us in Quarters.

"Wantage was then a toddling infant—a small thing with his great deformity. His mother became—as unattached women frequently will—one of the guards' harlots, and was killed in a drunken brawl before her son reached puberty."

"Whose nerves do you think this recitation steadies?" Fermour asked.

"In fear lies no expansion; our lives are only lent us," Marapper said. "See the shape of our poor Comrade's life. As so often happens, his end echoes his beginning; the wheel turns one full revolution, then breaks off. When he was a child, Wantage endured nothing but torment from the other boys—taunts because his mother was a bad lot, taunts because of his face. He came to identify the two as one woe. So he walked with his bad side to the wall, and deliberately submerged the memory of his mother. But being back in the tangle brought back his infant recollections. He was swamped by the shame of her, his mother. He was overwhelmed by infantile fears of darkness and insecurity."

"Now that our little object lesson in the benefits of self-confession is over," Complain said heavily, "perhaps you will recollect, Marapper, that Wantage is *not* dead. He still lives to be a danger to us.

"I'm just going to finish him," Marapper said. "Your torch a moment, dimly. We don't want him squealing like a pig."

Bending down gingerly, Complain fought a splitting headache as the blood flow into his skull increased. The impulse came to do just what Wantage had done: hurl away the discomforts of reason, and charge blindly into the ambushed thickets, screaming. It was only later that he questioned his blind obedience to the priest at this dangerous hour; for it was obvious on reflection that Marapper had found some sort of mental refuge from this crisis by turning to the routines of priesthood; his exhumation of Wantage's childhood had been a camouflaged seeking for his own.

"I think I'm going to sneeze again," Wantage remarked, in a reasonable voice, from the ground. He had regained consciousness without their knowing it.

His face, in the pencil of light squeezed between Complain's fingers, was scarcely recognizable. Normally pale and thin, the countenance was now swollen and suffused

100

with blood; it might have been a gorged vampire's mask, had the eyes not been hot, rather than chill with death. And as the light of Complain's torch fell upon him, Wantage jumped.

Unprepared, Complain went down under a frontal attack. But, arms and legs flailing, Wantage paused only to knock his previous assailant out of the way. Then he was off through the tangles, crashing away from the little party.

Marapper's torch came on, picking at the greenery, settling dimly on Wantage's retreating back.

"Put it out, you crazy fool priest!" Fermour bellowed.

"I'm going to get him with my dazer," Marapper shouted.

But he did not. Wantage had burst only a short way into the tangle when he paused and swung about. Complain heard distinctly the curious whistling noise he made. For a second, everything was still. Then Wantage made the whistling noise again and staggered back into range of Marapper's torch. He tripped, collapsed, tried to make his way to them on hands and knees.

Two yards from Marapper, he rolled over, twitched and lay still. His blank eye stared incredulously at the arrow sticking out of his solar plexus.

They were still peering stupidly at the body when the armed guards of Forwards slid from the shadows and confronted them.

Part III

FORWARDS

I

Forwards was a region like none Roy Complain had seen before. The grandeur of Sternstairs, the cosy squalor of Quarters, the hideous wilderness of Deadways, even the spectacle of that macabre sea where the Giants had captured him—none of them prepared him for the *differentness* of Forwards. Although his hands, like Fermour's and Marapper's, were tied behind his back, his hunter's eye was keenly active as their small party was marched into the camp.

One radical distinction between Forwards and the villages lost in the festering continent of Deadways soon became obvious. Whereas the Greene tribe and others like it were always slowly on the move, Forwards was firmly established, its boundaries fixed and unchanging. It looked the result of organization rather than accident. Complain's conception of it had always been vague; in his mind it had featured as a place of dread, the more dreadful for being vague. Now he saw it was immensely larger than a village. It was almost a region in its own right.

Its very barriers differed from Quarters' make-shift affairs. The skirmishing party, as they pushed unceremoniously through the ponics, came first of all to a heavy curtain which, loaded with small bells, rang as they drew it aside. Beyond the curtain was a section of corridor, dirty and scarred but devoid of ponics, terminating in a barricade formed of desks and bunks, behind which Forwards guards stood ready with bows and arrows.

After an amount of hailing and calling, the skirmishing party—which numbered four men and two women—was allowed up to and past this last barricade. Beyond it was another curtain, this time of fine net, through which the hitherto ubiquitous midges, one of the scourges of Deadways, could not get. And beyond that lay Forwards proper.

For Complain, the incredible feature was the disappearance of ponic plants. Inside Quarters, of course, the thickets had been hacked or trampled down, but with indifferent enthusiasm and in the knowledge that the clearance was only temporary; often enough the old root system was allowed to remain covering the deck. And always there had been tokens of them about, from the sour-sweet miltex smell pervading the air to the dried staves used by men and the chitinous seeds played with by children.

Here the ponics had been swept away as if they had never been. The detritus and soil that attended them had been completely removed; even the scoured pattern the roots made on the hard deck had been erased. The lighting, no longer filtered through a welter of greedy foliage, shone out boldly. Everywhere wore such a strange aspect— so hard, bare and, above all, so geometrical—that some while was to elapse before Complain realized fully that these doors, corridors and decks were not an independent kingdom but, in fact, only an extension of their dingier counterparts elsewhere; the external appearance was so novel that it blinded him to its real conformity with the lay-out of Quarters.

The three prisoners were prodded into a small cell. All their equipment was removed and their hands freed. The door was slammed on them.

"O Consciousness!" Marapper groaned. "Here's a pretty state for a poor, innocent old priest to be in. Froyd rot their souls for a pack of dirty miltex-suckers!"

"At least they let you do the death rites for Wantage," said Fermour, trying to pick the filth out of his hair.

They looked at him curiously.

"What else would you expect?" Marapper asked. "The brutes are at least human. But that doesn't mean to say

104

that they won't be wearing our intestines around their necks before they eat again."

"If only they hadn't taken my dazer ... " Complain said. Not only their dazers, but their packs and all their possessions had been taken. He prowled helplessly around the little room. Like many apartments in Quarters, it was all but featureless. By the door, two broken dials were set into a wall, a bunk was fixed into another wall, a grille in the ceiling provided a slight current of air. Nothing offered itself as a weapon.

The trio had to possess themselves in uneasy patience until the guards came back. For some while, the silence was broken only by an uneasy whine deep in the priest's intestines. Then all three began to fidget.

Marapper tried to remove some clotted filth from his cloak. Working half-heartedly, he looked up with eagerness when the door was opened and two men appeared in the open doorway; pushing roughly past Fermour, the priest strode over to them.

"Take me to your Lieutenant and expansion to your egos," he said. "It is important I see him as soon as possible. I am not a man to be kept waiting."

"You will all come with us," one of the pair said firmly. "We have our orders."

Wisely, Marapper saw fit to obey at once, although he kept up a flow of indignant protest as they were ushered into the corridor. They were led deeper into Forwards, passing several curious bystanders on their way. Complain noticed these people stared at them angrily; one middle-aged woman called, "You curs, you killed my Frank! Now they'll kill you."

His senses nicely stimulated by a scent of danger, Complain took in every detail of their route. Here, as throughout Deadways, what Marapper had called the Main Corridor was blocked at each deck, and they followed a circuitous detour around the curving corridors and through the inter-deck doors. In effect, it meant that to go further forward they took, not the straight course a bullet takes to leave a rifle, but the tight spiral traced by the rifling in the barrel.

By this method they traversed two decks. Complain saw with wild surprise the notice "Deck 22" stencilled against the inter-deck door; it was a link with all the seemingly unending deck numbers which had punctuated their trek; and it implied, unless Deadways began again on the other side of Forwards, that Forwards itself covered twenty-four decks.

This was too much for Complain to believe. He had to remind himself forcibly how much he was incapable of crediting which had actually been proved to be. But— what lay beyond Deck 1? He could picture only a wilderness of super-ponics, growing out into what Myra, his mother, had called the great stretch of other darkness, where strange lanterns burned. Even the priest's theory of the Ship, backed as it was by printed evidence, had little power to thrust out that image he had known since childhood. With a certain pleasure, he balanced the two theories against each other; never before in his life had he felt anything but discomfort at the contemplation of intangibles. He was rapidly sloughing the dry husk that limited Greene tribe thinking.

Complain's interior monologue was interrupted by their guards, who now pushed him with Fermour and the priest into a large compartment, entering themselves and shutting the door. Two other guards were already in the room.

A couple of unusual features distinguished the room from any other Complain had been in. One was a plant bearing bright flowers which stood in a tub, as if for some purpose—though what purpose, the hunter could not guess. The other unusual feature was a girl; she stood regarding them from behind a desk, dressed in a neat grey uniform and with her hands restfully down at her sides. Her hair fell straight and neat about her neck. The hair was black, and her eyes were gray; her face was thin, pale and intense, the exact curve of her cheek down to her mouth holding, Complain felt compulsively, a message he longed to understand. Although she was young and her brow magnificent, the impression she gave was not so much of beauty as of gentleness—until one's gaze dropped to her jaw. There lay delicate but unmistakable warning that it might be uncomfortable to know this girl too well.

She surveyed each of the prisoners in turn.

Complain experienced a strange *frisson* as her eyes

engaged his; and something tense in Fermour's attitude revealed that he, too, felt an attraction to her. That her direct gaze defied a strict Quarters' taboo only made it the more disturbing.

"So you're Gregg's ruffians," she said finally. Now she had seen them, she was obviously inclined to look at them no more; she tilted her neat head up and studied a patch of wall. "It is good that we have caught some of you at last. You have caused us much unnecessary irritation. Now you will be handed over to the torturers; we have to extract information from you. Or do you wish to surrender it voluntarily here and now?"

Her voice had been cold and detached, using the tone the proud employ to the criminal. Torture, it was implied, was the natural disinfectant for their sort.

Fermour spoke.

"We beg you, as you are a kind woman, to spare us from torture!"

"It is neither my business nor my intention to be kind," she replied. "As for my sex—that, I think, lies outside the scope of your concerns. My name is Inspector Vyann; I investigate all captives brought into Forwards, and those who are coy about talking go on the presses. You ruffians in particular deserve nothing better. We need to know how to get to the leader of your band himself."

Marapper spread his hands wide.

"You may take it from me we know nothing of this leader," he said, "nor of the ruffians who serve him. We three are completely independent; our tribe lies many decks away. As I am a humble priest, I would not lie to you."

"Humble, are you?" she asked, thrusting the little chin out. "What were you doing so near Forwards? Do you not know our perimeters are dangerous?"

"We did not realize we were so near Forwards," said the priest. "The ponics were thick. We have come a long way."

"Where exactly have you come from?"

This was the first question of a series that Inspector Vyann thrust at them. Marapper answered them greasily and unhappily; he was not permitted to deviate. Whether she spoke or listened, the girl in gray looked slightly away from them. They might have been three performing dogs hustled before her, so detachedly did she ignore them as people; the two silent figures and the third, Marapper, standing slightly ahead of his companions, gesticulating, protesting, shifting his weight from one leg to the other, were for her mere random elements in a problem awaiting solution.

The direction of her interrogation soon made it obvious that she began by believing them to be members of a marauding gang, and ended by doubting it. The gang, it became apparent, had been carrying out raids on Forwards from a nearby base at a time when other—as yet unspecified—problems pressed.

Vyann's natural disappointment at finding the trio less exciting than hoped for chilled her manner still further. The thicker grew the ice, the more voluble grew Marapper. His violent imagination, easily stimulated, pictured for him the ease with which this impervious young woman might snap her fingers and launch him on his Long Journey. At last he stepped forward, placing one hand gently on her desk.

"What you have failed to realize, madam," he said impressively, "is this: that we are no ordinary captives. When your skirmishers waylaid us, we were on our way to Forwards with important news."

"Is that so?" Her raised eyebrows were triumph. "You were telling me a moment ago you were only a humble priest from an obscure village. These contradictions bore us."

"Knowledge!" Marapper said. "Why question where it comes from? I warn you seriously, I am valuable."

Vyann permitted herself a small, frosty smile.

"So your lives should be spared because you hold some vital information between you. Is that it, priest?"

"I said *I* had the knowledge," Marapper pointed out craftily, puffing up his cheeks. "If you also deign to spare the breath of my poor, ignorant friends here, I should, of course, be everlastingly delighted."

"So?" For the first time, she sat down behind the desk, a hint of humor lurking around her mouth, softening it. She pointed to Complain.

You," she said. "If you have no knowledge to pour into our ears, what can you offer?"

"I am a hunter," Complain said. "My friend Fermour here is a farmer. If we have no knowledge, we can serve you with our strength."

Vyann folded her quiet hands on the desk, not really bothering to look at him. "Your priest has the right idea, I think: intelligence could bribe us, muscle could not. There is plenty of muscle in Forwards already."

She turned her eyes to Fermour, saying, "And you, big fellow, you've hardly had a word to say for yourself. What gift do *you* offer?"

Fermour looked steadily at her before dropping his gaze.

"My silence only covered my disturbed thoughts, madam," he said gently. "In our small tribe we had no ladies who rivaled you in any way."

"That sort of thing is not acceptable as a bribe, either," Vyann said levelly. "Well, Priest, I hope your information is interesting. Suppose you tell me what it is?"

It was a small moment of triumph for Marapper. He stuck his hands beneath his tattered cloak and shook his head firmly.

"I will keep it for someone in authority," he said. "I regret, madam, I cannot trust you with it."

She seemed not to be offended. It was a measure, possibly, of her self-assurance that her hands never moved on the desk top.

"I will have my superior brought here at once," she said. One of the guards was sent out; he was away only a short while, returning with a brisk middle-aged man.

The newcomer was instantly impressive. Deep lines ran down his face like water runnels down a slope, and this eroded appearance was increased by the inroads of gray into his still yellow hair. His eyes were wide-awake, his mouth autocratic. He relaxed his aggressive expression to smile at Vyann, and conferred quietly with her in one corner, thrusting occasional glances at Marapper as he listened to what she was saying.

"How about making a dash for it?" Fermour whispered to Complain, in a choked voice.

"Don't be a fool," Complain whispered back. "We'd

never get out of this room, never mind past the barrier guards."

Fermour muttered something inaudible, looking almost as if he might attempt a break on his own. But at that moment the man conferring with Vyann stepped forward and spoke.

"We have certain tests we wish to carry out on the three of you," he said mildly. "You will shortly be called back here, Priest. Meanwhile—guards, remove these prisoners to Cell Three, will you?"

The guards were prompt to obey. Despite protests from Fermour, he and Complain and Marapper were hustled out of the room and into another only a few yards down the corridor, where the door was shut on them. Marapper looked embarrassed, realizing that his recent attempt to extricate himself at their expense might have cost him a little goodwill; he began straightway to try to retain his position by cheering them up.

"Well, well, my children," he said, extending his arms to them, "the Long Journey has always begun, as the scripture puts it. These people of Forwards are more civilized than we, and will certainly have a horrible fate awaiting us. Let me intone some last rite for you."

Complain turned away and sat down in a far corner of the room. Fermour did likewise. The priest followed them, squatting on his massive haunches and resting his arms on his knees.

"Keep away from me, Priest!" Complain said. "Leave me in peace!"

"Have you no guts, no reverence?" the priest asked him. His voice became as thick as cool treacle. "Do you think the Teaching allows you *peace* in your last hours? You must be stirred into Consciousness for the final time. Why should you slump here, despairing? What is your wretched, sordid life to care a curse over? Where in your mind is anything so precious that it should not be carelessly extinguished? You are sick, Roy Complain, you need my ministrations."

"Just take it I'm not in your parish any more, will you?" Complain said wearily. "I can look after myself."

The priest made a face and turned to Fermour.

"You, my friend, what have you to say?" he asked.

Fermour smiled. He was in control of himself again.

"I'd just like an hour alone with that luscious Inspector Vyann—then I'd travel happy," he said. "Can you arrange that for me, Marapper?"

Before Marapper had time to choose a suitably moral answer, the door opened and an ugly face peered in; a hand followed it, beckoning to the priest. Marapper rose, smoothing his clothes self-consciously.

"I'll put in a word for you, children," he said, and stalked with dignity into the passage behind the guard. A minute later, he was facing the inspector and her superior again. The latter, perched on a corner of the desk, began to speak at once.

"Expansions to you. You are Henry Marapper, a priest, I believe? My name is Scoyt, Master Scoyt, and I am in charge of alien investigation. Anybody brought into Forwards comes before me and Inspector Vyann. If you are what you claim, you will not be harmed—but some strange things emerge from Deadways, and must be guarded against. I understand you came here especially to bring us some information?"

"I have come a long way, through many decks," Marapper said, "and do not appreciate my reception now I am here."

Master Scoyt inclined his head.

"What is this information you have?" he asked.

"I can divulge it only to the Captain."

"Captain? What Captain? The captain of the guard? There is no other captain."

This put Marapper in an awkward position, since he did not wish to use the word "ship" before the moment was ripe.

"Who is your superior?" he asked.

"Inspector Vyann and I answer only to the Council of Five," Scoyt said, with anger in his tone. "It is impossible for you to see the Council until we have assessed the importance of your information. Come, Priest—other matters are on hand! Patience is an old-fashioned virtue I don't possess. What is this intelligence you set so much store by?"

Marapper hesitated. The moment was definitely not

ripe. Scoyt had risen almost as if to go, Vyann looked restless. All the same, he could hedge no more.

"This world," he began impressively, "all Forwards and Deadways to the far regions of Sternstairs is one body, the Ship. And the Ship is man-made, and moves in a medium called space. Of this I have proof." He paused to take in their expressions. Scoyt's was one of ambiguity. Marapper continued, explaining the ramifications of his theory with eloquence. He finished by saying, "If you will trust me, trust me and give me power, I will set this Ship—for such you may be assured it is—at its destination, and we will all be free of it and its oppression for ever."

He faltered to a stop. Their faces were full of harsh amusement. They looked at each other and laughed briefly, almost without humor. Marapper rubbed his jowls uneasily.

"You have no faith in me because I come from a small tribe," he muttered.

"No, Priest," the girl said. She came and stood before him. "You see—in Forwards we have known of the ship and its journey through space for a long while."

Marapper's jaw dropped.

"Then—the Captain of the ship—you have found him?" he managed to say.

"The Captain does not exist. He must have made the Long Journey generations ago."

"Then—the Control Cabin—you have found that?"

"It does not exist either," the girl said. "We have a legend of it, no more."

"Oh?" said Marapper, suddenly wary and excited. "In our tribe even the legend of it had faded—presumably because we were further from its supposed position than you. But it *must* exist! You have looked for it?'"

Again Scoyt and Vyann looked at each other; Scoyt nodded in answer to an unspoken question.

"Since you appear to have stumbled on part of the secret," Vyann told Marapper, "we may as well tell you the whole of it. Understand this is not general knowledge even among the people of Forwards—we of the *élite* keep it to ourselves in case it causes madness and unrest. As the proverb has it, the truth never set anyone free. The Ship is a ship, as you rightly say. There is no Captain. The

112

ship is plunging on unguided through space, non-stop. We can only presume it is lost. We presume it will travel for ever, till all aboard have made the Long Journey. It cannot be stopped—for though we have searched all Forwards for the Control Room, it does not exist!"

She was silent, looking at Marapper with sympathy as he digested this unpalatable information; it was almost too ghastly to accept.

". . . some terrible wrong of our forefathers," he murmured, drawing his right index finger superstitiously across his throat. Then he pulled himself together. "But at least the Control Room exists," he said. "Look, I have proof!"

From under his dirty tunic, he drew the book of circuit diagrams and waved it at them.

"You were searched at the barriers," Scoyt said. "How did you manage to retain that?"

"Shall we say—thanks to a luxuriant growth of underarm hair?" the priest asked, winking at Vyann. He had them impressed again, and was at once back on form. Now he spread the small book on the Inspector's desk and pointed dramatically to the diagram he had previously shown Complain; the little bubble of the Control Room was clearly indicated at the front of the ship. As the other two stared, he explained how he came by the book.

"This book was made by the Giants," he said. "They undoubtedly owned the ship."

"We know that much," Scoyt said. "But this book is valuable. Now we have a definite location to check for the Control Room. Come on, Vyann, my dear, let's go and look at once."

She pulled open a deep drawer in her desk, picked out a dazer and belt and strapped them around her slender waist. It was the first dazer Marapper had seen here: they were evidently in short supply. He recalled that the Greene tribe was so well armed only because old Bergass's father had stumbled on a supply of them in Deadways, many decks from Forwards.

They were about to leave when the door opened and a tall man entered. He was dressed in a good robe and his hair was worn long and neat. As if respect were due to him, Scoyt and Vyann drew themselves up deferentially.

"Word has come to me that you have prisoners, Master

113

Scoyt," the newcomer said slowly. "Have we caught some of Gregg's men at last?"

"I fear not, Councilor Deight," Scoyt said. "They are only three wanderers from Deadways. This is one of them."

The councilor looked hard at Marapper, who looked away.

"The other two?" the councilor prompted.

"They are in Cell Three, Councilor," Scoyt said. "We shall question them later. Inspector Vyann and I are testing this prisoner now."

For a moment, the councilor seemed to hesitate. Then he nodded and quietly withdrew. The priest, impressed, stared after him—and it was rarely the priest was impressed.

"That," Scoyt said for Marapper's benefit, "was Councilor Zac Deight, one of our Council of Five. Watch your manners in front of any of them, and particularly in front of Deight."

Vyann pocketed the priest's circuit book. They left the room in time to see the old councilor disappear around the curve of the corridor. Then began a long march toward the extremity of Forwards, where the diagram indicated the controls to be; it would have taken them several sleep-wakes to make the distance had it been uncharted and overgrown with ponics and their attendant obstacles.

Marapper, engrossed though he was with future plans— for the discovery of the ship's controls would undoubtedly put him in a strong position—kept an interested eye on his surroundings. He soon realized that Forwards was far from being the wonderful place that Deadways' rumor painted, or that he had supposed at first sight. They passed many people, of whom a good proportion were children. Everyone wore less than in Quarters; the few clothes they had looked washed and neat, and the general standard of cleanliness was good, but bodies were lean, running to bone. Food was obviously short. Marapper surmised shrewdly that being less in contact with the tangles, Forwards could count on fewer hunters than Quarters, and those perhaps of inferior quality. He found also, as they progressed, that though all Forwards, from the barriers at Deck 24 to the dead end at Deck 1, was under Forwards' sway, only Decks 22 to 11 were occupied, and they but partially.

As they passed beyond Deck 11, the priest saw part of the explanation for this. For three entire decks, the lighting circuits had failed. Master Scoyt switched on a light at his belt, and the three proceeded in semi-darkness. If darkness had been oppressive in Deadways, it was doubly so here, where footsteps rang hollow and nothing stirred. When they circled into Deck 7, and light shone falteringly again, the prospect was no more cheerful. The echo still followed them and devastation lay on all sides.

"Look at that!" Scoyt exclaimed, pointing to where a section of wall had been cut entirely away and curled back against the bulkheads. "There were once weapons on the ship which could do that! I wish we had something that would cut through a wall. We should soon find our way into space then."

"If only windows had been built somewhere, the original purpose of the ship might not have been forgotten," Vyann said.

"According to the plan," Marapper remarked, "there are large enough windows in the Control Room."

They fell silent. The surroundings were dreary enough to annihilate all conversation. Most doors stood open; the rooms they revealed became increasingly full of machines, silent, broken, smothered under the dust of generations.

"Many strange things of which we have no knowledge happen in this ship," Scoyt said gloomily. "Ghosts are among us, working against us."

"Ghosts?" Marapper asked. "You believe in them, Master Scoyt?"

"What Roger means," Vyann said, "is that we are confronted with two problems here. There is the problem of the Ship, where it is going, how it is to be stopped; that is the background problem, always with us. The other problem grows; it did not face our great-grandfathers: there is a strange race on this ship that was not here before."

The priest stared at her. She was glancing carefully into each doorway as they went by; Scoyt was being as cautious. He felt the hair on his neck bristle uncomfortably.

"You mean—the Outsiders?" he asked.

She nodded. "A supernatural race masquerading as men . . ." she said. "You know, better than we, that three-quarters of the ship is jungle. In the hot muck of the tangles, somewhere, somehow, a new race has been born, masquerading as men. They are not men; they are enemies; they come in from their secret places to spy on us and kill us."

"We have to be always on the look-out," Scoyt said.

From then on, Marapper also looked in every doorway.

Now the layout changed. The three concentric corridors on each deck became two, their curvature sharpened. Deck 2 consisted of one corridor only with one ring of rooms around it, and in the middle the great hatch at the beginning of Main Corridor, sealed forever. Scoyt tapped it lightly.

"If this corridor, the only straight one in the ship, were opened up," he said, "we could walk to Sternstairs at the other end of the ship in less than a wake!"

A closed spiral staircase was now the sole way forward. Heart beating heavily, Marapper led them up it; the Control Room should be at the top if his diagram spoke truth.

At the top, a dim light showed them a small circular room, completely unfurnished, floor bare, walls also bare. Nothing else. Marapper flung himself at the walls, searching for a door. Nothing. He burst into furious tears.

"They lied!" he shouted. "They lied! We're all victims of a monstrous . . . a monstrous. . . ."

But he could think of no word big enough.

II

Roy Complain yawned boredly and changed his position on the cell floor for the twentieth time. Bob Fermour sat with his back to the wall, rotating a heavy ring endlessly around a finger of his right hand. They had nothing to say to each other; there was nothing to say, nothing to think. It was a relief when the pug-ugly on guard outside thrust his head around the door and summoned Complain with a few well-chosen words of abuse.

"See you on the Journey," Fermour said cheeringly as the other got up to go.

Complain waved to him and followed the guard, his heart beginning to beat more rapidly. He was led, not to the room where Inspector Vyann had interviewed them, but back along the way he had first been brought, into an office on Deck 24, near the barricades. The ugly guard stayed outside and slammed the door on him.

Complain was alone with Master Scoyt. The alien investigator, under the increasing pressure of the trouble piling up about them, looked more eroded than ever. As if his cheeks ached, he supported them with long fingers; they were not reassuring fingers; they could be cruel with artistry, although at present, resting against that haggard countenance, they seemed more the hands of a self-torturer.

"Expansion to you," he said heavily.

"Expansion," Complain replied. He knew he was to be tested, but most of his concern went on the fact that the girl Vyann was absent.

"I have some questions to ask you," Scoyt said. "It is advisable to answer them properly, for various reasons. First, where were you born?"

"In Quarters."

"That is what you call your village? Have you any brothers and sisters?"

"In Quarters we obeyed the Teaching," said Complain defiantly. "We do not recognize brothers and sisters after we are waist high to our mothers."

"To the hull with the T—" Scoyt stopped himself abruptly, smoothing his brow as one who keeps himself in control only by effort. Without looking up, he said tiredly, "How many brothers and sisters would you have to recognize now if you did recognize them?"

"Only three sisters."

"No brothers?"

"There was one. He ran amok long ago."

"What proof have you you were born in Quarters?"

"Proof!" Complain echoed. "If you want proof, go and catch my mother. She still lives. She'd love to tell you all about it."

Scoyt stood up.

"Understand this," he said. "I haven't time to coddle civil answers out of you. Everyone on shipboard is in a damn beastly situation. It's a ship, you see, and it's headed nobody-knows-where, and it's old and creaking, and it's thick with phantoms and mysteries and riddles and pain— and some poor bastard has got to sort it all out soon before it's too late, if it's not already too late!" He paused. He was giving himself away: in his mind, he was the poor bastard, shouldering the burden alone. More calmly, he continued. "What you've got to get into your head is that we're *all* expendable, and if you can't make yourself out to be any use, you're for the Long Journey."

"I'm sorry," Complain said. "I might be more co-operative if I knew which side I was on."

"You're on your own side. Didn't the Teaching teach you that much? 'The proper study of mankind is self'; you'll be serving yourself best by answering my questions."

Earlier, Complain might have submitted; now, more conscious of himself, he asked one more question: "Didn't Henry Marapper answer all you wanted to know?"

"The priest misled us," Scoyt said. "He has made the Journey. It's the usual penalty for trying my patience too far."

When his first stunned reaction to this news was over,

Complain began to wonder about its truth; he did not doubt the ruthlessness of Scoyt—the man who kills for a cause kills almost unthinkingly—but he could hardly bring himself to believe he would see the garrulous priest no more. His mind preoccupied, he answered Scoyt's questions. These mainly concerned their epic trek through Deadways; directly Complain began to explain about his capture by the Giants, the investigator, non-committal till now, pounced.

"The Giants do not exist!" he said. "They were extinct long ago. We inherited the ship from them."

Although openly skeptical, he then pressed as hard for details as Marapper once had, and it was obvious he slowly began to accept Complain's narrative for truth. His face clouded in thought, he tapped his long fingers on the desk.

"The Outsiders we have known for enemies," he said, "but the Giants we always regarded as our old allies, whose kingdom we took over with their approval. If they do still live somewhere in Deadways, why do they not show themselves—unless for a sinister reason? We already have quite enough trouble piled up against us."

As Complain pointed out, the Giants had not killed him when they might conveniently have done so; nor had they killed Ern Roffery, although what had become of the valuer remained a mystery. In all, their role in affairs was ambiguous.

"I'm inclined to believe your tale, Complain," Scoyt said finally, "because from time to time we receive rumors— people swear they've seen Giants. Rumors! Rumors! We get our hands on nothing tangible. But at least the Giants seem to be no threat to Forwards—and best of all, they don't seem to be in alliance with the Outsiders. If we can tackle them separately, that'll be something."

He lapsed into silence, then asked, "How far is it to this sea where the Giants caught you?"

"Many decks away—perhaps forty."

Master Scoyt threw up his hands in disgust.

"Too far!" he said. "I thought we might go there . . . but Forwards men do not love the ponics."

The door burst open. A panting guard stood on the threshhold and spoke without ceremony.

"An attack at the barriers, Master Scoyt!" he cried. "Come at once—you're needed."

Scoyt was up immediately, his face grim. Half-way to the door, he paused, turning back to Complain.

"Stay there," he commanded. "I'll be back when I can."

The door slammed. Complain was alone. As if unable to believe it, he looked slowly around. In the far wall, behind Scoyt's seat, was another door. Cautiously, he went over and tried it. It opened. Beyond was another room, a small antechamber, with another door on the far side of it. The antechamber boasted only a battered panel containing broken instruments on one wall, and on the floor, four packs. Complain recognized them at once as his, Marapper's, Bob Fermour's and Wantage's. All their meager belongings seemed to be still there, although it was evident the kit had been searched. Complain gave it only a brief glance, then crossed the room and opened the other door.

It led on to a side corridor. From one direction came the sound of voices; in the opposite direction, not many paces away, were—ponics. The way to them looked unguarded. His heart beating rapidly, Complain shut the door again, leaning against it to decide. Should he try to escape or not?

Marapper was killed; there was no evidence he also would not be as coolly disposed of. It might well be wise to leave—but for where? Quarters was too far away for a solitary man to reach. But nearer tribes would welcome a hunter. Complain recalled that Vyann had mistaken his group for members of some tribe that was raiding Forwards; in his preoccupation with their capture, Complain had scarcely taken note of what she said, but it might well be the same gang that was besieging the barricades now. They should appreciate a hunter with a slight knowledge of Forwards.

He swung his pack up on to his shoulder, opened the door, looked left and right, and dashed for the tangle.

All the other doors in the side corridor were shut, bar one. Instinctively, Complain glanced in as he passed—and stopped dead. He stood on the threshold, transfixed.

Lying on a couch just inside the room, relaxed as if it were merely sleeping, lay a body. It sprawled untidily, its

120

legs crossed, its shabby cloak rolled up to serve as pillow; its face wore the melancholy expression of an over-fed bulldog.

"Henry Marapper!" Complain exclaimed, eyes fixed on that familiar profile. The hair and temple were matted with blood. He leaned forward and gently touched the priest's arm. It was stone cold.

Instantly the old mental atmosphere of Quarters clicked into place around Complain. The Teaching was almost as instinctive as a reflex. He snapped without thought into the first gesture of prostration, going through the ritual of fear. Fear must not be allowed to penetrate to the subconscious, says the Teaching; it must be acted out of the system at once, in a complex ritual of expressions of terror. Between bow, bemoan, obeisance, Complain forgot all zest for escape.

"I'm afraid we must interrupt this efficient demonstration," a chilly female voice said behind him. Startled, Complain straightened and looked around. Dazer leveled, two guards at her side, there stood Vyann. Her lips were beautiful, but her smile was not inviting.

So ended Complain's test.

It was Fermour's turn to be ushered into the room on Deck 24. Master Scoyt sat there as he had done with Complain, but his manner was openly more abrupt now. He began, as he had with Complain, by asking where Fermour was born.

"Somewhere in the tangles," Fermour said, in his usual unhurried way. "I never knew where exactly."

"Why weren't you born in a tribe?"

"My parents were fugitives from their tribe. It was one of the little Midway tribes—smaller than Quarters."

"When did you join the Greene tribe?"

"After my parents died," Fermour said. "They had the trailing rot. By then I was full grown."

Scoyt's mouth, naturally heavy, had now elongated itself into a slit. A rubber cosh had appeared, and was lightly balanced between Scoyt's hands. He began to pace up and down in front of Fermour, watching him closely.

"Have you any proof of all this stuff you tell me?" he asked.

121

Fermour was pale, tensed, incessantly twisting the heavy ring on his finger.

"What sort of proof?" he asked, dry-mouthed.

"Any sort. Anything about your origins we can check on. We aren't just a rag-taggle village in Deadways, Fermour. When you drift in from the tangles, we have to know who or what you are. . . . Well?"

"Marapper the priest will vouch for me."

"Marapper's dead. Besides, I'm interested in someone who knew you as a child: anyone." He swung around so that they were face to face. "In short, Fermour, we want something you seem unable to give—proof that you're human!"

"I'm more human than you, you little—" As he spoke, Fermour jumped, his fist swinging.

Nimbly, Scoyt skipped back and brought the cosh hard across Fermour's wrist. Numbness shooting up his arm, Fermour subsided deflatedly, face sour with malice.

"Your reflexes are too slow," Scoyt said severely. "You should easily have taken me by surprise then."

"I was always called slow in Quarters," Fermour muttered, clutching his sleeve.

"How long have you been with the Greene tribe?" Scoyt demanded, coming closer to Fermour again and waggling the cosh as if keen to try out another blow.

"Oh, I lose track of time. Twice a hundred dozen sleep-wakes."

"We do not use your primitive method of calculating time in Forwards, Fermour. We call four sleep-wakes one day. That would make your stay with the tribe . . . six hundred days. A long time in a man's life."

He stood looking at Fermour as if waiting for something. The door was pushed roughly open and a guard appeared on the threshold, panting.

"There's an attack at the barriers, Master Scoyt," he cried. "Please come at once—you're needed."

On his way to the door, Scoyt paused and turned back toward Fermour, grim-faced.

"Stay there!" he ordered. "I'll be back as soon as possible."

In the next room, Complain turned slowly to Vyann. Her dazer had gone back in its holster at her waist.

"So that tale about the attack at the barriers is just a trick to get Master Scoyt out of the room, is it?" he said.

"That's right," she said steadily. "See what Fermour does now."

For a long moment, Complain stood looking into her eyes, caught by them. He was close to her, alone in what she had called the observation room, next to the room in which Fermour now was and Complain had been earlier. Then, pulling himself away in case his heart might be read in his face, Complain turned and fixed his gaze through the peephole again.

He was in time to see Fermour grab a small stool from the side of the room, drag it into the middle, stand on it, and reach up towards the grille that here, as in most apartments, was a feature of the ceiling. His fingers curled helplessly a few inches below the grille. After a few fruitless attempts to jump and stand on tip-toe, Fermour looked around the room in desperation and noticed the other door beyond which lay his pack. Kicking the stool away, he hurried through it, so vanishing from Complain's sight.

"He has gone, just as I went," Complain said, turning to brave the gray eyes again.

"My men will pick him up before he gets to the ponics," Vyann said carelessly. "I have little doubt your friend Fermour is an Outsider, but we shall be certain in a few minutes."

"Bob Fermour! He couldn't be!"

"We'll argue about that later," she said. "In the meantime, Roy Complain, you are a free man—as far as any of us are free. Since you have knowledge and experience, I hope you will help us attack some of our troubles."

She was so much more beautiful and frightening than Gwenny had ever been. His voice betraying his nervous excitement, Complain said, "I will help you in any way I can."

"Master Scoyt will be grateful," she said, moving away with a sudden sharpness in her voice. It brought him back to realities, and he asked with an equal sharpness what the Outsiders did that made them so feared; for though they had been dreaded by the Greene tribe, it was only because they were strange, and not like men.

"Isn't that enough?" she said. And then she told him of the powers of Outsiders. A few had been caught by Master Scoyt's various testing methods—and all but one had escaped. They had been thrown into cells bound hand and foot, and sometimes unconscious as well—there to vanish completely; if guards had been in the cells with them, they had been found unconscious without a mark on their bodies.

"And the Outsider who did not escape?" Complain asked.

"He died under torture on the presses. We got nothing from him, except that he came from the ponics."

She led him from the room. He humped his pack on to his back, walking tiredly by her side, occasionally glancing at her profile, sharp and bright as torchlight. No longer did she appear as friendly as she had a moment ago; her moods seemed capricious, and he hardened himself against her, trying to recall the old Quarters' attitude to women—but Quarters seemed a thousand sleep-wakes out of date.

On Deck 21, Vyann paused.

"There is an apartment for you here," she said. "My apartment is three doors further along, and Roger Scoyt's is opposite mine. He or I will collect you for a meal shortly."

Opening the door, Complain looked in.

"I've never seen a room like this before," he said impressed.

"You've had all the disadvantages, haven't you?" she said ironically, and left him. Complain watched that retreating figure, took off his grimy shoes and went into the room.

It held little luxury, beyond a basin with a tap which actually yielded a slight flow of water and a bed made of coarse fabric rather than leaves. What chiefly impressed him was a picture on the wall, a bright swirl of color, non-representational, but with a meaning of its own. There was also a mirror, in which Complain found another picture; this one was of a rough creatured smirched with dirt, its hair festooned with dried miltex, its clothes torn.

He set to work to change all that, grimly wondering what Vyann must have thought of such a barbarous figure. He scrubbed himself, put on clean clothes from his

124

pack, and collapsed exhausted on the bed—exhausted, but unable to sleep; for at once his brain started racing.

Gwenny had gone, Roffery had gone, Wantage, Marapper, now Fermour, had gone; Complain was on his own. The prospect of a new start offered itself—and the prospect was thrilling. Only the thought of Marapper's face, gleaming with unction and bonhomie, brought regret.

His mind was still churning when Master Scoyt looked around the door.

"Come and eat," he said simply.

Complain went with him, watching carefully to gauge the other's attitude toward him, but the investigator seemed too preoccupied to register any attitude at all. Then, looking up and catching Complain's eye on him, he said, "Well, your friend Fermour is proved an Outsider. When he was making for the ponics, he saw the body of your priest and kept straight on. Our sentries had an ambush for him and caught him easily."

Shaking his head impatiently at Complain's puzzled look, Scoyt explained, "He is not an ordinary human, bred in an ordinary part of the ship, otherwise he would have stopped automatically and made the genuflections of fear before the body of a friend; that ceremony is drummed into every human child from birth. It was your doing that which finally convinced us you were human."

He sank back into silence until they reached the dining-hall, scarcely greeting the several men and women who spoke to him on the way. In the hall, a few officers were seated, eating. At a table on her own sat Vyann. Seeing her, Scoyt instantly brightened, went over to her and put a hand on her shoulder.

"Laur, my dear," he said. "How refreshing to find you waiting for us. I must get some ale—we have to celebrate the capture of another Outsider—and this one won't get away."

Smiling at him, she said, "I hope you're also going to eat, Roger."

"You know my foolish stomach," he said, beckoning an orderly and beginning to tell her at once the details of Fermour's capture. Not very happily, Complain took a seat by them; he could not help feeling jealous of Scoyt's easy way with Vyann, although the investigator was twice her age. Ale was set before them, and food, a strange white meat that tasted excellent; it was wonderful too, to eat without being surrounded with midges, which in Deadways formed an unwanted sauce to many a mouthful; but Complain picked at his plate with little more enthusiasm than Scoyt showed.

"You look dejected," Vyann remarked, interrupting Scoyt, "when you should be feeling cheerful. It is better here, isn't it, than locked up in a cell with Fermour?"

"Fermour was a friend," Complain said, using the first excuse for his unhappiness that entered his head.

"He was also an Outsider," Scoyt said heavily. "He exhibited all their characteristics. He was slow, rather on the weighty side, saying little ... I'm beginning to be able to detect them as soon as I look at them."

"You're brilliant, Roger," Vyann said, laughing. "How about eating your fish?" And she put a hand over his affectionately.

Perhaps it was that which sparked Complain off. He flung his fork down.

"Rot your brilliance!" he said. "What about Marapper?—he was no alien and you killed him. Do you think I can forget that? Why should you expect any help from me after killing him?"

Waiting tensely for trouble to start, Complain could see other people turning from their meal to look at him. Scoyt opened his mouth and then shut it again, staring beyond Complain as a heavy hand fell on the latter's shoulder.

"Mourning for me is not only foolish but premature," a familiar voice said. "Still taking on the world single-handed, eh, Roy?"

Complain turned, amazed, and there stood the priest, beaming, scowling, rubbing his hands. He clutched Marapper's arm incredulously.

"Yes, I, Roy, and no other: the great subconscious rejected me—and left me confoundedly cold. I hope your scheme worked, Master Scoyt?"

"Excellently, Priest," Scoyt said. "Eat some of this beastly indigestible food and explain yourself to your friend, so that he will look at us less angrily."

"You were dead!" Complain said.

"Only a short Journey," Marapper said, seating himself

126

and stretching out for the ale jug. "This witch doctor, Master Scoyt here, thought up an uncomfortable way of testing you and Fermour. He painted my head with rat's blood and laid me out with some beastly drug to stage a death scene for your benefit."

"Just a slight overdose of chloral hydrate," said Scoyt, with a secretive smile.

"But I touched you—you were cold," Complain protested.

"I still am," Marapper said. "It's the effects of the drug. And what would be that beastly antidote your men shot into me?"

"Strychnine, I believe it's called," Scoyt said.

"Very unpleasant. I'm a hero, no less, Roy: always a saint, and now a hero as well. The schemers also condescended to give me a hot coffee when I came around; I never tasted anything so good in Quarters. . . . But this ale is better."

His eyes met Complain's still dazed ones over the rim of the mug. He winked, and belched with charming deliberation.

"I'm no ghost, Roy," he said. "Ghosts don't drink."

Before they had finished the meal, Master Scoyt was looking fretful. With a muttered apology, he left them.

"He works too hard," Vyann said, her eyes following him out of the hall. "We must all work hard. Before we sleep, you must be put in the picture and told our plans, for we shall be busy next wake."

"Ah," Marapper said eagerly, clearing his bowl, "that is what I want to hear. You understand my interest in this whole matter is purely theological, but what I'd like to know is, what do I get out of it?"

"First we are going to exorcise the Outsiders," she smiled. "Suitably questioned, Fermour should yield up their secret hiding place. We go there and kill them, and then we are free to concentrate on unravelling the riddles of the ship."

This she said quickly, as if anxious to avoid questioning on that point, and went on at once to usher them out of the dining-room and along several corridors. Marapper, now fully himself again, took the chance to tell Complain of their abortive search for the Control Room.

"So much has changed," Vyann complained. They were passing through a steel companionway whose double doors, now open, allowed egress from deck to deck. She indicated them lightly, saying: "These doors, for instance—in some places they are open, in some closed. And all the ones along Main Corridor are closed—which is fortunate, otherwise every marauder aboard ship would make straight for Forwards. But we cannot open or shut the doors at will, as the Giants must have been able to do when they owned the ship. As they stand now, so they have stood for generations; but *somewhere* must be a lever which controls them all. We are so helpless. We control nothing."

Her face was tense, the pugnacity of her jaw more noticeable. With a flash of intuition which surprised him, Complain thought, "She's getting an occupational disease like Scoyt's, because she's identifying her job with him." Then he doubted his own perceptions and, with a terrifying mental picture of the great ship with them all in it hurtling forever on its journey, had to admit the facts were enough to worry anyone. But it was still with the idea of checking her reactions that he asked Vyann, "Are you and Master Scoyt the only ones working on this problem?"

"For hem's sake, no!" she said. "We're only subordinates. A group calling itself the Survival Team has recently been constituted, and it and all other Forwards officers apart from guard officers are also devoting attention to the problem. In addition, two of the Council of Five are in charge of it; one of them you met, Priest—Councilor Zac Deight, the tall, long-haired man. The other of them I'm taking you to see now—Councilor Tregonnin. He is the librarian. He must explain the world to you."

So it was that Roy Complain and the priest came to their first astronomy lesson. Tregonnin, as he talked to them, hopped about the room from object to object; he was almost ludicrously small and nervous. Although he was neat in a womanish way, the room he ruled over was heaped with books and miscellaneous bric-à-brac in disorderly fashion. Confusion had here been brought to a fine art. Tregonnin explained first that until very recently in Forwards—as was the rule still in Quarters—anything like a book or a printed page had been destroyed, either from superstition or from a desire to preserve the power of the rulers by maintaining the ignorance of the ruled.

"That, no doubt, was how the idea of the ship became lost to begin with," Tregonnin said, strutting in front of them. "And that is why what you see assembled around you represents almost all the records intact in the area of Forwards. The rest has perished. What remains allows us only a fragment of the truth."

As the councilor began his narrative, Complain forgot the odd gestures with which he accompanied it. He forgot everything but the wonder of the tale as it had been pieced together, the mighty history patched up in this little room.

Through the space in which their world moved, other worlds also moved—two other sorts of worlds, one called sun, from which sprang heat and light, one called planet. The planets depended on the suns for heat and light. At one planet attached to a sun called Sol lived men; this planet was called Earth and the men lived all over the outside of it, because the inside was solid and had no light.

"The men did not fall off it, even when they lived on the bottom of it," Tregonnin explained. "For they had discovered a force called gravity. It is gravity which enables us to walk all the way around a circular deck without falling off."

Many other secrets the men discovered. They found a way to leave their planet and visit the other planets attached to their sun. This must have been a difficult secret, for it took them a long while. The other planets were different from theirs, and had either too little light and heat or too much. Because of this, there were no men living on them. This distressed the men of Earth.

Eventually they decided they would visit the planets of other suns, to see what they could find there, as their Earth was becoming exceptionally crowded. Here the scanty records in Tregonnin's possession became confusing, because while some said that space was very empty, others said it contained thousands of suns—stars, they were sometimes called.

For some lost reason, men found it hard to decide which sun to go to, but eventually, with the aid of instruments in which they were cunning, they picked on a bright sun called Procyon to which planets were attached, and which was only a distance called eleven light years away. To cross this distance was a considerable undertaking even for the ingenious men, since space had neither heat nor air, and the journey would be very long: so long that several generations of men would live and die before it was completed.

Accordingly, men built this ship in which they now were, built it of inexhaustible metal in eighty-four decks, filled it with everything needful, stocked it with their knowledge, powered it with charged particles called ions.

Tregonnin crossed rapidly to a corner.

"See!" he exclaimed. "Here is a model of the planet our ancestors left long ago—Earth!"

He held up a globe above his head. Chipped by careless handlers, obnubilated by the steep passage of time, it still retained on its surface the imprint of seas and continents.

Moved, he hardly knew why, Complain turned to look at Marapper. Tears were pouring down the old priest's cheeks.

"What ... what a beautiful story," Marapper sobbed. "You are a wise man, Councilor, and I believe it all, every word of it. What power those men had, what power! I am only a poor old provincial priest, jeezers nose, I know nothing, but. ..."

"Stop dramatizing yourself, man," Tregonnin said with unexpected severity. "Take your mind off your ego and concentrate on what I am telling you. Facts are the thing—facts, and not emotions!"

"You're used to the magnificence of the tale, I'm not," Marapper sobbed, unabashed. "To think of all that power. ..."

Tregonnin put the globe carefully down and said in a petulant tone to Vyann, "Inspector, if this objectionable fellow doesn't stop sniffing, you will have to take him away. I cannot stand sniffing. You know I cannot."

"When do we get to this Procyon's planets?" asked

Complain quickly. He could not bear the thought of leaving here till everything had been told him.

"A sound question, young man," Tregonnin said, looking at him for what was practically the first time. "And I'll try to give you a sound answer. It seems that the flight to Procyon's planets had two main objectives. The ship was made so big because not only would the confinement of a small ship be unendurable on such a long journey, but it had to carry a number of people called colonists. These colonists were to land on the new planet and live there, increasing and multiplying; the ship transported a lot of machines for them—we have found inventories of some of the things—tractors, concrete mixers, pile drivers—those are some of the names I recall.

"The second objective was to collect information on the new planet and samples from it, and bring it all back for the men of Earth to study."

In his jerky fashion, Councilor Tregonnin moved to a cupboard and fumbled about inside it. He brought out a metal rack containing a dozen round tins small enough to fit in a man's hand. He opened one. Crisp broken flakes like transparent nail parings fell out.

"Microfilm!" Tregonnin said, sweeping the flakes under a table with his foot. "It was brought in to me from a far corner of Forwards. Damp has ruined it, but even if it were intact it would be of no use to us: it needs a machine to make it readable."

"Then I don't see—" Complain began puzzledly, but the councilor held up a hand.

"I'll read you the labels on the tins," he said. "Then you'll understand. Only the labels survive. This one says, 'FILM: Survey New Earth, Aerial, Stratospheric, Orbital. Mid-Summer, N. Hemisphere.' This one says, 'FILM: Flora and Fauna Continent A, New Earth'. And so on."

He put the cans down, paused impressively and added, "So there, young man, is the answer to your question; on the evidence of these tins, it is obvious the ship reached Procyon's planets successfully. We are now traveling back to Earth."

In the untidy room deep silence fell, as each struggled alone to the very limits of his imagination. At last Vyann rose, shaking herself out of a spell, and said they should be going.

"Wait!" Complain said. "You've told us so much, yet you've told us so little. If we are traveling back to Earth, when do we get there? How can we know?"

"My dear fellow," Tregonnin began, then sighed and changed his mind about what he was going to say. "My dear fellow, don't you see, so much has been destroyed. ... The answers aren't always clear. Sometimes even the *questions* have been lost, if you follow my meaning. Let me answer you like this: we know the distance from New Earth, as the colonists called it, to Earth; it is eleven light years, as I have said. But we have not been able to find out how fast the ship is traveling."

"But one thing at least we do know," Vyann interposed. "Tell Roy Complain about the Forwards Roll, Councilor."

"Yes, I was just about to," Tregonnin said, with a touch of asperity. "Until we of the Council of Five took over command of Forwards, it was ruled by a succession of men calling themselves Governors. Under them, Forwards grew from a pitiful tribe to the powerful state it now is. Those Governors took care to hand down to each other a Roll or Testament, and this Roll or Testament the last Governor handed over to my keeping before he died. It is little more than a list of Governor's names. But under the *first* Governor's name it says—" he shut his eyes and waved a delicate hand to help him recite—" 'I am the fourth homeward-bound Captain of this ship, but since the title is only an irony now, I prefer to call myself Governor, if even that is not too grand a name'."

The councilor opened his eyes and said, "So you see, although the names of the first three men are lost, we have in the Roll a record of how many generations have lived aboard this ship since it started back for Earth. The number is twenty-three."

Marapper had not spoken for a long while. Now he asked, "Then that is a long time. When do we reach Earth?"

"That is the question your friend asked," Tregonnin said. "I can only answer that I know for how many generations we have been traveling. But no man knows

132

now when or how we stop. In the days before the first Governor, came the catastrophe—whatever that was—and since then the ship goes on and on non-stop through space, without captain, without control. One might almost say: without hope."

For most of that sleep, tired though he was, Complain could not rest. His mind seethed and churned with fearfu' images, and fretted itself with conjecture. Over and over he ran through what the councilor had said, trying to digest it.

It was all disquieting enough. Yet, in the midst of it, one tiny, irrelevant detail of their visit to the library kept recurring to him like toothache. At the time, it had seemed so unimportant that Complain, who was the only one who noticed it, had said nothing; now, its significance grew till it eclipsed even the thought of stars.

While Tregonnin was delivering his lecture, Complain had chanced to glance up at the library ceiling. Through the grille there, alert as if listening and understanding, peered a tiny rat's face.

III

"Contraction take your ego, Roy!" Marapper exploded. "Don't start mixing yourself up with the ideas of Forwards. It's that girl who's doing it, I know—you mark my words, she's playing her own game with you! You're so busy dreaming about the spicy secrets of her skirts, you can't see the wood for the ponics. Just remember: we came here with our own objectives, and they're still our objectives."

Complain shook his head. He and the priest were eating alone early the next wake. Officers crowded the dining-hall, but Vyann and Scoyt had not yet appeared. Now Marapper was making his old appeal, that they should try for power together.

"You're out of date, Marapper," he said shortly. "And you can leave Inspector Vyann out of it. These Forwards people have a cause beyond any petty seeking for power. Besides, what if you killed the lot of them? What good would it do? Would it help the ship?"

"To the hull with the ship. Look, Roy, trust your old priest who never let you down yet. These people are using us for their own ends; it's only common sense to do the same ourselves. And don't forget the Teaching tells you always to seek for yourself so that you may be freed from inner conflict."

"You're forgetting something," Complain said. "The Litany ends 'And the ship brought home'; it's one of the main tenets of the Teaching. You were always a shockingly bad priest, Marapper."

They were interrupted by the appearance of Vyann, looking fresh and attractive. She said she had already taken breakfast. With more irritation than he usually showed, Marapper excused himself. Something in Vyann's

134

manner told Complain she was happy enough to let him go; it suited him well also.

"Has Fermour been questioned yet?" he asked.

"No. One of the Council of Five, Zac Deight, has seen him, but that's all. Roger—that is, Master Scoyt—will question him later, but at present he is involved with some other, unexpected business."

He did not ask what this business might be. Seeing her so close again overpowered him, so that he could hardly think of anything to say. Mainly, he longed to tell her that nothing less than a miracle could have arranged her dark hair as it was. Instead, and with an effort, he asked what he was required to do.

"You are going to relax," she said brightly. "I have come to show you around Forwards."

It proved an impressive tour. Many rooms, here as in Quarters, were barren and empty; Vyann explained that this must be because their contents had been left on Procyon's planet, New Earth. Others had been turned into farms far surpassing Quarters' in scale. Many varieties of animal Complain had never seen before. He saw fish for the first time, swimming in tanks—here Vyann told him that they yielded the white meat he had enjoyed. There were amazing varieties of crops, some grown under special lighting. Cultivated ponics grew also, and brightly flowering shrubs. In one long room fruit grew, trees against the walls, bushes and plants in raised trenches in the middle; Complain inspected his first grapefruit here. The temperature was high in this room, the gardeners working naked to the waist. Sweat stood out on Complain's face, and he noticed Vyann's blouse sticking to her breasts; for him they were the sweetest fruits aboard the ship.

Many men and women worked on these agricultural decks, at humble tasks and complicated ones. Essentially a peaceful community, Forwards regarded agriculture as its chief occupation. Yet, despite all the trouble lavished on them, Vyann said, harvests mysteriously failed, animals died without apparent cause. Starvation remained a constant threat.

They moved to other decks. Sometimes the way was dark, the walls scarred with tokens of unguessable and forgotten weapons: souvenirs of the catastrophe. They came, feeling lonely now, to the Drive Floors, which Vyann said were strictly forbidden to all but a few officers. Here nobody lived; all was left to the silence and the dust.

"Sometimes I imagine this as it must once have been," Vyann whispered, sweeping her torch to left and right. "It must have been so busy. . . . This was the part of the ship where the actual force that made the ship go was produced. Many men must have worked here."

The doors which stood open along their way were doors with heavy wheels set in them, quite unlike the ordinary metal ship's doors. They passed through a last archway and were in a colossal chamber several floors high. The cone of the torch's beam picked out massed banks of strange shapes to either side, and in between, cumbrous structures on wheels, with grapnels and scoops and metal hands.

"Once it was alive: now it's all dead!" Vyann whispered. There was no echo here; the brutal undulations of metal sucked up every sound. "This is what the Control Room would control if we could find it."

They retreated, and Vyann led the way into another chamber much like the first, but smaller, though it too was enormous by ordinary standards. Here, though the dust was as thick, a deep and constant note filled the air.

"You see—the force is not dead!" the girl said. "It still lives behind these steel walls. Come and look here!"

She led into an adjoining room, almost filled with the gigantic bulk of a machine. The machine, completely panelled over, was shaped like three immense wheels set hub to hub, with a pipe many feet in diameter emerging from either side and curving up into bulkheads. At Vyann's behest, Complain set his hand on the pipe. It vibrated. In the side of one of the great wheels was an inspection panel; Vyann unlatched and opened it, and at once the organ note increased, like a proslambanomenos implementing a sustained chord.

The girl shone her torch into the aperture.

Complain stared fascinated. Within the darkness, flickering and illusory, something spun and reflected the light, droning deeply as it did so. At the heart of it, a small pipe drip, drip, dripped liquid continually on to a whirling hub.

"Is this space?" he asked Vyann breathlessly.

"No," she said, as she closed the panel again. "This is one of three tremendous fans. The little pipe in the middle lubricates it. Those fans never stop; they circulate air to the whole ship."

"How do you know?"

"Because Roger brought me down here and explained to me."

Immediately, Complain's present surroundings meant nothing to him. Before he could think of stopping the words, he said, "What is Roger Scoyt to you, Vyann?"

"I love him very much," she said tensely. "I am an orphan—my mother and father both made the Journey when I was very young. They caught the trailing rot. Roger Scoyt and his wife, who was barren, adopted me; and since she was killed in a raid on Forwards many watches ago, he has trained me and looked after me constantly."

In the upsurge of relief that buoyed Complain, he seized Vyann's hand. At once, she clicked off her torch and pulled away from him, laughing mockingly in the dark.

"I didn't bring you down here to flirt, sir," she said. "You must prove yourself before trying that sort of thing with me."

He tried to grab her, but in the darkness banged his head, whereupon she at once switched on the torch. At his lack of success he was angry and sulky, turning away from her, rubbing his sore skull.

"Why did you bring me down here?" he asked. "Why be friendly to me at all?"

"You take the Teaching too seriously—it's what I might expect from someone out of a provincial tribe!" she said pettishly. Then, relenting a little, she said. "But come, don't look so cross. You need not think because someone shows friendliness they mean you harm. That old-fashioned idea is more worthy of your friend Priest Marapper."

Complain was not so easily teased out of his mood, especially as mention of Marapper's name recalled the priest's warning. He lapsed into a gloomy silence which Vyann was too haughty to break, and they made their way back rather dejectedly. Once or twice, Complain looked half-imploringly at her profile, willing her to speak. Finally she did—without looking at him.

"There was something I had to ask you," she said in a reluctant voice. "The lair of the Outsiders must be found; a tribe of raiders has to be destroyed. Because our people are mainly agriculturalists, we have no hunters. Even our trained guards will not venture far into the tangles—certainly they could not cover the vast areas you did on your way here. Roy—we need you to lead us against our enemies. We hoped to show you enough to convince you they were your enemies too."

Now she was regarding Complain. She smiled kindly, plaintively.

"When you look at me like that, I could get out and walk to Earth!" he exclaimed.

"We shall not ask that of you," she said, still smiling, and for once the reserve completely left her. "Now we must go and see how Roger's business is coming along. I'm sure he has been taking the work of the entire ship on his shoulders. I told you about the Outsiders; he can explain about Gregg's band of raiders."

Pressing on keenly, she missed the expression of surprise on Complain's face.

Master Scoyt had been more than busy; he had been successful. For once, feeling he was achieving something, his brow was clear; he greeted Complain like an old friend.

The interrogation of Fermour, who was still under surveillance in a nearby cell, had been postponed because of a rumpus in Deadways. Forwards scouts, hearing a commotion among the tangles, had ventured as far as Deck 29 (which, it transpired, was the deck on which Complain and Marapper had been caught). This deck, only two beyond the frontiers of Forwards, was badly damaged, and the scouts never dared to go beyond it. They had returned empty-handed, reporting a fight of some sort, punctuated by the shrill screams of men and women, taking place on Deck 30.

There the whole matter might have ended. But shortly after this episode, one of Gregg's ruffians had approached the barriers, calling for truce and begging to see someone in authority.

"I've got him in the next cell," Scoyt told Vyann and Complain. "He's a queer creature called Hawl, but beyond referring to his boss as 'the Captain', he seems sane enough."

"What does he want?" Vyann asked. "Is he a deserter?"

"Better even than that, Laur," Scoyt said. "This fight our scouts reported in Deadways was between Gregg's and another gang. Hawl won't say why, but the episode has seriously put the shakes up them. So much so, that Gregg is suing for peace with us through this fellow Hawl, and wants to bring his tribe to live in Forwards for protection."

"It's a ruse!" Vyann exclaimed, "a trick to get in here!"

"No, I don't think so," Scoyt said. "Hawl is obviously quite sincere. The only snag is that Gregg, knowing the sort of reputation he has with us, wants a Forwards official to go to him as a token of good faith to arrange terms. Whoever is chosen goes back with Hawl."

"Sounds fishy to me," Vyann said.

"Well, you'd better come and see him. But prepare yourself for a shock. He is not a very lovely specimen of humanity."

Two Forwards officers were with Hawl, supposedly guarding him. They had plainly been beating the hull out of him with knotted ropes. Scoyt dismissed them sharply, but for some while could get no sense out of Hawl, who lay face down, groaning, until the offer of another thrashing made him sit up. He was a startling creature, as near a mutant as made no difference. Madarosis had left him completely hairless, so that neither beard nor eyebrows sprouted from his flesh; he was also toothless; and an unfortunate congenital deformity had given his face a crazed top-heaviness, for while he was so undershot that his upper gum hung in air, his forehead was so distended by exostosis that it all but hid his eyes. Yet Hawl's chief peculiarity was that these minor oddities were set above a normal-sized body on a skull no bigger than a man's two fists clenched one atop the other.

As far as could be judged, he was of middle age. Taking

in Vyann's and Complain's awed gaze, he muttered a fragment of scripture.

"May my neuroses not offend. . . . "

"Now, Shameface," Master Scoyt said genially. "What guarantee does your good master offer our representative—*if* we send him one—of getting back here in safety?"

"If I get back safely to the Captain," Hawl mumbled, "your man shall get back safely to you. This we swear."

"How far is it to this brigand you call the Captain?"

"That your man will know when he comes with me," Hawl replied.

"Very true. Or we could drag it out of you here."

"You couldn't!" There was something in the strange creature's tone which compelled respect. Scoyt evidently felt it, for he told the man to get up and dust himself down and take a drink of water. While he did so, Scoyt asked. "How many men in Gregg's gang?"

Hawl put the drinking utensil down and stood defiantly with hands on hips.

"That your man will be told when he comes with me to arrange terms," he said. "Now I've said all I'm going to say, and you'll have to make up your minds whether you agree or not. But remember this—if we come here, we shall be no trouble. And we shall fight for you rather than against. This also we swear."

Scoyt and Vyann looked at each other.

"It's worth trying if we can get a foolhardy volunteer," he said.

"It'll have to go to the Council," she said.

Complain had not spoken yet, awaiting his opportunity. Now he addressed Hawl.

"This man you call Captain," he said. "Has he another name than Gregg?"

"You can ask him that when you're arranging terms," Hawl repeated.

"Look at me carefully, fellow. Do I resemble your Captain in any way? Answer."

"The Captain has a beard," Hawl said evasively.

"He should give it you to cover your head with!" Complain snapped. "What do you say to this then?—I had a brother who ran amok into Deadways long ago. His

140

name was Gregg—Gregg Complain. Is that your Captain, man?"

"Gord's guts!" Hawl said. "To think the Captain has a brother lounging in this bed of pansies!"

Complain turned excitedly to Master Scoyt, whose heavy face creased with surprise. "I volunteer to go with this man to Gregg," he said.

The suggestion suited Master Scoyt well. He immediately turned his vast energy to get Complain on his way as soon as possible. The full force of his persuasiveness, genial but relentless, was applied to the elders of the Council of Five, who convened at once under his direction; Tregonnin was urged reluctantly from the library, Zac Deight disentangled from a theological argument with Marapper, and Billyoe, Dupont and Ruskin, the other three of the Council, lured from their various interests. After a private discussion, they had Complain brought before them, instructed him on the terms to lay down before Gregg, and dismissed him with their expansions. He would have to hurry to be back before the next dark sleep-wake descended upon them.

Though the disadvantages of having Gregg's band in Forwards were obvious, the Council was keen to welcome them in; it would mean an end to most of the skirmishing on Forwards' perimeter and the acquiring of an experienced ally to fight against the Outsiders.

An orderly returned Complain's dazer and torch to him. He was in his room strapping them on when Vyann entered, closing the door behind her. On her face was a comically defiant expression.

"I'm coming with you," she said, without preamble.

Complain crossed to her, protesting. She was not used to the ponics, danger might lurk there, Gregg might well play them false, she was a woman—She cut him short.

"It's no good arguing," she said. "This is Council's orders."

"You got around them! You arranged it!" he said. He could see he guessed rightly, and was suddenly deliriously glad. Seizing her wrist, he asked, "What made you wish to come?"

The answer was not as flattering as he might have wished. Vyann had always wanted to hunt in the ponics, she said; this was the next best thing. And suddenly Complain was reminded—without pleasure—of Gwenny and her passion for the hunt.

"You'll have to behave yourself," he said severely, wishing her reason for joining him could have been more personal.

Marapper appeared before they left, seeking a word alone with Complain. He had found a mission in life: the people of Forwards needed to be reconverted to the Teaching; since the more lenient rule of the Council began, the Teaching had lost its grip. Zac Deight in particular was against it—hence Marapper's argument with him.

"I don't like that man," the priest grumbled. "There's something horribly *sincere* about him."

"Don't stir up trouble here, please," Complain begged, "just when these people have got around to accepting us. For hem sake relax, Marapper. Stop being yourself!"

Marapper shook his head so sadly his cheeks wobbled.

"You also are falling among the unbelievers, Roy," he said. "I must stir up trouble: turmoil in the id—it must out! There lies our salvation, and of course if the people rally around me at the same time, so much the better. Ah, my friend, we have come so far together, only to find a girl to corrupt you."

"If you mean Vyann, Priest," Complain said, "have a care to leave her out of this. I've warned you before, she's nothing to do with you."

His voice was challenging, but Marapper was as bland as butter in return.

"Don't think I object to her, Roy. Though as a priest I cannot condone, as a man, believe me, I envy."

He looked forlorn as Complain and Vyann made for the barriers, where Hawl awaited them. His old boisterousness had been muted by Forwards, where everyone was a stranger to him; undoubtedly, for Marapper, to be a big fish in a small pool was better than being a small fish in a big pool. Where Complain had found himself, the priest was beginning to lose himself.

Hawl, his incredibly tiny head cocked, looked only too glad to get back into the ponics; the reception Forwards had given him had not been notably cordial. Once the

142

little party of three were seen through the barricades, he loped ahead professionally, Vyann behind him, Complain bringing up the rear. No longer a mere freak, Hawl moved with an ability the hunter in Complain could only admire; the fellow hardly seemed to stir a leaf. Complain wondered what could have alarmed a man of his stamp so much that he was willing to forsake his natural element for the unfamiliar disciplines of Forwards.

Having only two decks to cover, they were not long in the ponics. This, in Vyann's view at least, was all to the good; the tangles, she found, were not romantic; merely drab, irritating and full of tiny black midges. She stopped gratefully when Hawl did, and peered ahead through the thinning stalks.

"I recognize this stretch!" Complain exclaimed. "It's near where Marapper and I were captured."

A black and ruinous length of corridor lay ahead, the walls pock-marked and scarred, the roof ripped wide with the force of some bygone explosion. It was here the explorers from Quarters had run into the eerie weightlessness. Hawl shone a light ahead and let out a fluttering whistle. Almost at once, a rope floated out of the hole in the roof.

"If you go and grab hold of that, they'll pull you up," Hawl said. "Just walk slowly to it and catch hold. It's simple enough."

It could, despite this reassurance, have been simpler. Vyann gave a gasp of alarm as the lightness seized her, but Complain, more prepared, took her waist and steadied her. Without too much loss of dignity, they got to the rope and were at once hauled up. They were hauled through the roof, and through the roof of the level above that— the damage had been extensive. Hawl, scorning the aid of ropes, dived up head first and landed nonchalantly before they did.

Four ragged men greeted them, crouched over a desultory game of Travel-Up. Vyann and Complain stood in a shattered room, still almost weightless. A miscellany of furniture was ranged around the hole from which they emerged, obviously acting as a shelter for anyone needing to guard the hole in the event of an attack. Complain expected to be relieved of his dazer, but instead Hawl, having exchanged a few words with his tattered friends, led them out to another corridor. Here their weight immediately returned.

The corridor was filled with wounded men and women lying on piles of dead ponics, most of them with face or legs bandaged; they were presumably the victims of the recent battle. Hawl hurried past them clucking sympathetically and pushed into another apartment filled with stores and men, most of them patched, bandaged or torn. Among them was Gregg Complain.

It was unmistakably Gregg. The old look of dissatisfaction, manifesting itself around the eyes and the thin lips, was not altered by his heavy beard, or by an angry scar on his temple. He stood up as Complain and Vyann approached.

"This is the Captain," Hawl announced. "I brought your brother and his fine lady to parley with you, Captain."

Gregg moved over to them, eyes searching them as if his life depended on it. He had lost the old Quarters' habit of not looking anyone in the eye. As he scanned them, his expression never changed. They might have been blocks of wood; he might have been a block of wood; the blood relationship meant nothing to him.

"You've come officially from Forwards?" he finally asked his younger brother.

"Yes," Complain said.

"You didn't take long to get yourself into their favors, did you?"

"What do you know of that?" Complain challenged. The surly independence of his brother had, from all appearances, grown stronger since his violent withdrawal from Quarters long ago.

"I know a lot of what goes on in Deadways," Gregg said, "I'm captain of Deadways, if nowhere else. I knew you were heading for Forwards. How I knew, never mind—let's get down to business. What did you bring a woman with you for? To wipe your nose?"

"As you said, let's get down to business," Complain said sharply.

"I suppose she's come to keep an eye on you to see you behave yourself," Gregg muttered. "That seems a likely Forwards arrangement. You'd better follow me; there's

144

too much moaning going on in here. . . . Hawl, you come too. Davies, you're in charge here now—keep 'em quiet if you can."

Following Gregg's burly back, Complain and Vyann were led into a room of indescribable chaos. All over its scanty furnishings, bloody rags and clothes had been tossed; red-soaked bandages lay over the floor like so many broken jam rolls. A remnant of manners still lurked in Gregg, for seeing the look of distaste on Vyann's face, he apologized for the muddle.

"My woman was killed in the fight last night," he said. "She was torn to bits—ugh, you never heard such screams! I couldn't get to her. I just couldn't get to her. She'd have cleaned this muck up by now. Perhaps you'd like to do it for me?"

"We will discuss your proposals and then leave as soon as possible," Vyann said tightly.

"What was it about this fight that has scared you so, Gregg?" Complain asked.

" 'Captain' to you," his brother said. "Nobody calls me Gregg to my face. And understand, I'm not scared: nothing's ever scared me yet. I'm only thinking of my tribe. If we stay here we'll be killed, sure as shame. We've got to move, and Forwards is as safe a place as any to move to. So—" he sat wearily on the bed and waved to his brother to do the same—"It's not safe here any more. Men we can fight, but not rats."

"Rats?" Vyann echoed.

"Rats, yes, my beauty," Gregg said, baring his fangs for emphasis. "Great big dirty rats, that can think and plan and organize like men. Do you know what I'm talking about, Roy?"

Complain was pale.

"Yes," he said. "I've had them running over me. They signal to each other, and dress in rags, and capture other animals."

"Oh, you know them, do you? Surprising. . . . You know more than I credited you with. They're the menace, the rat packs, the biggest menace on the ship. They've learned to co-operate and attack in formation—that's what they did last sleep when they fought us—that's why we're

145

getting out. We wouldn't be able to beat them off again if they came in strength."

"This is extraordinary!" Vyann exclaimed. "We've had no such attacks in Forwards."

"Maybe not. Forwards is not the world," Gregg said grimly. He told them his theory, that the rat packs kept to Deadways because there they found the solitary humans whom they could attack and destroy without interference. Their latest raid was partly evidence of increasing organization, partly an accident because they had not at the outset realized the strength of Gregg's band. Deciding he had said enough, Gregg changed the subject abruptly.

His plans for coming into Forwards were simple, he said. He would retain his group, numbering about fifty, as an autonomous unit which would not mix with the people of Forwards; they would spend their wakes as they spent them now, skirmishing through Deadways, returning only for sleep. They would be responsible for the guarding of Forwards from Outsiders, Giants, rats and other raiders.

"And in return?" Complain asked.

"In return, I must keep the right to punish my own folk," Gregg said. "And everyone must address me as Captain."

"Surely rather a childish stipulation?"

"You think so? You never knew what was good for you. I've got here in my possession an old diary which proves that I—and you, of course—are descended from a Captain of this ship. His name was Captain Complain—Captain Gregory Complain. He owned the whole ship. Imagine that if you can. . . ."

Gregg's face was suddenly lit with wonder, then the curtain of surliness fell again. Behind it was a glimpse of a human trying to come to terms with the world. Then he was once more a scruffy brute, sitting on bandages. When Vyann asked him how old the diary was, he shrugged his shoulders, said he did not know, said he had never read more than the title page of the thing—and that, Complain guessed shrewdly, would have taken him some while.

"The diary's in the locker behind you," Gregg said. "I'll show it you sometime—if we come to terms. Have you decided about that?"

"You really offer us little to make the bargain attractive,

146

Brother," Complain replied. "This rat menace, for instance—for your own motives you are over-estimating it."

"You think so?" Gregg stood up. "Then come and have a look here. Hawl, you stay and keep an eye on the lady—what we're going to see is no sight for her."

He led Complain along a desolate muddle of corridor, saying as they went how sorry he was to have to leave this hideout. The ancient explosion and a chance arrangement of closed inter-deck doors had given his band a fortress only approachable through the gashed roof by which Complain and Vyann had entered. Still talking—and now beyond his habitual surliness were tokens that he felt some pleasure at the sight of his brother—Gregg burst into a cupboard-like room.

"Here's an old pal for you," he said, with a sweeping gesture of introduction.

The announcement left Complain unprepared for what he saw. On a rough and dirty couch lay Ern Roffery, the valuer. He was barely recognizable. Three fingers were missing, and half the flesh of his face; one eye was gone. Most of the superb moustache had been chewed away. It needed nobody to tell Complain that this was the work of the rats—he could see their teeth-marks on a protruding cheek bone. The valuer did not move.

"Shouldn't be surprised if he's made the Journey," Gregg said carelessly. "Poor cur's been in continual pain. Half his chest is eaten away."

He shook Roffery's shoulder roughly, raised his head and let it drop back on the pillow.

"Still warm—probably unconscious," he said. "But this'll show you what we're up against. We picked this hero up last wake, several decks away. He said the rats had finished him. It was from him I heard about you—he recognized me, poor cur. Not a bad fellow."

"One of the best," Complain said. His throat was so tight he could scarcely speak; his imagination was at work—involuntarily—picturing this horrible thing happening. He could not drag his eyes from Roffery's ravaged face. In a daze he stood there while his brother kept talking. The rats had picked Roffery up in the swimming pool; while he was still helpless from the effects of the Giants' gassing, they had loaded him on to a sort of stretcher and dragged him to their warrens. And there he had been questioned, under torture.

The warren was between broken decks, where no man could reach. It was packed stiff with rats, and with an extraordinary variety of bric-à-brac they had scavenged and built into dens and caves. Roffery saw their captive animals, existing under appalling conditions. Many of these helpless beasts were deformed, like human mutations, and some of them had the ability to probe with their minds into other minds. These mutated creatures were set by the rats to question Roffery.

Complain shuddered. He recalled his disgust when the rabbit had bubbled its insane interrogations into his mind. Roffery's experience, long protracted, had been infinitely worse. Whatever they learned from him—and they must have acquired much knowledge of the ways of men— Roffery learned something from them: the rats knew the ship as no man ever had, at least since the catastrophe; the tangles were no obstacle to them, for they traveled by the low roads between decks, which was why men saw them rarely, traveled by the ten thousand pipes and sewers and tubes that were the great ship's arteries.

"Now you see why I'm not happy here," Gregg said. "I don't want my flesh chewed off my skull. These rats are the end as far as I'm concerned. Let's go back to your woman. You picked lucky with her, brother. My woman was no beauty—the cartilage in her legs was all bone, so she could not bend her knees. But ... it didn't worry her in bed."

Vyann seemed content when they returned to her; she was drinking a hot liquid. Only Hawl looked guilty and saw fit to explain that the bloody bandages had made her ill, so he had gone to fetch her a drink.

"There's a drop left for you, Captain," the small-head added. "Drain it off like a good fellow."

As Gregg drank, Complain made to go. He was still feeling shaken at the sight of Roffery.

"We'll put your proposition to the Council," he said. "They should accept it when they hear about the rats. I'll come back and report to you what they say. Now we must get back: the next sleep-wake is a dark, and there is much to be done before that."

Gregg looked hard at his brother. Beneath the morose indifference of his expression, uneasiness stirred; undoubtedly he was anxious to get his band to Forwards as soon as possible. Perhaps he realized for the first time that his younger brother was a force to reckon with.

"Here's a present for you to take with you," he said clumsily, picking up something from the bed and thrusting it at Complain. "It's a sort of dazer I took off a Giant we speared two wakes back. It kills by heat. It's awkward to handle, and you'll burn yourself if you aren't careful, but it was a useful enough weapon against the rats."

The "sort of dazer" was a stubby metal object, as cumbrous as Gregg had said; he pressed the button, and a fan of almost invisible heat spread from the front. Even standing away from it, Complain could feel its heat, but its range was obviously short. Nevertheless, Complain accepted it gratefully, and he parted from his brother on an unexpectedly cordial note. It felt funny, he thought, to be pleased by a personal relationship like that.

Vyann and Complain made their way back to Forwards unescorted, the latter with more anxiety than when they had set out, keeping his senses alert for rats. They arrived safely, only to find Forwards in an uproar.

IV

A Giant had entered Forwards. He had not come through any of the barriers, which of course were guarded continually, but had suddenly appeared before a home-ward-bound labouring girl on Deck 14. Before she could cry out, the unfortunate girl had been seized, gagged and bound; she was in no way molested, and as soon as the Giant had finished tying her up, he disappeared. Without much delay, the girl managed to bite off the gag and call for help.

Police and guards had started a search for the invader at once. Their alarm at this confirmation of the existence of Giants, if confirmation still was needed in Forwards, was increased by the apparent pointlessness of his action; obviously some sinister move was afoot. General concensus of opinion was that the Giants were returning from their long sleep to take back the ship. In the pursuit that followed, Master Scoyt and most of his staff joined, and were at present scouring all levels near the scene of the incident.

This Vyann and Complain learned from an excited sentry at the barriers. As they made for their own apart-ments, distant whistles could be heard; the corridors were almost empty—evidently most people had joined in the chase. A diversion was always as welcome in Forwards as it had been in Quarters.

Vyann breathed a sigh of relief.

"This gives us a lull," she said. "I didn't want to face the Council before I had talked to you. I don't know how you feel, but I'm sure of one thing: we can't have your brother's mob here—they'd be unmanageable."

Complain had known instinctively how she felt. Inclined

to agree, he nevertheless said, "Do you feel happy about leaving them to the rats?"

"Gregg's deliberately over-estimating the abilities of the rats, as a lever to get himself in here. If he's really so anxious about them he can move further into Deadways. He certainly can't come here: our organization would collapse."

Vyann had the stubborn look about her mouth again. She was so self-possessed that a wave of rebellion ran through Complain. Catching the defiance in his eyes, Vyann smiled slightly and said, "Come into my room and talk, Roy."

It was an apartment much like Complain's, rather bare, rather military, except for a bright rug on the floor. Vyann shut the door behind them and said, "I shall have to recommend to Roger and the Council that we keep Gregg out at all costs. You may have noticed that half his men had some sort of deformity; I suppose he has to pick what recruits he can from the freaks of Deadways, but we can't possibly allow that sort here."

"He has more knowledge of that area of the ship than anyone here," Complain said, stung by the contempt in her voice. "For any forays into the ponics he'd be invaluable."

She waved a hand gently, bringing it to rest on his arm. "Let us not quarrel. The Council can decide the matter. Anyhow I have something to show you—"

"Before we change the subject," Complain interrupted, "Gregg made a remark that worried me. He thought you came with me to keep an eye on me, was that true?"

She looked at Complain searchingly and said, her seriousness dissolving, "Supposing I like keeping an eye on you?"

He had reached one of those points there could be no retreat from; already his blood hammered with a mysterious foreknowledge of what he was bound to do. He dropped the cumbrous weapon Gregg had given him on to the bed. Any rebuff was worth this delirious event of putting his hands behind her back and pulling her—her, the dark, unattainable Vyann!—towards him, and kissing her on the lips. There was no rebuff; when she opened her eyes again they were full of an excitement as wild as his.

" 'Home is the hunter, home from the hull . . .'," Vyann whispered, quoting from a poem she had learned in childhood. "You'll stay in Forwards, now, won't you, Roy?"

"Do you need to ask?" he exclaimed, putting his hand up to touch the hair that had always so compelled him. They stood together for a long while, just looking at each other, just living, until at last Vyann said, "This will not do. Come and see what I've got to show you—something thrilling! With any luck it will tell us a great deal we need to know about the ship."

Vyann was back to business; it took Complain somewhat longer to recover. She sat down on the bed. As Complain sat beside her, she unbuttoned her tunic and pulled out a narrow black book, handing it to him. It was warm from her body heat. Dropping it, he put his hand on her blouse, tracing the arable contours of her breasts.

"Laur, darling—" This was the first time he had spoken her first name aloud, "—must we look at this wretched book just now?"

Vyann put the book playfully but firmly back into his hands.

"Yes, we must," she said. "It was written by an ancestor of yours. I stole it from Gregg's locker when I had sent that dreadful monster Hawl out to get me a drink. It's the diary of Gregory Complain, sometime Captain of this ship."

The instinct which prompted Vyann to steal the diary was a sure one; although the entries were comparatively few, the vistas they opened up came like a revelation. Because Vyann read more quickly than he, Complain soon gave up, lying with his head in her lap as she read aloud. Neither of them could have been more fascinated, even if they had known of the lucky flukes to which, over the years, the little book owed its continued existence.

At first the account was difficult to follow, by virtue of its reference to things of which Vyann and Complain had no knowledge; but they soon grew to understand the alarming predicament in which the writer of the diary and his contemporaries found themselves. That ancient crisis seemed suddenly very near, although it had happened so long ago; for Captain Gregory—as Vyann soon discovered

—had been the first captain on the ship's journey home from Procyon.

An illuminating entry occurred only a few pages after the diary began:

"28.xi.2521. More trouble from Agricultural Bay (the long-dead Captain Gregory had written). Watkins, I/C Floriculture was up to see me after morning watch. He reports that the chlorosis afflicting many species of plants is no better, despite constant iron treatments. Advance spectrum output has been increased two degrees. Lt. Stover—I understand the ratings call him 'Noah'—was up shortly afterwards. He is I/C Animal Insemination, and is no happier about his lower animals than Watkins is about his higher plants. Apparently the mice are breeding at a significantly faster rate, but bearing undeveloped foetuses; guinea pigs show similar tendencies. This is hardly a major worry. Most of these creatures went offboard at New Earth (Procyon V's fancy name) as planned; the few we have are concessions to Noah's sentimentality—though his argument that they may be useful for laboratory experiments has something to commend it.

"30.xi.2521. Last night was our usual monthly ball. My dear wife, Yvonne, who always organizes these things, had gone to great pains over it; she looked lovely—but of course the years tell on us both—it's hard to realize Frank is eighteen! Unfortunately the dance was a complete failure. This was our first dance since leaving Orbit X, and the absence of the colonists made itself felt. So few people seem left aboard. We are now ten days out from Procyon V. The monotonous years stretch like dead weight before us.

"Went amidships this morning to see Floriculture. Watkins and Montgomery, the hydroponics specialist, look more cheerful. Though many of the crops appear in worse fettle than before, those essential plants, the five cultures which provide us with our air, are picking up again; the iron dosages evidently did the trick. Less cheer from 'Noah' Stover—they have a lot of sick animals on their hands.

153

"2.xii2521. We are now on full acceleration. The long journey home may be said to have begun in earnest: as if any one felt excited about that. Morale is low. ... Yvonne and Frank are being splendid, partly, I suppose, to try and forget that Joy—so recently our baby girl!—is now several a.u.'s behind. A nefarious 'No More Procreation' club has been formed in crew's quarters, I am told by Internal Relations; the basic human drives can cope with that one, I think. More difficult to deal with is poor Bassitt. . . . He was an Aviarist Second Class, but now that all birds except a handful of sparrows have been released on the New World, time hangs heavy for him. He has evolved a dismal religion of his own, mugged it up out of old psychology textbooks, which he insists on preaching up and down Main Corridor. Amazing thing is, people seem inclined to listen. Sign of the times, I suppose.

"These are minor matters. I was about to deal with a more serious one—the animals—when I was called. More later.

"5.xii.2521. No time for diary writing. A curse has fallen upon us! Hardly an animal aboard ship is now on its feet; many are dead. The rest lie stiffly with eyes glazed, occasional muscular spasms providing their only sign of life. The head of Fauniculture, Distaff—who went to school with me—is sick, but his underlings and Noah are doing good work. Drugs, however, seem ineffective on the suffering creatures. If only they could talk! Agritechnics are co-operating full blast with the Laboratory Deck, trying to find what plague has descended on us. Curse of God, I say! ... All this is grist for Bassitt's mill, of course.

"10.xii.2521. Among the stack of routine reports on my desk every morning is the sick report. On the 8th there were nine sick, yesterday nineteen, today forty-one—and a request, which I hardly needed, from Senior M.O. Toynbee, to see me. I went straight down to Sick Bay to see him. He says the trouble is a food poisoning of some still unidentified kind. Toynbee, as usual, was rather pompous and learned, but without definite knowledge; obviously, as he explains, whatever got into the animals has got into his patients. They were a pathetic lot, a high

154

percentage of them children. Like the animals, they lie rigidly, occasionally undergoing muscular twitch; high temperatures, vocal chords apparently paralyzed. Sick Bay out of bounds to visitors.

"14.xii.2521. Every child and adolescent aboard now lies locked in pain in Sick Bay. Adults also affected. Total sick: 109. This is nearly a quarter of our company; fortunately—at least as far as manning the ship is concerned—the older people seem more immune. Distaff died yesterday, but he was sick anyway. No deaths from the strange paralysis reported. Anxious faces everywhere. I can hardly bear to look at them.

"17.xii.2521. Oh Lord, if You did not from its launching turn Your face from this ship, look upon us all now. It is nine days since the first nine sicknesses were reported. Eight of them died today. We had thought, and Toynbee assured me, they were recovering. The stiffness lasted a week; for the last two days, the patients were relaxed, although still running temperatures. Three spoke up intelligently and said they felt better, the other six seemed delirious. The deaths occurred quietly, without struggle. Laboratory Deck has post-mortems on hand, Sheila Simpson is the only survivor of this first batch, a girl of thirteen; her temperature is lower, she may live.

"The nine day cycle will be up for ten more cases tomorrow. Infinite foreboding fills me.

"One hundred and eighty-eight people are now in bed, many lying in their respective rooms, the Sick Bay being full. Power staff are being drafted as orderlies. Bassitt in demand! A deputation of twenty officers, all very respectful, and headed by Watkins, came to see me after lunch; they requested that we turn back to New Earth before it is too late. Of course I had to dissuade them; poor Cruikshank of Ship's Press was among them—his son was one of the eight who died this morning.

"18.xii.2521. Could not sleep. Frank was taken early this morning, dear lad. He lies as rigid as a corpse, staring at—what? Yet he was only one of twenty fresh cases; the older people are getting it now. Have been forced to modify the ship's routine: another few days and it must be abandoned altogether. Thank heaven most devices are automatic and self-servicing.

"Of the ten patients whose nine day cycle finished today, seven have died. The other three remain on the threshold of consciousness. No change in young Sheila. All anyone talks about now is what is called the 'Nine Day Ague'. Had Bassitt put in the cells on a charge of spreading depression.

"I am tired after a prolonged inspection of Agriculture with, among others, Watkins, who was rather stiff after the failure of his deputation yesterday. Ninety-five per cent of all livestock took the Ague, Noah tells me. About 45 per cent of those recovered—wish human figures looked as good! Unfortunately, the bigger animals came off worst; no horses survived and, more serious, no cows. Sheep fared badly, pigs and dogs comparatively well. The mice and rats are fully recovered, their reproductive capacities unimpaired.

"Ordinary earth-grown plants have shown roughly similar percentages of survival. Back-breaking work had gone on here; the depleted staffs have coped nobly with the job of cleaning the acres of beds.

"In the adjacent chambers, Montgomery showed me his hydroponics with pride. Completely recovered from chlorosis—if it was chlorosis—they are more vigorous than ever, and seem almost to have benefited from their version of the Nine Day Ague. Five types of oxygenator are grown: two 'wet,' one 'semi-wet' and two 'dry' varieties. One of these dry varieties in particular, an edible variety modified centuries ago from ground elder, is growing luxuriantly and shows a tendency to flow out from its gravel beds over the deck. Temperatures in Floriculture are being kept high; Mongomery thinks it helps.

"Phoned Laboratories. Research promise (as they have before) to produce a cure for our plague tomorrow; unfortunately most of the scientists there are down with the Ague, and a woman called Payne is trying to run things.

"21.xii.2521. I have left the Control Room—perhaps for good. The shutters have been closed against the ghastly stars. Gloom lies thick over the ship. Over half our population has the Nine Day Ague; out of sixty-six who have completed the full cycle, forty-six have died. The percentage of deaths is dropping daily, but the survivors seem comatose. Sheila Simpson, for instance, hardly stirs.

"Managing any sort of organization becomes increasingly hard. Contact with further parts of the ship is virtually lost, since all the switchboard team has the Ague. Everywhere, groups of men and women huddle together, waiting. Licentiousness vies with apathy for upper hand. I have visions of us all dying, this dreadful tomb speeding on perhaps for millenia until it is captured by a sun.

"This pessimism is weakness: even Yvonne cannot cheer me.

"Research now knows the cause of the Ague; somehow that seems of small importance. The knowledge comes too late. For what it is worth, here are their findings. Before leaving the new planet, we completely rewatered. All stocks of water aboard were evacuated into orbit, and fresh supplies ferried up. The automatic processes which claim moisture from the air and feed it back into the hull tanks have always been efficient; but naturally such water, used over and over, had become—to use a mild word—insipid.

"The new water, ferried up from the streams of Procyon V, tasted good. It had, of course, been tested for microscopic life and filtered; but perhaps we were not as thorough as we should have been—scientific method has naturally stagnated over the generations. However, apportioning blame is irrelevant in our present extremity. In simple terms, proteins were suspended in the water in molecular solutions, and so slipped through our filters.

"June Payne, in Research, a bright and conceited young thing whose hyper-agarophobia rendered her unable to join her husband on Procyon V, explained the whole chain of events to me in words of one syllable. Proteins are complex condensation forms of amino acids; amino acids are the basics, and link together to form proteins in peptic chains. Though the known amino acids number only twenty-five, the combinations of proteins they can form is infinite; unfortunately a twenty-sixth amino acid turned up in the water from Procyon V.

157

"In the tanks, the proteins soon hydrolyzed back into their constituents, as doubtless they would have done on the planet. Meanwhile, the ship's quota of human beings, livestock and plants absorb many gallons of water per day; their systems build up the amino acids back into proteins, which are transferred to the body cells, where they are used as fuel and, in the combustive processes of metabolism, dissolved back into aminos again. That's the usual way it happens.

"The twenty-sixth amino acid disrupts this sequence. It combines into too complex a protein for any system—vegetable or animal—to handle. This is the point at which rigidity of the limbs sets in. As Payne explained, the denser peptic linkage may partially be due to the heavier gravity of New Earth; we know very little about the sustained effects of gravity on free-building molecules.

"By now, the settlement on the new world must be in as sad a state as we. At least they have the privilege of dying in the open air.

"22.xii.2521. I had no time to finish yesterday. Today there seems to be all the time in the world. Fourteen more deaths reported this morning by a tired Toynbee. The Nine Day Ague is undisputed master of the ship: my dear Yvonne is its latest victim. I have tucked her in bed but cannot look at her—too terrible. I have ceased to pray.

"Let me finish what young Payne told me. She was guardedly optimistic about the ultimate survival of a percentage of our population. The bodies of Ague victims are inactive while their internal forces cope with the overcomplex proteins; they will eventually break them down if the constitution concerned is elastic enough: 'another little protein won't do us any harm', Miss Payne pertly quotes. Proteins are present already in all living cells and, after a danger period, another protein, differing but slightly, may be tolerated. The new amino, christened *paynine* (this bright young creature smoothly informs me!), has been isolated; like leucine and lysine, which are already known, it has an effect on growth—what effect, only long-term research will establish, and I doubt that we have that much time.

'The short-term results are before us. The plants have mainly adapted to paynine and, once adapted, seem to thrive. The animals, varying with their species, have adapted, though only the pig colony actually seems exhuberant. All survivals, Payne says, may be regarded as mutations—what she calls 'low-level mutations'. It seems the heat in Agriculture may have helped them; so I have ordered a ten degree temperature increase from Inboard Power for the whole ship. That is literally the only step we have been able to take to help. . . .

"It looks as if the more complex the organism, the more difficulty it has in adjusting to the new proteins. Bad luck on man: in particular, us.

"24.xi.2521. Toynbee has the Ague. So has Mongomery. They are two of only five new victims this morning. The freak proteins seem to have done the worst of their work. Trying to analyze the reports Sick Bay still heroically send in, I find that the older the person, the better he holds out to begin with and the less chance he stands of surviving once the ague has him. I asked Payne about this when she came, quite voluntarily, to see me (she has made herself I/C Research, and I can only bless her efficiency); she thinks the figures are not significant—the young survive most things better than older people.

"Little Sheila Simpson has recovered! Hers was one of the first cases, sixteen long days ago. I went down and saw her; she seems perfectly all right, although quick and nervous in her actions. Temperature still high. Still, she is our first cure.

"Feel absurdly optimistic about this. If only 100 men and women came through, they might multiply, and their descendants get the ship home. Is there not a lower limit to the number who can avoid extinction? No doubt the answer lurks somewhere in the library, perhaps among those dreary tomes written and printed by past occupants of this ship. . . .

"There was a mutiny today, a stupid affair, led by a Sergeant Tugsten of Ship's Police and 'Spud' Murphy, the surviving armourer. They ran amok with the few hand-atomic weapons not landed on P.V., killing six of their companions and causing severe damage amidships.

Strangely enough, they weren't after me! I had them disarmed and thrown into the brig—it will give Bassitt someone to preach at. And all weapons apart from the neurolethea, or 'dazers' as they are popularly called, have been collected and destroyed, to prevent further menace to the ship; the 'dazers', acting only on living nervous systems, have no effect on inorganic material.

"25.xii.2521. Another attempt at mutiny. I was down in Agriculture when it all blew up. As one of the essential ship's services, the farm must be kept running at all costs. The oxygenators in Hydroponics have been left, as they can manage themselves; one of them, the dry variety mentioned before, has proliferated over the floor and seems almost as if it could sustain itself. While I was looking at it, 'Noah' Stover came in with a 'dazer', a lot of worried young women with him. He fired a mild charge at me.

"When I revived, they had carried me up into the Control Room, there threatening me with death if I did not turn the ship around and head back for New Earth! It took some time to make them understand that the maneuver of deflecting the ship through 180 degrees when it is traveling at its present speed of roughly 1328·5 times EV (Earth) would take about five years. Finally, by demonstrating stream factors on paper, I made them understand; then they were so frustrated they were going to kill me anyhow.

"Who saved me? Not my other officers, I regret to tell, but June Payne, single-handed—my little heroine from Research! So furiously did she rant at them, that they finally slunk off, Noah in the lead. I can hear them now, rampaging around the low-number decks. They've got at the liquor supplies.

"26.xii.2521. We have now what may be termed six complete recoveries, including little Sheila. They all have temperatures and act with nervous speed, but claim to feel fit; mercifully, they have no memory of any pain they underwent. Meanwhile, the Ague still claims its victims. Reports from Sick Bay have ceased to come in, but I estimate that under fifty people are still in action. Fifty! Their—my—time of immunity is fast running out. Ultimately, there can be no avoiding the protein pile-up, but since the freak linkages are random factors, some of us dodge a critical congestion in our tissues longer than others.

"So at least says June Payne. She has been with me again; of course I am grateful for her help. And I suppose I am lonely. I found myself kissing her passionately; she is physically attractive, and about fifteen years my junior. It was all foolishness on my part. She said—oh, the old argument needs no repeating—she was alone, frightened, we had so little time, why did we not make love together? I dismissed her, my sudden anger an indication of how she tempted me; now I'm sorry I was so abrupt—it was just that I kept thinking of Yvonne, stretched out in dumb suffering a few yards away in the next room.

"Must arm myself and make some sort of inspection of the ship tomorrow.

"27.xii.2521. Found two junior officers, John Hall and Margaret Prestellan to accompany me around ship. Men very orderly. Noah running a nursing service to feed those who come out of the Nine Day Ague. What will the long term repercussions of this catastrophe be?

"Someone has let Bassitt loose. He is raving mad—and yet compelling. I could almost believe his teaching myself. In this morgue, it is easier to put faith in psycho-analysis than God.

"We went down to Agriculture. It's a shambles, the livestock loose among the crops. And the hydroponics! The dry oxygenator mentioned here before has wildly mutated under the paynine influence. It has invaded the corridors near the Hydroponics section, its root system sweeping a supply of soil before it, almost as if the plant had developed an intelligence of its own. With somewhat absurd visions of the thing growing and choking the whole ship, I went up to the Control Room and flung the lever which closes the inter-deck doors all along Main Corridor. That should cramp the plant's style.

"Frank broke out of his stiffness today. He did not recognize me; I will see him again tomorrow.

"June was taken with the Ague today. Bright and living June! Prestellan showed her to me—motionless in suffering even as she had predicted. Somehow, treacherously, the sight of her hurt me more than the sight of Yvonne had done. I wish—but what does it matter what I wish? MY TURN NEXT.

"28.xii.2521. Prestellan reminded me that Christmas has come and gone; I had forgotten that mockery. That was what the drunken mutineers were celebrating, poor devils!

"Frank recognized me today; I could tell by his eyes, although he could not speak. If he ever becomes Captain, it will be of a very different ship.

"Twenty recoveries to date. An improvement—room for hope.

"Adversity makes thinkers of us all. Only now, when the long journey means no more than a retreat into darkness, do I begin to question the sanity behind the whole conception of inter-stellar travel. How many hapless men and women must have questioned it on the way out to Procyon, imprisoned in these eternal walls! For the sake of that grandiose idea, their lives guttered uselessly, as many more must do before our descendants step on Earth again. Earth! I pray that there men's hearts have changed, grown less like the hard metals they have loved and served so long. Nothing but the full flowering of a technological age, such as the Twenty-fourth Century knew, could have launched this miraculous ship; yet the miracle was sterile, cruel. Only a technological age could condemn unborn generations to exist in it, as if man were mere protoplasm, without emotion or aspiration.

"At the beginning of the technological age—a fitting token, to my mind—stands the memory of Belsen; what can we do but hope that this more protracted agony stands at its end: its end for ever, on Earth, and on the new world of Procyon V."

There the diary ended.

During the reading of it, Vyann had been forced to pause several times and master her voice. Her usual rather military bearing had deserted her, leaving her just a girl on a bed, close to tears. And when she had finished reading, she forced herself to turn back and re-read a sentence on the first page which had escaped Complain's notice. In the spiky writing of Captain Gregory Complain were the words: "We head for Earth in the knowledge that the men who will see those skies will not be born until six generations have died." Vyann read it aloud in a shaky voice before finally breaking into a storm of tears.

"Don't you see!" she cried. "Oh, Roy—the Journey was only meant to take seven generations! And we are the twenty-third generation! The *twenty-third*! We must be far past Earth—nothing can ever save us now."

Hopelessly, wordlessly, Complain tried to console her, but human love had no power to soften the inhumanity of the trap they were in. At last, when Vyann's sobbing had partly subsided, Complain began to talk. He could hear his voice creaking with numbness, forced out in an attempt to distract her—to distract both of them—from the basic plight.

"This diary explains so much, Laur," he said. "We must try and be grateful for knowing. Above all, it explains the catastrophe; it's not a frightening legend any more, it's something we might be able to deal with. Perhaps we shall never know if Captain Gregory survived, but his son must have done, to carry on the name. Perhaps June Payne survived—somehow she reminds me of you ... At least it's obvious enough people survived—little groups, forming tribes ... And by then the hydroponics had almost filled the ship."

"Who would have thought," she whispered, "that the ponics weren't really meant to be there. They're ... they're part of the natural order of things! It seems so—"

"Laur! Laur!" he exclaimed, suddenly interrupting. He sat up and seized the strange weapon his brother had given him. "This weapon! The diary said all weapons except dazers had been destroyed. So this thing must be something other than a weapon!"

"Perhaps they missed one," she said wearily.

"Perhaps. Or perhaps not. It's a heat device. It must have a special use. It must be able to do something we don't know about. Let me try it—"

"Roy! Be careful!" Vyann cried. "You'll have a fire!"

"I'll try it on something that doesn't burn. We're on to something, Laur, I swear it!"

He picked the gun up carefully, training the nozzle

towards the wall; it had an indicator and a button on the smooth top surface. He pressed the button, as Gregg had done earlier. A narrow fan of intense heat, almost invisible, splayed out and touched the wall. On the matt metal of the wall, a bright line appeared. It loosened, widened. Two cherry-red lips grew, parting in a smile. Hastily, Complain pressed the button again. The heat died, the lips lost their color, turned maroon, hardened into a gaping black mouth; through it, they could see the corridor.

Vyann and Complain stared at each other, thunderstruck.

"We must tell the Council," Complain said finally, in an awed voice.

"Wait!" she said. "Roy, darling, there's somewhere I want us to try that weapon. Will you come with me before we say a word to anyone?"

They found, with some surprise, when they got into the corridors, that the hunt for the Giant was still on. It was fast approaching the time when the darkness that would cover the next sleep-wake fell; everyone not engaged in the hunt was preparing for sleep, behind closed doors. The ship seemed deserted, looking as it must have looked long ago, when half its occupants lay dying under the rule of the Nine Day Ague. Vyann and Complain hurried along unnoticed. When the dark came down, the girl flashed on the torch at her belt without comment.

Complain could only admire her refusal to admit defeat; he was not enough of a self-analyst to see it was a quality he had a fair measure of himself. The uneasy notion that they might meet rats or Giants or Outsiders, or a combination of all three, obsessed him, and he kept the heat gun ready in one hand and his dazer in the other. But their progress was uneventful, and they came safely to Deck 1 and the closed spiral staircase.

"According to your friend Marapper's plan," Vyann said, "the Control Room should be at the top of these stairs. On the plan, the Control Room is shown large: yet at the top there is only a small room with featureless circular walls. Supposing those walls have been put up to keep people out of the Control Room?"

"You mean—by Captain Gregory?"

164

"Not necessarily. Probably, by someone later," she said. "Come and aim your gun at the walls. . . ."

They climbed the enclosed stairs and faced the circle of metal walls, with a hushed sensation of confronting a mystery. Vyann's grip on his arm was painfully tight.

"Try there!" she whispered, pointing at random.

She switched her torch off as he switched the gun on.

In the dark, beyond the leveled nozzle, a ruddy glow was born, woke to brightness, moved under Complain's control until it formed a radiant square. Rapidly the sides of the square sagged; the metal within it peeled back like a piece of skin, leaving them room to climb through. An acrid smell in their nostrils, the two waited impatiently for the heat to subside. Beyond it, in a great chamber dimly revealed, they could see a narrow outline of something, something indefinable because beyond their experience.

When the square was cool enough to climb through, they made by common consent for that beckoning line.

The great shutters which, when closed, covered the magnificent 270 degree sweep of the observation blister, were exactly as Captain Gregory Complain had left them long since, even down to a carelessly abandoned spanner whose positioning on a sill prevented one panel of shutter from closing properly. It was the gap between this panel and its neighbor which drew Complain and the girl, as surely as ponics seek the light.

Through the narrow chink, which continued almost from ground level to far above their heads, they could glimpse a ribbon of space. How many pointless years had passed since the last inhabitant of the ship had looked out at that mighty void? Heads together, Complain and the girl stared through the impervious hyaline tungsten of the window, trying to take in what they saw. Little, of course, could be seen, just a tiny wedge of universe with its due proportion of stars—not enough to dizzy them, only enough to fill them with courage and hope.

"What does it matter if the ship is past Earth?" Vyann breathed. "We have found the controls! When we have learned how to use them, we can steer the ship down to the first planets we come to—Tregonnin told us most suns have planets. Oh, we can do it! I *know* we can! After this, the rest will be easy!"

In the faint, faint light, she saw a far-off gleam in Complain's eye, a look of dumb-struck speculation. She put her arms round him, suddenly anxious to protect him as she had always protected Scoyt; for the independence so unremittingly fostered in Quarters had momentarily left Complain.

"For the first time," he said, "I've realized—fully realized, right down inside me—that we are on a ship." His legs were like water.

It was as if she interpreted the words as a personal challenge.

"Your ancestor brought the ship from New Earth," she said. "You shall land it on a Newer Earth!"

And she flicked on her torch and swung its beam eagerly found the great array of controls, which up till now had remained in darkness. The phalanx on phalanx of dials which had once made this chamber the nerve center of the ship, the array of toggles, the soldier-like parade of indicators, levers, knobs and screens, which together provided the outward signs of the power still throbbing through the ship, had coagulated into a lava-like mess. On all sides, the boards of instruments resembled, and were as much use as, damp sherbet. Nothing had been left unmolested; though the torch beam flitted here and there with increasing pace, it picked out not a switch intact. The controls were utterly destroyed.

Part IV

THE BIG SOMETHING

I

Only the occasional stale glow of a pilot light illuminated the coiled miles of corridor. At one end of the ship, the ponics were beginning to collapse on to themselves in the death each dark sleep-wake inevitably brought; at the other end of the ship, Master Scoyt still drove his men in a torch-light search for the Giant. Scoyt's party, working along the lower levels of the Drive Floors, had drained the twenties decks of Forwards almost clear of life.

As the dark came down, it caught Henry Marapper, the priest, going from Counsilor Tregonnin's room to his own without a torch. Marapper had been carefully ingratiating himself into the librarian's favor, against the time when the Council of Five should be reconstituted as the Council of Six—Marapper, of course, visualizing himself as the sixth Counsellor. He walked now through the dimness warily, half afraid a Giant might pop up in front of him.

Which was almost exactly what did happen.

A door ahead of him was flung open, a wash of illumination pouring into the corridor. Startled, Marapper shrank back. The light eerily flapped and churned, transforming shadows into frightened bats as the bearer of the torch hustled about his nocturnal business in the room. Next moment, two great figures emerged, bearing between them a smaller figure who slumped as if ill. Undoubtedly, these were Giants: they were over six feet high.

The light, of exceptional brilliance, was worn as a fitting on one Giant's head; it sent the uneasy shadows scattering again as its wearer bent and half-carried the small figure. They went only half a dozen paces down the corridor before stopping in the middle of it, kneeling there with their faces away from Marapper. And now the light fell upon the face of the smaller man. It was Fermour!

With a word to the Giants, Fermour, leaning forward, put his knuckles to the deck in a curious gesture. His hand, finger-tips upward, was for a moment caught alone in the cone of torchlight; then a section of deck, responding to his pressure, rose and was seized by the Giants, seized and lifted to reveal a large manhole. The Giants helped Fermour down into it, climbed down themselves, and closed the hatch over their heads. The glow from a square pilot light on the wall was again the only illumination in a deserted corridor.

Then Marapper found his tongue.

"Help!" he bellowed. "Help! They're after me!"

He pounded on the nearest doors, flinging them open when no reply came. These were workers' apartments, mainly deserted by their owners, who were away following Scoyt and the Survival Team. In one room, Marapper discovered a mother suckling her babe by a dim light. She and the baby began to howl with fear.

The rumpus soon brought running feet and flashing torches. Marapper was surrounded by people and reduced to a state of coherence. These were mainly men who had been on the grand Giant-hunt, men with their blood roused by the unaccustomed excitement; they let out wilder cries than Marapper to hear that Giants had been here, right in their midst. The crowd swelled, the noise increased. Marapper found himself crushed against the wall, repeating his tale endlessly to a succession of officers, until an icy man called Pagwam, Co-Captain of the Survival Team, pushed his way through the group.

Pagwam rapidly cleared a space round Marapper.

"Show me this hole you say the Giants disappeared down," he ordered. "Point to it."

"This would have terrified a less brave man than I," Marapper said, still shaking. He pointed: a rectangular line in the deck outlined the Giants' exit. It was a hair-fine

168

crack, hardly noticeable. Inside the rectangle at one end was a curious octagonal indentation, not half an inch across; apart from that, there was nothing to distinguish the trap-door from the rest of the deck.

At Pagwam's orders, two men tried to lever open the trapdoor, but the crack was so fine they could do no more than poke their fingernails down it.

"It won't come up, sir," one of the men said.

"Thank hem for that!" Marapper exclaimed, visualizing a stream of Giants emerging upon them.

By this time, somebody had fetched Scoyt. The Master's face was harder set than ever; his long fingers restlessly caressed the runnels of his cheeks as he listened to Pagwam and Marapper. Though he looked tired, when he spoke he revealed that his brain was the widest awake of those present.

"You see what this means," he said. "These traps are set in the floor about a hundred paces apart throughout the ship; we've never recognized them as such because we could never open them, but the Giants can open them easily enough. We no longer need doubt, whatever we once thought to the contrary, that the Giants still exist. For reasons of their own, they have laid low for a long while: now they're coming back—and for what other purpose than to take over the ship again?"

"But this trap—" Marapper said.

"This trap," Scoyt interrupted, "is the key to the whole matter. Do you remember when your friend Complain was captured by Giants he said he was spirited into a hole and traveled in a low, confined space that sounded like no part of the ship we knew? Obviously, it was a space between decks, and he was taken down a trap just like this one. All traps must inter-communicate—and if the Giants can open one, they can open the lot!"

An uneasy babble of comment rose from the crowd in the corridor. Their eyes were bright, their torches dim; they seemed to press more closely together, as if for comfort. Marapper cleared his throat, inserting the tip of his little finger helplessly into his ear, as if that were the only thing in the world he could get clear.

"This means—jezers nose, this means our world is en-

169

tirely surrounded by a sort of thin world where the Giants can get and we can't," he said. "Is that so?"

Scoyt nodded curtly.

"Not a nice thought, Priest, eh?" he said.

When Pagwam touched his arm, Scoyt turned impatiently to find that three of the Counsel of Five, Billyoe, Dupont and Ruskin, had arrived behind him. They looked both unhappy and annoyed.

"Please say no more, Master Scoyt," Billyoe said. "We've heard most of this, and it hardly sounds the sort of thing which should be discussed in public. You'd better bring this—er, this priest along with you to the counsel room; we'll talk there."

Scoyt hardly hesitated.

"On the contrary, Counsellor Billyoe," he said distinctly. "This matter affects every man jack on board. Everyone must know about it as quickly as possible. I'm afraid we are being swept to a time of crisis."

Although he was contradicting the Counsel, Scoyt's face bore such a heavy look of pain that Billyoe wisely avoided making an issue of the matter. Instead, he asked, "Why do you say a crisis?"

Scoyt spread his hands.

"Look at it this way," he said. "A Giant suddenly appears on Deck 14 and ties up the first girl he finds in such a way that she escapes in no time. Why? So that an alarm could be given. Later he appears again down on the Drive Floors—at little risk to himself, let me add, because he can duck down one of these traps whenever he feels like it! Now: from time to time, we've had reports of sightings of Giants, but obviously in those cases the meeting was completely accidental; in this case, it looks as if it was not. For the first time, a Giant *wanted* himself to be seen; you can't explain the pointless tying up of the girl otherwise."

"But *why* should he want to be seen and hunted?" Counsellor Ruskin asked plaintively.

"*I* can see why, Counsellor," said Marapper. "The Giant wanted to create a diversion while these other Giants rescued Fermour from his cell."

"Exactly," agreed Scoyt, without pleasure. "This all happened just as we began to question Fermour; we had

170

scarcely started to soften him up. It was a ruse to get everyone out of the way while the Giants helped Fermour to escape. Now that the Giants know *we* know they are about, they'll be forced to do something—unless we do something first! Priest Marapper, get down on your hands and knees and show me exactly what you think it was that Fermour did to make the trap-door open."

Puffing, Marapper got down as directed. The light of every torch present centered on him. He scuffled to one corner of the trap, looking up dubiously.

"I think Fermour was about here," he said. "And then he leaned forward like this . . . and put his fist down on the deck like this—with his knuckles along the floor like this. And then—no, by hem, I know what he did! Scoyt, look!"

Marapper moved his clenched hand. A faint click sounded. The trap-door rose, and the way of the Giants lay open.

Laur Vyann and Roy Complain came slowly back to the inhabited part of Forwards. The shock of finding the controls ruined had been almost too much for both of them. Once again, but now more insistently than ever before, the desire to die had come over Complain; a realization of the total bleakness of his life swept through him like poison. The brief respite in Forwards, the happiness Vyann afforded him, were absolutely nothing beside the overriding frustration he had endured since birth.

As he sank down into this destroying sadness, one thing rescued him: the old Teaching of Quarters, which a little while ago he had told himself proudly he had eschewed.

Back to him echoed the voice of the priest: "We are the sons of cowards, our days are passed in fear. . . . The Long Journey has always begun: let us rage while we can, and by so discharging our morbid impulses we may be freed from inner conflict. . . ." Instinctively, Complain made the formal gesture of rage. He let the anger steam up from the recesses of his misery and warm him in the withering darkness. Vyann had begun to weep on his shoulder; that she should suffer too added fuel to his fury.

He foamed it all up inside him with increasing excitement, distorting his face, calling up all the injuries he and everyone else had undergone, churning them, creaming

171

them up together like batter in a bowl. Muddy, bloody, anger, keeping his heart a-beat.

After that, feeling much saner, he was able to comfort Vyann and lead her back to the regions of her own people.

As they approached the inhabited part, a curious clanging grew louder in their ears. It was an odd noise without rhythm, an ominous noise, at the sound of which they increased their pace, glancing at each other anxiously.

Almost the first person they met, a man of the farmer class, came up quickly to them.

"Inspector Vyann," he said, "Master Scoyt is looking for you; he's been shouting about everywhere!"

"It sounds as if he's pulling the ship apart for us," Vyann said wryly. "We're on our way, thank you."

They quickened their step, and so came upon Scoyt at Deck 20, from which Fermour had been rescued. Co-Captain Pagwam, with a squad of men, was pacing along the corridor, bending every so often and opening a series of traps in the deck. The heavy covers, flung aside, accounted for the strange clanging Vyann and Complain had heard. As each hole was revealed, a man was left to guard it while other men hurried on to the next trap.

Directing operations, Scoyt looking around saw Vyann. For once, no welcoming smile softened his mouth.

"Come in here," he said, opening the door nearest to him. Somebody's apartment, it happened to be empty just then. Scoyt shut the door when they were all three inside and confronted them angrily.

"I've a mind to have you both flung into cells," he said. "How long have you been back from Gregg's stronghold? Why did you not report straight back to me or the Counsel, as you were instructed to do? Where've you been together, I want to know?"

"But, Roger—" Vyann protested. "We haven't been back long! Besides, you were all out on a chase when we arrived. We didn't know the thing was so urgent, or we should have—"

"Just a minute, Laur," Scoyt interrupted. "You'd better save the excuses: we've a crisis on hand. Never mind all that, I'm not interested in the frills; just tell me about Gregg."

Seeing the hurt and angry look on Vyann's face, Complain stepped in and gave a brief account of their interview with his brother. At the end of it, Scoyt nodded, relaxing slightly.

"Better than I dared hope," he said. "We will send scouts to get Gregg's party here as soon as possible. It is expedient that they move in here at once."

"No, Roger," Vyann said quickly. "They can't come here. With all respects to Roy, his brother's nothing but a brigand! His followers are nothing but a mob. They and their wives are maimed and mutated. The whole pack would bring endless trouble on to our hands if we had them living with us. They are absolutely no good for anything but fighting."

"*That*", Scoyt said grimly, "is just what we want them for. You'd better get abreast with events, Laur." Rapidly, he told her what Marapper had seen and what was now going on.

"Had you hurt Fermour?" Complain asked.

"No—just a preliminary flogging to soften him up."

"He was used to that sort of thing in Quarters, poor devil" Complain said. His own back tingled in sympathetic memory.

"Why should all this make it so urgent to get Gregg's mob here?" Vyann said.

Master Scoyt sighed heavily and answered with emphasis.

"Because," he said, "here we have for the first time incontestible proof that the Outsiders and the Giants are in alliance—against us!"

He looked at them hard as this soaked in. "Nice position we're in, eh?" he said ironically. "That's why I'm going to have up every trap in the ship, and a man posted by it. Eventually we'll hunt the enemy out; I swear I won't rest till we do."

Complain whistled. "You'll certainly need Gregg's ruffians; manpower will be the crucial problem," he said. "But just how did Marapper manage to open that trap-door?"

"Simply because that fat priest is the man he is, I'd say," Scoyt remarked with a short laugh. "Back in your tribe, I suppose he was pretty much of a magpie?"

"Picked up anything he could get," Complain agreed, recalling the lumber in Marapper's room.

"One thing he picked up was a ring: a ring with an eight-sided stone, which someone must at some time have removed from a corpse. It's not a stone actually, it's some little mechanical device, and it fits exactly into a kind of keyhole in each trap-door: press it in and the trap opens at once. Originally—way back before the catastrophe—everybody whose duty it was to go down into these traps must have had one of these ring-keys. Counsellor Tregonnin, by the way, says these between-deck places are called inspection ways; he found a reference to them in his lumber; and that's just what we're going to do—inspect them! We're going to comb every inch of them. My men have Marapper's ring now and are opening up every trap aboard."

"And Bob Fermour had a similar ring to Marapper's!" Complain exclaimed. "I often remember seeing it on his finger."

"We think all Outsiders may wear them," Scoyt said. "If so, it explains how easily they elude us. It explains a lot—although it doesn't explain how in the past they've managed to spirit themselves out of cells carefully guarded on the outside. On the assumption that all who wear these rings are our enemies, I've got some of the Survival Team working through the entire population, looking for the giveaway. Anyone caught wearing that ring makes the Journey! Now I must go. Expansions!"

He ushered them back into the clanging corridor. At once he was surrounded by underlings wanting orders; he became gradually separated from Complain and Vyann. They heard him delegating a junior officer to bear the news to Gregg, then he turned away and his voice was lost.

"Union with Gregg. . . ." Vyann said, and shivered. "Now what do *we* do? It looks as if Roger intends to give me no more work."

"You're going to bed," Complain said. "You look exhausted."

"You don't think I could sleep with all this noise going on, do you?" she asked, smiling rather tiredly.

"I think you could try."

He was surprised with what submissiveness she let him lead her away, although she stiffened suddenly as they met Marapper loitering in a side corridor.

"You are the hero of the hour, priest, I understand," she said.

Marapper's face was ponderous with gloom; he wore injury around him like a cloak.

"Inspector," he said with a bitter dignity. "You are taunting me. For half my wretched lifetime I go about with a priceless secret on my finger without realizing it. And then when I do realize it—behold, in a moment of quite uncharacteristic panic, I give it away to your friend Scoyt for nothing!"

II

"We've got to get out of the ship somehow," Vyann murmured. Her eyes were shut as she spoke, her dark head down on the pillow. Softly, Complain crept from the dark room; she would be asleep before he closed the door, despite the chaos of sound two decks away. He stood outside Vyann's door, half afraid to go away, wondering if this was a good time to bother the Counsel or Scoyt with news of the ruined controls. Indecisively, he fingered the heat gun tucked in his belt, as gradually his thoughts wandered back to more personal considerations.

Complain could not help asking himself what part he was playing in the world about him; because he was undecided what he wanted from life, he seemed to drift on a tide of events. The people nearest to him appeared to have clear-cut objectives. Marapper cared for nothing but power; Scoyt seemed content to grapple with the endless problems of the ship; and Complain's beloved Laur wanted only to be free of the restraints of life aboard. And he? He desired her, but there was something else, the something he had promised himself as a kid without finding it, the something he could never put into words, the something too big to visualize. . . .

"Who's that?" he asked, roused suddenly by a close footstep.

A square pilot light near at hand revealed a tall man robed in white, a distinctive figure whose voice, when he spoke, was powerful and slow.

"I am Counsellor Zac Deight," he said. "Don't be startled. You are Roy Complain, the hunter from Deadways, are you not?"

Complain took in his melancholy face and white hair,

176

and liked the man instinctively. Instinct is not always the ally of intelligence.

"I am, sir," he answered.

"Your priest, Henry Marapper, spoke highly of you."

"Did he, by hem?" Marapper often did good by stealth, but it was invariably to himself.

"He did," Zac Deight said. Then his tone changed. "I believe you might know something about that hole I see in the corridor wall."

He pointed at the gap Complain and Vyann had made earlier in the wall of her room.

"Yes I do. It was made with this weapon here," Complain said, showing the weapon to the old Counsellor and wondering what was coming next.

"Have you told anyone else you have this?" Zac Deight asked, turning the heat gun over with interest.

"No. Only Laur—Inspector Vyann knows; she's asleep at present."

"It should have been handed to the Counsel for us to make the best use of we could," Zac Deight said gently. "You ought to have realized that. Will you come to my room and tell me all about it?"

"Well, there's not much to tell, sir. . . ." Complain began.

"You can surely see how dangerous this weapon could be in the wrong hands. . . ." There was something commanding in the old counsellor's tone. When he turned and made down the corridor, Complain followed that Gothic back—not happily, but without protest.

They took a lift down to the lower level, then walked five decks forward to the counsellor's apartment. It was absolutely deserted here, silent and dark. Bringing out an ordinary magnetic key, Zac Deight unlocked a door and stood aside for Complain to enter. Directly the latter had done so, the door slammed behind him. It was a trap!

Whirling around, Complain charged the door with all the fury of a wild animal—uselessly. He was too late, and Deight had the heat gun with which he might have burned his way to freedom. Savagely, Complain flashed on his torch and surveyed the room. It was a bedroom which had been disused for some while, to judge by the dust

177

everywhere; like most such rooms throughout the length of the ship, it was spartan, anonymous.

Complain picked up a chair and battered it to bits against the locked door, after which he felt better able to think. An image swam up to him of the time when he had first stood close to Vyann, watching through a spyhole when Scoyt left Fermour alone in the interrogation room; Fermour had jumped on to a stool and tried to reach the ceiling grille. Obviously, he had expected to find an escape route that way. Now supposing. . . .

He swung the bed into the center of the room, tossed a locker on top of it and climbed rapidly up to examine the grille. It was similar to every other grille in every other room of the ship; three feet square, latticed with thin bars widely enough spaced to allow a finger to be poked between them. The exploring torch revealed these spaces to be as silted up with sticky dust as rheumy eyes; such breeze as drained through into the room was faint indeed.

Complain heaved tentatively at the grille. It did not budge.

It had to budge. Fermour did not stand on that stool and stretch upwards just because he needed some physical jerks. Here too, if the grilles opened, would be an explanation of the way some of Scoyt's previously captured Outsiders had escaped from guarded cells. Complain stuck his fingers through the grille and felt along its inner edge, hope and fear scampering coldly through his veins.

His index finger soon met with a simple, tongued catch. Complain pressed it over. Similar catches lay on the upper surface of the other three sides of the grille. One by one, he flicked them over. The grille lifted easily up; Complain angled it sideways, brought it down and put it quietly on the bed. His heart beat rapidly.

Catching hold of the aperture, he drew himself up into it.

There was hardly space to stir. He had expected to find himself in the inspection ways; instead he was in the ventilation system. He guessed immediately that this pipe ran through the strange inter-deck world of the inspection ways. Clicking his torch off, he strained his eyes down the low duct, ignoring the breeze that sighed continuously into his face.

178

One light only lit the tunnel, filtering up from the next grating along. Struck with the idea that he must look much like a cork in a bottle, Complain dragged himself forward and peered through the grille.

He was staring down into Zac Deight's room. Zac Deight was there alone, talking into an instrument. A tall cupboard, standing now in the middle of the room, showed how the niche in the wall which housed the instrument was normally concealed. So fascinated was Complain with his novel viewpoint that for a moment he failed to hear what Zac Deight was speaking about. Then it registered with a rush.

" ... fellow Complain causing a lot of trouble," the Counsellor said into the phone. "You remember when your man Andrews lost his welder a few weeks back? Somehow it has now got into Complain's hands. I found out because I happened to come across a gaping hole in the wall of one of the compartments on Deck 22, Inspector Laur Vyann's room. ... Yes, Curtis, can you hear me? This line is worse than ever. ..."

For a moment, Deight was silent, as the man at the other end of the line spoke. Curtis! Complain exclaimed to himself—that was the name of the Giant in charge of the mob who captured him. Looking down on the counsellor, Complain suddenly noticed the give-away ring with the octagonal stone on Zac Deight's finger, and began to wonder what ghastly web of intrigue he had blundered into.

Deight was speaking again. "I had the chance of slipping into Vyann's room," he said, "while your diversion down on the Drive Floors was in full swing. And there I found something else the dizzies have got hold of: a diary we never knew existed, written by the first man to captain the ship on the way back from Procyon V. It contains far more than the dizzies should know; it'll set them questioning all sorts of things. By a stroke of luck, I have managed to get both diary and welder into my possession. ... Thanks. Even more luckily, nobody but Complain and this girl Vyann yet know anything about—or realize the significance of—either diary or welder. Now then, I know all about Little Dog's ideas on the sanctity of dizzy lives, but they're not up here coping with this problem, and it's getting more difficult hour by hour—if they want their precious secret kept, there is one easy way to do it. I've got Complain locked in next door to me now. . . . Of course not, no force; he just walked into the trap like an angel. Vyann is asleep in her room. What I'm asking you is this, Curtis: I want your sanction to kill Complain and Vyann. . . . Yes, I don't like it either, but it's the only way we can possibly retain the *status quo*, and I'm prepared to do it now before it's too late. . . ."

Zac Deight was silent, listening, an expression of impatience creeping over his long face.

"There isn't time to radio Little Dog," he said, evidently interrupting the speaker. "They'd procrastinate too long. You're in charge up here, Curtis, and all I need is your permission. . . . That's better. . . . Yes, I do consider it imperative. You don't think I enjoy the task? I shall gas them both through the air vents of their rooms, as we've done before in similar awkward cases. At least we know it's painless."

He rang off. He pushed the cupboard back into place. He stood for a while hesitating, gnawing his knuckles, his face seamed with distaste. He opened the cupboard and removed a long cylinder. He looked speculatively up at the ceiling grille. He took the blast of Complain's dazer right in his face.

The color fled from Zac Deight's brow. His head flopped on to his chest and he collapsed, sprawling, on the floor.

For a minute, Complain lay where he was, his mind attempting to adjust to events. He was brought back to the immediacy of the present by a horrible sensation. An alien thought had somehow drifted among his thoughts; it was as if somebody's thickly furred tongue licked his brain. Flipping on his torch, he found a tremendous moth hovering before his eyes. Its wing span was about five inches; the *tapetum lucidum* in its eyes reflected the light like two cerise pin points.

Sickened, he struck at it but missed. The moth fluttered rapidly away down the air duct. Complain recalled another moth in Deadways which had left a similar delicately dirty fingerprint on his mind. Now he thought, "This power the rabbits have—the moths must have it in a lesser degree. And the rats seem to be able to understand them . . . Perhaps these moths are a sort of airborne scouts for the rat-hordes!"

This notion scared him a great deal more than hearing Deight pronounce his death sentence had done.

In a sweat of panic, he flicked back the four tongues which kept Zac Deight's grille in place, slithered the grille along the duct and dropped down into the councillor's room. Pulling up a table, he climbed on to it and moved the grille back into its proper position. Then he felt safer.

Zac Deight was not dead: Complain's dazer had been turned only to half power; but he had been at close enough range to receive a shock of sufficient strength to keep him senseless for some while. He looked harmless, even benevolent, huddled on the deck with hair fallen over his ashen forehead. Complain took the councillor's keys without a stir of compunction, collected his heat gun, unlocked the door, and let himself out into the silent corridor.

At the last moment he paused, turning back into the room to flash his torch up at the grille. Sharp little pink hands grasped the bars, a dozen sharp faces hated down at him. Hair prickling up his neck, Complain gave them the daze. The little burning eyes lost their brilliance at once, the pink hands relaxed their grip.

Squeals following him down the corridor told Complain he had also winged concealed reinforcements.

His ideas flowed fast as he walked. One thing he stubbornly determined: Councillor Deight's role in this affair, and all that he had said on the strange instrument to Curtis (where *was* Curtis?) should be mentioned to nobody until he had discussed it with Vyann. They could no longer tell who was on their side and who was not.

"Just supposing Vyann . . ." he began aloud; but he quickly tucked that dread away. There was a point where distrust merged with insanity.

A practical item worried Complain, but he could not quite formulate it. It was something to do with the rescue of Fermour. . . . No, it would have to wait. He was too anxious to reason cooly; he would consider it later. Meanwhile, he wanted to give the heat gun, the welder, as

Deight had called it, over to somebody who could make best use of it: Master Scoyt.

The excitement around Scoyt had gloriously increased; he had transferred himself into the center of a whirlpool of activity.

The barriers between Forwards and Deadways had been broken down. Sweating men busily tore down the barricades, relishing the work of destruction.

"Take them away!" Scoyt shouted. "We thought they guarded our frontiers, but now that our frontiers are all around us, they are useless."

Through the broken barriers, the tribe of Gregg came. Ragged and filthy, male or female or hermaphrodite, well or wounded, on foot or on rough stretchers, they flocked excitedly among the watching Forwarders. They bore bundles and bedding rolls and boxes and panniers; some pulled crude sledges they had dragged through the ponics; one woman drove her belongings before her on the back of an emaciated sheep. With them all flew the black midges of Deadways. Such was the fever of excitement which simmered over Forwards, that this animated gaggle of squalor was greeted with welcoming smiles and an occasional cheer. The tattered legion waved back. Roffery had been left behind; he was considered near enough dead to make any trouble expended on his account worthless.

One thing at least was clear: the outcasts, wounded though many of them were from their encounter with the rats, were prepared to fight. Every man jack of them was loaded down with dazers, knives and improvised pikes.

Gregg himself, accompanied by his weird henchman, Hawl, was conferring with Scoyt, Pagwam and Councillor Ruskin behind a closed door when Complain arrived on the scene. Without ceremony, he thrust his way into the room. He savored an unprecedented confidence which even their shouts at his intrusion did not sap.

"I've come to help you," he said, facing Scoyt as the natural leader there. "I've two things for you, and the first is a bit of information. We've discovered that there are trapdoors on every level of every deck; that is only one way the Giants and Outsiders can escape. They also have a handy exit in every single room!"

He jumped up on to the table and demonstrated to

them how a grille opened. Climbing down again without comment, he enjoyed the surprised look on their faces.

"That's something else for you to watch, Master Scoyt," he said. And then the point about Fermour's escape that had been troubling him slid into his mind without effort; instantly, a slice more of the puzzle became clear.

"Somewhere in the ship, the Giants have a headquarters," he said. "They took me to it when they caught me, but I don't know where it is—I was gassed. But obviously it's in a part of a deck or level cut off from us, deliberately or by design. There are plenty such places in the ship—that's where we have to look."

"We've already decided that," said Gregg, impatiently. "The trouble is, things are in such a muddle, on most decks we don't know when a bit's cut off and when it isn't. An army could be hiding behind any bulkhead."

"I'll tell you one such place near at hand," Complain said tensely. "*Above the cell Fermour was kept in,* on Deck 21."

"What makes you think that, Complain?" Scoyt asked curiously.

"Deduction. The Giants, as we have realized, went to an enormous amount of trouble to lure everyone away from the corridors so that they could get Fermour and rescue him via the trap-doors. They could have spared themselves all that bother if they had simply pulled him up through the grille in his cell. It would not have taken them a minute, and they could have remained unseen. Why didn't they? My guess is, because they couldn't. Because something on the level above has collapsed, blocking that grille. In other words, there may be chambers up there we have no access to. We ought to see what's in them."

"I tell you there are a hundred such places—" Gregg began.

"It certainly sounds worth investigating—" Counsellor Ruskin said.

"Suppose you're right, Complain," Scoyt interrupted. "If the grille's blocked, how do we get through?"

"Like this!" Complain leveled the heat gun at the nearest wall, fanning it horizontally. The wall began to

183

drip away. He switched off power when a ragged archway had formed, and looked challengingly at them. For a moment all were silent.

"Gawd's blood!" Gregg croaked. "That's the thing *I* gave you."

"Yes. And that's how you use it. It's not a real weapon, as you thought—it's a flame projector."

Scoyt stood up. His face was flushed.

"Let's get down to Deck 21," he said. "Pagwam, keep your men pulling up trap-doors as fast as you can circulate that ring. Complain, you've done well. We'll try that gadget out at once."

They moved out in a body, Scoyt leading. He gripped Complain's arm gratefully.

"Given time, we can pull the damn ship apart with that weapon," he said. It was a remark which did not fully register on Complain until much later.

Chaos reigned on the middle level of Deck 21, where Fermour's cell was. All the manholes were exposed, each being now guarded by a sentry; their covers were flung aside in untidy piles. The few people who lived here— mostly men of the barriers and their families—were evacuating before further trouble came, straggling among the sentries, getting in everyone's way. Scoyt elbowed his way roughly through them, pushing squeaking children to right and left.

As they flung open Fermour's cell door, Complain felt a hand on his arm. He turned, and there was Vyann, fresh and bright of eye.

"I thought you were asleep!" he exclaimed, smiling with the delight of seeing her again.

"Do you realize it's within a watch of waking?" she said. "Besides, I'm told things are about to happen. I had to come and see that you didn't get into trouble."

Complain pressed her hand.

"I've been in and out of it while you were sleeping," he said cheerfully.

Gregg was already in the middle of the cell, standing on the battered crate which served here as a chair, peering up at the grille above his head.

"Roy's right!" he announced. "There's an obstruction on the other side of this thing. I can see some crumpled

184

metal up there. Hand me up that heat gun and let's try our luck."

"Stand from under!" Complain warned him. "Or you'll shower yourself with melted metal."

Nodding, Gregg aimed the weapon as Scoyt handed it up, and depressed the button. The glassy arc of heat bit into the ceiling, drawing a red weal on it. The weal broadened, the ceiling sagged, metal came gooing down like shreds of pulverized flesh. Through the livid hole, other metal showed; it too, began to glow lividly. Noise filled the room, smoke cascaded about them and out into the corridor, bitter smoke which rasped their eyeballs. Above the uproar came a crackling explosion, and just for a second the lights flashed on with unexpected brilliance then died away to nothing.

"That should do it!" Gregg exclaimed with immense satisfaction, climbing down from his perch and eyeing the gaping ruin above him. His beard twitched in excitement.

"I really think we ought to hold a full Council meeting before we do anything as drastic as this, Master Scoyt!" Councillor Ruskin said plaintively, surveying the ruin of the cell.

"We've done nothing but hold Counsel meetings for years," Scoyt said. "Now were going to act."

He ran into the corridor and bellowed furiously, producing in very short time a dozen armed men and a ladder.

Complain, who felt he had more experience of this kind of thing than the others, went to fetch a bucket of water from the nearby guards' quarters, flinging it up over the tortured metal to cool it. In the ensuing cloud of steam, Scoyt thrust the ladder into place and climbed up with his dazer ready. One by one, as quickly as possible, the others followed, Vyann keeping close to Complain. Soon the whole party stood in the strange room above the cell.

It was overwhelmingly hot; the air was hard to breathe. Their torches soon picked out the reason for the blocked grille and the collapsed inspection way below their feet: the floor of this chamber had undergone a terrific denting in some long-past explosion. A machine—perhaps left untended in the time of the Nine Day Ague, Complain thought—had blown up, ruining every article and wall in the place. A staggering quantity of splintered glass and wood was scattered all over the floor. The walls were pitted with shrapnel. But there was not a trace of a Giant.

"Come on!" Scoyt said, trampling ankle deep through the wreckage towards one of two doors. "Let's not waste time here."

The explosion had wedged the door tightly. They melted it with the heat gun and passed through. Night loomed menacingly at the end of their torch beam. The silence sang like a thrown knife.

"No sign of life . . ." Scoyt said. His voice held an echo of unease.

They stood in a side corridor, sealed off from the rest of the ship, entombed, scattering their torchlight about convulsively. It was so achingly hot they could hardly see over their cheek bones.

One end of the brief corridor finished in double doors on which a notice was stenciled. Crowding together, they shuffled to read what it said:

DUTYMEN ONLY
CARGO HATCH—AIR LOCK
DANGER!!

A locking wheel stood on either door with a notice printed beside it: "DO NOT ATTEMPT TO OPEN UNTIL YOU GET THE SIGNAL". They all stood there staring stupidly at the notices.

"What are you doing—waiting to get a signal?" Hawl grated at them. "Melt the door down, Captain!"

"Wait!" Scoyt said. "We ought to be careful here. What's an air lock, I'd like to know? We know magnetic locks and octagonal ring locks, but what's an air lock?"

"Never mind what it is. Melt it down!" Hawl repeated, waggling his grotesque head. "It's your lousy ship, Captain—make yourself at home!"

Gregg turned the heat on. The metal blushed a sad, dull rose, but did not run. Nor did an amount of cursing make any difference, and in the end Gregg put the weapon bewilderedly away.

"Must be special metal," he said.

One of the armed men pushed forward and spun the

wheel on one of the doors, whereupon the door slid easily back into a slot in the wall. Someone laughed sharply at the slackening of tension; Gregg had the grace to look abashed. They were free to move into the cargo air lock.

Instead of moving, they stood pixilated by a stream of light which beat remorselessly upon them. The air lock, although only a medium-sized chamber, had, set in its opposite wall, something none of them had ever seen before, something which to their awed eyes extended the length of the lock to infinity: a window: a window looking into space.

This was not the meager pinch of space Vyann and Complain had seen in the Control Room; this was a broad square. But their previous experience had prepared them for this in some measure. They were the first to be drawn across the deep dust floor to the glory itself; the others of the party remained rooted in the entrance.

Beyond the window, with stars tossed prodigiously into it like jewels into an emperor's sack, roared the unending stillness of space. It was something beyond the comprehension to gaze upon, the mightiest paradox of all, for although it gave an impression of unyielding blackness, every last pocket of it glistened with multi-colored pangs of light.

Nobody spoke, swallowing the spectacle as if dumb.

Though all of them were fit to weep before the serenity of space, it was what floated in space that commanded their eyes, that ultimately held them: a sweet crescent of a planet, as bright blind blue as a new-born kitten's eyes, looking larger than a sickle held at arm's length. It scintillated into dazzling white at its center, where a sun seemed to rise out of it. And the sun, wreathed in its terrible corona, eclipsed everything else in grandeur.

Still nobody spoke. They were silent as the crescent crept wider and the splendid sun broke free from behind it. They could not speak one word for the miracle of it. They were struck dumb, deaf and dizzy by its sublimity.

At last it was Vyann who spoke.

"Oh, Roy darling," she whispered. "We have arrived somewhere, after all! There's still a hope for us, there's still some sort of hope."

Complain turned to look at her then, to force his choked throat to answer. And then he could not answer. He suddenly knew what the big something was he had wanted all his life.

It was nothing big at all. It was a small thing. It was just to see Laur's face—by sunlight.

III

W ithin a watch, distorted versions of the great news had circulated to every man, woman and child in Forwards. Everyone wanted to discuss it with everyone else; everyone, that is, except Master Scoyt. For him, the incident was a mere irrelevance, almost a set-back in the priority task of hunting down the Giants and their allies, the Outsiders. He had found no Giants; now he returned full of a new scheme which, after snatching a cat-nap and some food, he proceeded to put into action.

The scheme was simple; that it involved a terrifying amount of damage to the ship did not deter Scoyt in the least. He was going entirely to dismantle Deck 25.

Deck 25 was the first deck of Deadways beyond Forwards. Remove it, and you would have a perfect no-man's-land nothing could cross unseen. Once this giant equivalent of a ditch had been created, and a strong guard set over it, a hunt could be started down all the inspection ways and the Giants would be unable to escape.

Work on the job commenced at once. Volunteers flocked to Scoyt's aid, willing to do anything they could to help. Human chains worked feverishly, passing back every movable item on the doomed deck to others who smashed it or, if smashing were not possible, flung it into other vacant rooms. Ahead of the chain, sweating warriors, many of them Gregg's men, who had experience of such tasks, attacked the ponics, hacking them down, rooting them up; just behind them came the clearance men, looting, gutting and filleting the place.

And so as soon as a room was cleared, Master Scoyt himself came with the heat gun, blazing around the sides of the walls till the walls came tumbling down; they were carted off directly they were cool enough to touch. The heat gun did not melt the metal which actually divided deck from deck—that metal was the same, evidently, as the metal of which the air lock doors were built, something extra tough—but everything else fell away before it.

Soon after the work began, a rat hideout was discovered in a big room marked "Laundry". Splitting open a boiler, two of Gregg's men revealed a crazy little maze of rat buildings, a rodent village. Different levels and flights of a bewildering complexity of design had been constructed inside the boiler from bones and rubble and cans and filth. There were tiny cages here containing starving creatures, mice, hamsters, rabbits, even a bird; there were moths living here, rising up in a storm; and there were the rats, in nurseries and studs and armories and slaughter houses. As Scoyt thrust the heat gun into the miniature city and it crackled up in flames, the rodents poured out savagely, leaping to the attack.

Scoyt saved himself with the gun, warding them off as he fell back. Gregg's two men had their throats bitten through before reinforcements could dash up with dazers and beat off the little furies. The bodies went back along the human chain, and demolition continued.

By now, the corridors of decks 24 to 13 had been completely stripped of trap-doors on all three levels. Each hole was guarded.

"The ship is rapidly becoming uninhabitable," Councillor Tregonnin protested. "This is destroying for destroying's sake."

He was presiding over a meeting to which everyone of importance had been called. Councillors Billyoe, Dupont and Ruskin were present. Pagwam and other officers of the Security Team were present. Gregg and Hawl were present. So were Complain and Vyann. Even Marapper had managed to wangle his way in. Only Scoyt and Zac Deight were missing.

By the messengers which had been dispatched to bring him to the meeting, Scoyt had sent back word that he was "too busy". Marapper, going down at Tregonnin's request to fetch up Zac Deight, had returned to say simply that the councillor was not in his rooms; at that, Complain and Vyann, who now knew of Deight's sinister part in affairs, exchanged glances but said nothing. It would have been a

190

relief to burst out with the news that Deight was a traitor—but might there not be other traitors here, whom it would be wiser not to warn?

"The ship must be pulled apart before the Giants pull us apart," Hawl shouted. "That's obvious enough; why make an issue of it?"

"You do not understand. We shall die if the ship is pulled apart!" Councillor Dupont protested.

"It would get rid of the rats, anyway," Hawl said, and cackled with laughter.

Right from the start, he and Gregg were quietly at loggerheads with the members of the Council; neither side liked the other's manners. The meeting was disorganized for another reason: nobody could decide whether they wanted most to discuss the steps Scoyt was taking or the discovery of the strange planet.

At last, Tregonnin himself tried to integrate these two facets of the situation.

"What it amounts to", he said, "is this. Scoyt's policy can be approved if it succeeds. To succeed, not only must the Giants be captured but, when captured, they must be able to tell us how to get the ship down on to the surface of this planet.

There was a general murmur of agreement at this.

"Obviously, the Giants must have such knowledge," Billyoe said, "since they built the ship in the first place."

"Then let's get on with it, and go and give Scoyt some support," Gregg said, standing up.

"There is just one other thing I would like to say before you go," Tregonnin said, "and that is, that our discussion has been on purely material lines. But I think we have also moral justification for our action. The ship is a sacred object for us; we may destroy it only under one condition: that the Long Journey be done. That condition, happily, is fulfilled. I am confident that the planet some of you have seen beyond the ship is Earth."

The pious tone of this speech brought derision from Gregg and some of the Survival Team. It brought applause and excitement from others. Marapper was heard to exclaim that Tregonnin should have been a priest.

Complain's voice cut through the uproar.

"The planet is not Earth!" he said. "I'm sorry to disappoint you, but I have certain information the rest of you do not know. We must be far away from Earth—twenty-three generations have passed on this ship: Earth should have been reached in seven!"

He was besieged by voices, angry, pitiful and demanding.

He had decided that everyone ought to know and face the situation exactly as it was; they must be told everything—about the ruined controls, about Captain Gregory Complain's journal, about Zac Deight. They must be told everything—the problem had grown far too urgent for any one man to cope with it. But before he could utter another word, the door of the council chamber was flung open. Two men stood there, faces distorted with fear.

"The Giants are attacking!" they shouted.

Stinking, blinding, smoke coiled through the decks of Forwards. The piled rubbish evacuated from Deck 25 on to Decks 24 and 23 had been set alight. Nobody cared; everyone was suddenly a pyromaniac. Automatic devices throughout most of the ship had a simple way of coping with outbreaks of fire: they closed off the room in which the fire began and exhausted the air from it. Unluckily, this fire was started in a room where the devices had failed, and in the open corridors.

Scoyt and his fellow destroyers worked on uncomplainingly in the smoke. An impartial observer, seeing these men, would have known that an inner fury possessed them; that a life-long hatred of the ship which imprisoned them had at last found expression and was working itself out with uncheckable force.

The Giants struck cleverly.

Scoyt had just burned around one wall of a small washroom and was resting while three of his men removed the wall, so that it shielded him momentarily from the view of the others. At that instant, the grille overhead was whipped away, and a Giant fired a gas pellet at Scoyt. It caught the Master in the face. He collapsed without a sound.

A cord ladder snaked down from the grille. One of the Giants skipped down it and seized the heat gun from Scoyt's limp grasp. As he did so, the severed wall toppled over on top of him and stunned him: the three handlers had been careless and did not mean to let it go. They stared in utter surprise at the Giant. As they did so, three more Giants dropped down the ladder, fired at them, picked up their mate and the heat gun and attempted to get back to safety.

Despite the smoke, other people had seen this foray. One of Gregg's ablest assassins, a fellow called Black, sprang forward. The hindmost Giant, who had just reached the grille, came crashing down again with a knife stuck in his back; the heat gun rolled from his grasp. Shouting for assistance, Black retrieved his knife and bounded up the ladder. He, too, fell back to the floor with a face full of gas. Others were behind him. Jumping him, they pressed on, swarming up the ladder and through the grille.

Then began a terrific running fight in the cramped space of the inspection ways. The Giants had cut through the actual air duct to get into the inspection way proper, but were hampered in their retreat by their injured companion. Reinforcements arrived for them on one of the low inspection trucks which had once carried Complain. Meanwhile, around pipes and stanchions, the Forwarders harried them in increasing numbers.

It was a strange world to fight in. The inspection ways ran around every level and between each deck. They were unlit; the torches which now erratically lit them produced a weird web of shadows among the girders. For a solitary sniper, the place was ideal; for a pack of them, it was hell: friend could no longer be told from foe.

At this stage in affairs, Gregg arrived from the counsel room to take control. He soon produced order out of the random give and take. Even the Forwarders obeyed him now Scoyt was temporarily out of action.

"Somebody bring me that heat gun," he bellowed. "Everyone else follow me back to Deck 20. If we get down the inspection hatches there, we can take the Giants from the rear."

It was an excellent idea. The only drawback—and it explained how the Giants still managed to move unseen from deck to deck, despite the removal of all trap-doors— was that the inspection ways extended right around the circumference of the ship, just inside the hull, thus surrounding the rooms of all upper levels. Until this was realized, the Giants' movements could never be blocked. The ship was more complex than Gregg had bargained for. His men, streaming wildly down the trap-doors, could not find the enemy.

Gregg did as his wild nature dictated. He blazed a way ahead with the heat gun, turning molten every obstacle in his path.

Never before had the inspection ways been open to the inhabitants of the ship; never before had a madly brandished welder played among all those delicate capillaries of the vessel.

Within three minutes of switching on power, Gregg ruptured a sewer sluice and a main water pipe. The water jetted out and knocked a crawling man flat, playing wildly over him, drowning him, streaming and cascading over everything, seething between the metal sandwich of decks.

"Switch that thing off, you crazy loon!" one of the Forwards men, sensing danger, yelled at Gregg.

For answer, Gregg turned the heat on him.

A power cable went next. Sizzling, rearing like a cobra, live wire flashed across the rails the inspection trucks ran on; two men died without a chirp.

The gravity blew. Over that entire deck, free fall suddenly snapped into being. Nothing so quickly produces panic as the sensation of falling. The stampede which followed in that constricted area only made matters worse. Gregg himself, though he had had experience of zero gravity, lost his head and dropped the gun. It rebounded gently up at him. Screaming, his beard flaming, he punched away the blazing muzzle with his fist. . . .

During this pandemonium, Complain and Vyann stood by Master Scoyt, who had just been brought up on a stretcher to his own room. Having had a taste of the gas himself, Complain could sympathize with the still unconscious Master.

He could smell the gas lingering in Scoyt's hair: he could also smell burning. A glance upwards showed him a tendril of smoke probing through the overhead grilles.

"That fire the fools started two decks down—the air

194

duct system is going to carry the smoke everywhere!" he exclaimed to Vyann. "It ought to be stopped."

"If we could only close the inter-deck doors . . ." she said. "Ought we to get Roger out of here?"

Even as she spoke, Scoyt stirred and groaned. Plunging water over his face, massaging his arms, they were too busy to notice the shouts in the corridor; there had been so much shouting that a little more went unremarked until, the door suddenly crashing open, Councillor Tregonnin entered.

"Mutiny!" he said. "Mutiny! I feared as much. Oh hem, what will happen to us all? I said from the start that that Deadways gang should never be allowed in here. Can't you rouse Scoyt? He'd know what to do! I'm not *supposed* to be a man of action."

Complain fixed him with a surly eye. The little librarian was almost dancing on his toes, his face gawky with excitement.

"What seems to be the trouble?" he asked.

With a visible effort, Tregonnin pulled himself up before that contemptuous stare.

"The ship is being wrecked," he said, more steadily. "That madman Hawl—the fellow with the little head—has the heat gun. Your brother was injured. Now most of his gang—and many of our men—are simply pulling everywhere to bits. I ordered them to stop and surrender the gun, but they just laughed at me."

"They'll obey Scoyt," Complain said grimly. He began shaking Scoyt insistently.

"I'm afraid, Roy. I can't help feeling something terrible is going to happen," Vyann said.

One glance at her face told Complain how worried she was. He stood up beside her, stroking her upper arm.

"Keep working on Master Scoyt, Councillor," he told Tregonnin. "He'll soon be lively enough to solve all your problems for you. We'll be back."

He hustled a surprised Vyann out into the corridor. A thin dribble of water crept along the deck, dripping into the manholes.

"Now what?" she asked him.

"I was a fool not to think of this before," he said. "We've got to risk pulling the place down about our heads to get to the Giants—unless there is another way. And there *is* another way. Zac Deight has an instrument in his room by which he spoke to Curtis, the Giants' leader."

"Don't you remember, Roy, Marapper said Zac Deight had gone?" she said.

"We may be able to find the way to work the instrument without him," Complain replied. "Or we may find something else there that will be useful to us. We are doing no good here, that's sure."

He spoke ironically, as six Forwards men, pelting silently along, brushed past him. Everyone seemed to be on the run, splashing down the corridors; no doubt the spiked stench of burning hustled them on. Taking Vyann's soft hand, Complain led her rapidly along to Deck 17 and down to the lower level. The trap-door covers lay about like discarded gravestones, but already the guards over them had deserted their posts to seek excitement elsewhere.

Halting before the room in which he had left the dazed councillor, Complain leveled his torch and flung open the door.

Zac Deight was there, sitting on a metal stool. So was Marapper, his bulky body eased into a chair; he had a dazer clamped in his hand.

"Expansions to your egos, children," he said. "Come in, Roy, come in. And you too, Inspector Vyann, my dear!"

IV

"What the hull do you think you're doing here, Marapper, you oily old villain?" Complain asked in surprise.

The priest, ignoring this unpleasant form of address, which Complain would never have employed in the old days, was as usual only too ready to explain. He was here, he said, with the express purpose of torturing the last secret of the ship out of Zac Deight, but had hardly begun to do so since, although he had been here some while, he had only just managed to pull the councillor back to consciousness.

"But you told the council meeting he was not here when you came to look for him," Vyann said.

"I didn't want them pulling Deight to bits for being an Outsider before I got at him," Marapper said.

"How long have you known he was an Outsider?" Complain asked suspiciously.

"Since I came in and found him on the ground—with an octagonal ring on his finger," Marapper said, with a certain amount of smugness in his tone. "And I've so far elicited one thing from him, with the help of a knife under his fingernails. The Outsiders and Giants come from the planet you saw outside; but they can't get back there till a ship comes up to get them. This ship can't go down there."

"Of course it can't, it's out of control," Vyann said. "Priest Marapper, you are wasting your time. I also cannot allow you to torture this councillor, whom I have known since I was a girl."

"Don't forget he was going to kill us!" Complain reminded her. She made no answer beyond looking stubbornly at him, knowing, woman-like, that she had an argument superior to reason.

"I had no alternative but to try and remove you both," Zac Deight said huskily. "If you will save me from this horrible creature I will do anything—within reason."

There are few more awkward situations in the world than to be dragged into a three-cornered argument between a priest and a girl; Complain did not enjoy the position. He would have been contented enough to let Marapper wring information out of Deight by any means possible, but with Vyann present he could not do it; nor could he explain his sudden sensitivity to the priest. They began a wrangle. It was interrupted by a noise nearby, a curious noise, a scraping rustle, frightening because it was unidentifiable. It grew louder. Suddenly, it was overhead.

Rats were on the move! They drummed along the air duct above this level; across the grille Complain had recently climbed through, pattering pink feet came and went, as the tribe thundered by. Dust showered down into the room, and with the dust came smoke.

"That sort of thing'll be happening all over the ship," Complain told Zac Deight gravely, when the stampede had gone by. "The fire is driving the rats out of their holes. Given time, the men will gut the place absolutely. They'll find your secret hideout in the end, if they kill us all doing it. If you know what's good for you, Deight, you'll get on that instrument and tell Curtis to come out with his hands up."

"If I did, they would never obey," Zac Deight said. His hands, paper-thin, rustled together on his lap.

"That's my worry," Complain said. "Where is this Little Dog?—Down on the outside of the planet?"

Zac Deight nodded confirmation miserably. He kept clearing his throat, a nervous trick which betrayed the strain he was undergoing.

"Get up and tell Curtis to speak to Little Dog double quick and make them send a ship up here for us," Complain said. He drew his dazer, aiming it steadily at Deight.

"I'm the only one who flashes dazers here!" Marapper shouted. "Deight's my captive." Jumping up, he came towards Complain with his own weapon raised. Savagely, Complain booted it out of his hand.

"We can't afford to have three sides in this argument, priest," he said. "If you're going to stay in on this, stay quiet. Otherwise, get out. Now then, Deight, have you made up your mind?"

Zac Deight stood up helplessly, twisting his face with indecision.

"I don't know what to do. You don't understand the position at all," he said. "I really would help you if I could. You seem a reasonable man, Complain, at heart; if only you and I—"

"I'm not reasonable" Complain shouted. "I'm anything but reasonable! Get on to Curtis! Go on, you old fox, move! Get a ship up here!"

"Inspector Vyann, can't you—" Zac Deight said.

"Yes, Roy, please—" Vyann began.

"No!" Complain roared. It was hell the way everyone had wills of their own, even women. "These beggars are responsible for all our miseries. Now they're going to get us out of trouble or else."

Seizing one end of the bookcase, he pulled it angrily away from the wall. The phone stood there on its niche, neutral and silent, ready to convey any message spoken into it.

"This time my dazer's at 'lethal', Deight," Complain said. "You have the count of three to begin talking. One ... two ..."

Tears stood in Zac Deight's eyes as he lifted the receiver. It shook in his grasp.

"Get me Crane Curtis, will you?" he said, when a voice spoke at the other end. Possessed as he was, Complain could not restrain a thrill shooting through him, to think that this instrument was now connected with the secret stronghold in the ship.

When Curtis came on, all four in the room could hear his voice distinctly. It was pitched high with anxiety; he talked so rapidly he hardly sounded like a Giant. He began speaking at once, before the old councillor could get a word in.

"Deight? You've slipped up somewhere," he said. "I always said you were too old for this job! The damned dizzies have got that welder in action. I thought you told me *you* had it? They're running amok with it—absolutely berserk. Some of the boys tried to get it back but failed, and now the ship's on fire near us. This is your doing! You're going to take the responsibility for this. . . ."

During this flow of words, Zac Deight subtly changed, slipping back into something like his old dignity. The receiver steadied in his hand.

"Curtis!" he said. The command in his tone brought a sudden pause on the line. "Curtis, pull yourself together. This is no time for recriminations. Bigger matters are at stake. You'll have to get Little Dog and tell them——"

"Little Dog!" Curtis cried. He went back into full spate again. "I *can't* get on to Little Dog. Why don't you listen to what I've got to say? Some crazy dizzie, monkeying with the welder, has severed a power cable on the middle level of Deck 20, just below us here. The structure's live all around us. Four of our men are out cold with shock. It's blown our wireless and our lighting. We're stuck. We can't raise Little Dog and we can't get out. . . ."

Zac Deight groaned. He turned hopelessly away from the phone, gesturing at Complain.

"We're finished," he said. "You heard that."

Complain poked the dazer into his thin ribs. "Keep quiet," he hissed. "Curtis hasn't finished speaking yet."

The phone was still barking.

"Are you there, Deight? Why don't you answer?"

"I'm here," Deight replied wearily.

"Then answer. Do you think I'm talking for fun?" Curtis snapped. "There's just one chance for us all. Up in the personnel hatch on Deck 10, there's an emergency transmitter. Got that? We're all bottled up here like lobsters in a pot. We can't get out. *You're* out. You've got to get to that transmitter and radio Little Dog for help. Can you do that?"

The dazer was eager at Zac Deight's ribs now.

"I'll try," he said.

"You'd better try! It's our only hope. And, Deight . . ."
"Yes?"

"For God's sake tell 'em to come armed—and quick."
"All right."

"Get into inspectionways and take a trolley."
"All right, Curtis."

"And hurry, man. For heaven's sake hurry."

200

A long, fruity silence followed Zac Deight's switching off.

"Are you going to let me get to that radio?" Deight asked.

Complain nodded.

"I'm coming with you," he said. "We've got to get a ship to us." He turned to Vyann. She had brought the old counsellor a beaker of water which he accepted gratefully.

"Laur," Complain said, "will you please go back and tell Roger Scoyt, who should be revived by now, that the Giants' hideout is somewhere on the upper level of Deck 20. Tell him to wipe them all out as soon as possible. Tell him to go carefully: there's danger of some sort there. Tell him—tell him there's one particular Giant called Curtis who ought to be launched very *slowly* on the Long Journey. Take care of yourself, Laur. I'll be back as soon as I can."

Vyann said: "Couldn't Marapper go instead of——"

"I'd like the message to arrive straight," Complain said bluntly.

"Do be careful," she begged him.

"He'll be all right," Marapper said roughly. "Despite the insults, I'm going with him. My bladder tells me something very nasty is brewing."

In the corridor, the square pilot lights greeted them. Their intermittent blue patches did little to make the darkness less creepy, and Complain watched Laur Vyann go off with some misgivings. Reluctantly, he turned to splash after Marapper and Zac Deight; the latter was already lowering himself down an open trap while the priest hovered unhappily over him.

"Wait!" Marapper said. "What about the rats down there?"

"You and Complain have dazers," Zac Deight said mildly.

The remark did not seem entirely to remove Marapper's uneasiness.

"Alas, I fear that trap-door is too small for me to squeeze down!" he exclaimed. "I am a large man, Roy."

"You're a bigger liar," Complain said. "Go on, get down. We'll have to keep our eyes open for the rats. With luck, they'll be too busy to worry about us now."

They bundled down into the inspection ways, crawling on hands and knees over to the double rail which carried the low trucks belonging to this level from one end of the ship to the other. No truck was there. They crawled along the tracks, through the narrow opening in the inter-deck metal which, even here, stood between one deck and another, and on into a third deck until they found a truck. Under Zac Deight's direction, they climbed on to its platform and lay flat.

With a touch at the controls, they were off, gathering speed quickly. The deck intersections flicked by only a few inches above their heads. Marapper groaned as he attempted to draw in his stomach, but in a short time they slowed, arriving at Deck 10. The counsellor stopped the truck and they got off again.

In this far end of the ship, evidence of rats abounded. Droppings and shreds of fabric littered the floor. Marapper kept his torch constantly swinging from side to side.

Having stopped the truck just inside the deck, they could stand up. Above and around them, four feet wide, the inspection ways here became a washer between two wheels of deck, its width crossed by a veritable entanglement of girders, braces, pipes and ducts, and by the immense tubes which carried the ship's corridors. A steel ladder ran up into the darkness over their heads.

"The personnel lock, of course, is on the upper level," Zac Deight said. Taking hold of the rungs of the ladder, he began to climb.

As he followed, Complain noted many signs of damage on either side of them, as if, in the rooms between which they now ascended, ancient detonations had occurred. Even as he thought the thought-picture "detonation", a bellow of sound vibrated through the inspection ways, setting up resonances and groans in a variety of pipes until the place sang like an orchestra.

"Your people are still wrecking the ship," Zac Deight said coldly.

"Let's hope they kill off a few squadrons of Giants at the same time," Marapper said.

"Squadrons!" Deight exclaimed. "Just how many 'Giants', as you call them, do you reckon are aboard ship?"

When the priest did not reply, Deight answered himself. "There are exactly twelve of them, poor devils," he said. "Thirteen including Curtis."

For an instant, Complain nearly succeeded in viewing the situation through the eyes of a man he had never seen, through Curtis's eyes. He saw that worried official boxed up somewhere in ruined rooms, in darkness, while everyone else in the ship hunted savagely for his place of concealment. It was not a grand picture.

No time was left for further thought. They reached the upper level, crawling horizontally once more to the nearest trap-door. Zac Deight inserted his octagonal ring in it and it opened above their heads. As they climbed out, a spray of tiny moths burst around their shoulders, hovered, then fluttered off down the dark corridor. Quickly Complain whipped up his dazer and fired at them; by the light of Marapper's torch, he had the satisfaction of seeing most of them drop to the deck.

"I just hope none got away," he said. "I'll swear those things act as scouts for the rats."

The damage in this region was as bad as any Complain and Marapper had seen so far. Hardly a wall stood straight in any direction. Glass and debris lay thickly everywhere, except where it had been brushed away to make a narrow path. Down this path they walked, every sense alert.

"What *was* this place?" Complain asked curiously. "I mean, when it was a place."

Zac Deight continued to walk forward without replying, his face bleak and absorbed.

"What was this place, Deight?" Complain repeated.

"Oh. . . . Most of the deck was Medical Research," Deight said, in a pre-occupied fashion. "In the end, I believe, a neglected computor blew itself to bits. You can't reach this part by the ordinary lifts and corridors of the ship; it's completely sealed off. A tomb within a tomb."

Complain felt a thrill inside him. Medical Research! This was where, twenty-three generations ago, June Payne, the discoverer of paynine, had worked. He tried to visualize her bent over a bench, but could only think of Laur.

So they came to the personnel air lock. It looked much

203

like a smaller edition of the cargo lock, with similar-looking wheels and danger notices. Zac Deight crossed to one of the wheels, still with his abstracted look.

"Wait!" Marapper said urgently. "Roy, as guile's my guide, I swear this wretch has something tricky up his stinking sleeves for us. He's leading us into danger."

"If there's anyone waiting in here, Deight," Complain said, "they and you make the Journey without delay. I'm warning you."

Deight turned to face them. The look of unbearable strain clenched over his countenance might have won him pity in a quieter moment, from other company.

"There's nobody there," he said, clearing his throat. "You need not be afraid."

"The . . . radio thing is in here?" Complain asked.

"Yes."

Marapper seized Complain's arm, keeping his torch burning in Deight's face.

"You're not really going to let him talk to this Little Dog place, are you, and tell them to come up here armed?"

"You needn't think me a fool, priest," Complain said, "just because I happened to be born in your parish. Deight will give the message *we* tell him to. Open up, Counselor!"

The door swung open, and there was the lock, about five paces square, with six metal space suits standing like suits of armor against one wall. Except for the suits, there was only one other object in the room: the radio, a small, portable job with carrying straps and telescopic aerial.

Like the cargo lock, this lock had a window. The four personnel and two cargo locks distributed down the length of the ship carried, apart from the now shuttered blister of the Control Room, the only ports in the ship. Having a different co-efficient of expansion from the rest of the great outer envelope, they naturally represented a weakness, and as such had been constructed only where it might be strictly necessary to see out. For Marapper, it was the first time he had had such a view.

He was as overwhelmed with awe as the others had

been. Breathlessly, he gazed out at the mighty void, for once completely robbed of words.

The planet now showed a wider crescent than the last time Complain had seen it. Mixed with the blinding blue of it were whites and greens, glistening under its casing of atmosphere as no colors had ever glistened before. Some distance from this compelling crescent, tiny by comparison, the sun burned brighter than life itself.

Marapper pointed at it in fascination.

"What's that? A sun?" he asked.

Complain nodded.

"Holy smother!" Marapper exclaimed, staggered. "It's round! Somehow I'd always expected it would be square— like a big pilot light!"

Zac Deight had gone over to the radio. As he picked it up, tremblingly, he turned to the others.

"You may as well know now," he said. "Whatever happens, I may as well tell you. That planet—it's Earth!"

"What?" Complain said. A rush of questions assailed him. "You're lying, Deight! You must be. It can't be Earth! We know it can't be Earth!"

The old man was suddenly weeping, the long salt tears raining down his cheeks. He hardly tried to check them.

"You ought to be told," he said. "You've all suffered so much . . . too much. That's Earth out there—but you can't go to it. The Long Journey . . . the Long Journey has got to go on forever. It's just one of those cruel things."

Complain grabbed him by his scrawny throat.

"Listen to me, Deight," he snarled. "If that's Earth, why aren't we down there, and who are you—and the Outsiders—and the Giants? Who are you all, eh? Who are you?"

"We're—we're from Earth," Zac Deight husked. He waved his hands fruitlessly before Complain's contorted face; he was being shaken like an uprooted ponic stalk. Marapper was shouting in Complain's ear and wrenching at his shoulder. They were all shouting together, Deight's face growing crimson under Complain's tightening grasp. They barged into the space suits and sent two crashing to the floor, sprawling on top of them. Then finally the priest managed to pry Complain's fingers away from the counselor's throat.

"You're crazy, Roy!" he gasped. "You've gone crazy! You were throttling him to death."

"Didn't you hear what he said?" Complain shouted. "We're victims of some dreadful conspiracy——"

"Make him speak to Little Dog first—make him speak first—he's the only one who can work this radio thing! Make him speak, Roy. You can kill him and ask questions after."

Gradually the words filtered into Complain's comprehension. The blinding anger and frustration ebbed like a crimson tide for his mind. Marapper, as always canny where his own safety was concerned, had spoken wisely. With an effort, Complain gained control of himself again. He stood up and dragged Deight roughly to his feet.

"What is Little Dog?" he asked.

"It's ... It's the code name for an institute on the planet, set up to study the inmates of this ship," Zac Deight said, rubbing his throat.

"To study! ... Well, get on to them right quick and say —say some of your men are ill and they've got to send a ship straight away to fetch them down to Earth. And don't say anything else or we'll tear you apart and feed you to the rats. Go on!"

"Ah!" Marapper rubbed his hands in appreciation and gave his cloak a tug down at the back. "That's spoken like a true believer, Roy. You're my favorite sinner. And when the ship gets here, we overpower the crew and go back to Earth in it. Everyone goes! *Everyone*! Every man, woman and mutant from here to Sternstairs!"

Zac Deight cradled the set in his arm, switching on power. Then, braving their anger, he mustered his courage and turned to face them.

"Let me just say this to you both," he said, with dignity. "Whatever happens—and I greatly fear the outcome of all this terrible affair—I'd like you to remember what I am telling you. You feel cheated, rightly. Your lives are enclosed in suffering by the narrow walls of this ship. But wherever you lived, in whatsoever place or time, your lives would not be free of pain. For everyone in the universe, life is a long, hard journey. If you——"

"That'll do, Deight," Complain said. "We're not asking

for paradise: we're demanding to choose where we suffer. Start talking to Little Dog."

Resignedly, his face pale, Zac Deight started to call, all too aware of the dazer a yard from his face. In a moment, a clear voice from the metal box said: "Hullo, Big Dog. Little Dog here, receiving you loud and clear. Back."

"Hullo, Little Dog," Zac Deight said, then stopped. He painfully cleared his throat. The sweat coursed down his forehead. As he paused, Complain's weapon jerked under his nose, and he began again, staring momentarily out at the sun in anguish. "Hullo, Little Dog," he said. "Will you please send up a ship to us at once—*the dizzies are loose!* Help! Help! The dizzies are loose! Come armed! The dizzies—aaargh! . . ."

He took Complain's blast in the teeth, Marapper's in the small of his back. He crumpled over, the radio chattering as it fell with him. He did not even twitch. He was dead before he hit the deck. Marapper seized the instrument up from the floor.

"All right!" he bawled into it. "Come and get us, you stinking scab-devourers! Come and get us!"

With a heave of his arm, the priest sent the set shattering against the bulkhead. Then, with characteristic change of mood, he fell on his knees before Zac Deight's body, in the first gesture of prostration, and began the last obsequies over it.

Fists clenched, Complain stared numbly out at the planet. He could not join the priest. The compulsion to perform ritual gestures over the dead had left him; he seemed to have grown beyond superstition. But what transfixed him was a realization which evidently had not occurred to Marapper, a realization which canceled all their hopes.

After a thousand delays, they had found Earth was near. Earth was their true home. And Earth, on Zac Deight's admission, had been taken over by Giants and Outsiders. It was again that revelation Complain had burned his anger in vain.

V

L aur Vyann stood silent and helpless, watching the furious activity on Deck 20. She managed to stand by wedging herself in a broken doorway: the gravity lines on this deck had been severed in the assaults on Master Scoyt's stormtroopers. Now directions in the three concentric levels had gone crazy; ups and downs existed that had never existed before, and for the first time Vyann realized just how ingeniously the engineers who designed the ship had worked. Half the deck, under these conditions, would be impossible to live in: the rooms were built on the ceilings.

Near Vyann, equally silent, were a cluster of Forwards women, some of them clutching children. They watched, many of them, the destruction of their homes.

Scoyt, clad only in a pair of shorts, black as a pot, had fully recovered from his gassing and was now dismantling the entire deck, as earlier he had begun to dismantle Deck 25. On receiving Complain's message from Vyann, he had flung himself into the work with a ferocity terrible to watch.

His first move had been to have executed without further ado the two women and four men whom Pagwam, with some of the Survival Team, had found wearing the octagonal ring of the Outsiders. Under his insensate direction, as Complain had predicted, the turbulence of Hawl and his fellow brigands had been curbed—or, rather, canalized into less randomly destructive paths. With Gregg, his face and arm stump bandaged, out of the way, Hawl readily took his place; his shrunken face gleamed with pleasure as he worked the heat gun. The rest of Gregg's mob worked willingly with him, unhampered by the lack of gravity. It was not that they obeyed Hawl, but that his demoniac will was theirs.

What had once been a neat honeycomb of corridor and living accommodation, now, in the light of many torches, looked like a scene from some fantastic everglades, cast in bronze. Throughout the cleared space—cleared though much of the metal was live enough with runaway voltage to make five dead men—girders of tough hull metal, the very skeleton of the ship, jutted solidly in all directions. From them projected icicles of lighter metals which had melted, dripped and then again solidified. And through all this chaos ran the water from burst mains.

Perhaps of the whole wild scene, the sight of the water was the strangest. Although its momentum carried it forward, bursting out into non-gravity, it showed an inclination to go nowhere and form into globules. But the conflagration started on decks 23 and 24 was now an inferno, which set up on either side of it waves of air within whose eddies the globules whirled and elongated like crazy glass fish.

"I think we got 'em Giants cornered there, my boys!" Hawl shouted. "There's blood to fill your supper bowls with this sleep." With practiced aim he sliced down one more partition. Shouts of excitement went up from the men around him. They worked tirelessly, swooping among the iron carcass.

Vyann could not stay there watching Scoyt. The lines on his face, rendered terrible by torch- and fire-light, had not softened under the breakdown of gravity. They looked now deeper than ever; for Scoyt, this dissection of the body in which he lived was a traumatic experience. This was what his relentless pursuit of a foe had crumbled to, and in the little frenzied Hawl it found external incarnation.

Profoundly saddened, the girl turned away. She glanced about for Tregonnin; he was nowhere to be seen. Perhaps he was fluttering alone in his apartments, a little man who knew truth without being able to convey it. She had to go to Roy Complain; the way she felt at the moment, only his face still wore the mask of humanity. Amid the clamor of demolition, quietly, she saw why she loved Complain; it was because (and this was something both were aware of, though neither spoke of it) Complain had changed, Vyann being both a witness of and a factor in the change. In this hour, many people—Scoyt for one—were changing, sloughing off the ancient molds of repression even as Complain had done: but whereas they were changing into lower beings, Roy Complain's metamorphosis lifted him to a higher sphere.

Decks 19 and 18 were packed with people, all ominously waiting for a climax they could but dimly sense. Beyond them, Vyann found the upper levels deserted as she made her way forward. Although the dark sleep-wake was over, the lights of the ship—hitherto as dependable as the sunrise—had failed to come on again; Vyann switched on the torch at her belt and carried her dazer in her hand.

On Deck 15, she paused.

A dim, rosy light filled the corridor, very subtle and soft. It emanated from one of the open trap-doors in the deck. As Vyann looked at the trap, a creature emerged slowly and painfully: a rat. At some time past, its back had been broken; now, a kind of rough sledge, on which its hind legs rested, was lashed across its rump. It pulled itself along with its forelegs, the sledge easing its progress.

Vyann thought, surprising herself: 'How long before they discover the wheel?"

Just after the rat emerged from the trap, the glow burst into brightness. A pillar of fire leapt out of the hole, fell, and then rose more steadily. Frightened, Vyann skirted it, hurrying on, keeping pace with the rat who, after one glance at her, pressed on without interest. A poignant illusion of mutual torment relieved Vyann's customary revulsion for the creatures.

Naked fire was not a thing the ship's company much concerned themselves with. Now, for the first time, Vyann realized it could destroy them utterly—and nobody was doing a thing about it. It was spreading between levels, like a cancerous finger; when they realized its danger, it would be too late. She walked more rapidly, gnawing her ripe lower lip, feeling the deck hot beneath her feet.

Suddenly, the crippled rat, not two yards ahead of her, coughed and lay still.

"Vyann!" a voice said behind her.

She wheeled like a startled deer.

Gregg stood there, putting away his dazer. Following her silently down the corridor, he had been unable to resist killing the rat. With his head swathed in bandages, he was hardly recognizable; the remnant of his left arm was also bandaged and strapped across his shirt. In the ruddy dark, he did not make a companionable figure.

Vyann could not repress a shiver of fright at the stealth of his appearance. If she, for any reason, should wish to cry for help, nobody would hear her in this lost corner of the ship.

He came up and touched her arm. She could see his lips among the swathes of bandage.

"I want to come with you, Inspector," he said. "I followed you through the crowd—I was no use back there like this."

"Why did you follow me?" she asked, withdrawing her arm.

She thought he smiled beneath his lint visor.

"Something's gone wrong," he said, very quietly. When he saw she did not understand, he added, "In the ship, I mean. We're all for it now. This is Lights Out. You can feel it down in your bones. . . . Let me come with you, Laur; you're so. . . . Oh, come on, it's getting hot."

She moved ahead without speaking. For some reason, her eyes stung with tears; they were, after all, in the same boat.

While Marapper was making his prostrations over the burned-out body of Zac Deight, Complain roved around the air lock, gauging its possibilities. If the Giants were coming up from Earth in force, this place had to be defended, and that must be the first thing to worry about. A flush-fitting door, leading to ante-room in the lock, stood in one wall; Complain pulled it open. It was a mere cubicle from which control could be kept over what came and went in the lock itself. Now, a man lay in it on a rough bunk.

It was Bob Fermour!

He greeted his ex-companion with terror, having heard through an open air valve all that had transpired on the other side of the door. The gentle interrogations of Scoyt and his friends, rapidly interrupted though they had been by the Giants coming to his deliverance, had removed

211

most of the skin from Fermour's back, as well as a percentage of his moral fiber. He had been left cowering here, while his rescuers returned to Curtis, to wait for a relief ship to come and take him home; now he was convinced he was about to make the Long Journey.

"Don't hurt me, Roy!" he begged. "I'll tell you everything you need to know—things you never guessed. Then you won't want to kill me!"

"I can't wait to hear," Complain said grimly. "But you're coming straight back to the Counsel to tell *them*: I find it dangerous to be the only one who receives these confidences."

"Not back into the ship, Roy, please, I beg you. I've had enough of it all. I can't face it again."

"Get up!" Complain said. Seizing Fermour by the wrist, he swung him up and pushed him into the air lock. Then he kicked Marapper gently in his ample, episcopal buttocks.

"You ought to have grown out of that mumbo jumbo, priest," he said. "Besides, we've no time to waste. We shall have to get Scoyt and Gregg and everyone here to this deck for a mass attack when the Giants arrive. Our only hope, that I can see, is to seize their ship when it comes."

Red-faced, the priest rose, dusting off his knees and banging dandruff from his shoulders. He maneuvered so that Complain stood between him and Fermour, avoiding the latter as if he had been a ghost.

"I suppose you're right," he said to Complain. "Although as a man of peace, I greatly regret all this bloodshed. We must pray to Consciousness that the blood may be theirs, rather than ours."

Leaving the old counselor to lie where he had fallen, they prodded Fermour out of the lock and back towards the trap-door in the littered corridor. As they went, a strange noise haunted their ears. At the trap, halting in apprehension, they found the origin of the sound. Beneath their feet, swarming along the inspection way, was a host of rats. Some of them glanced pinkly up at Marapper's torch; none faltered in their rapid advance towards the bow of the ship. Brown rats, small rats, gray rats, tawny rats, some with belongings strapped to their backs, hurried to the pipe of fear.

"We can't get down there!" Complain said. His stomach twisted at the idea.

The ominous thing was the determined way the swarm moved as if nothing could divert it. It looked as if it might pour on beneath their feet forever.

"Something really devastating must be happening in the ship!" Fermour exclaimed. In that ghastly fur river, he drowned his last fear of those who had once been his friends. This united them again.

"There's a tool kit in the air lock cubicle," he said. "I'll go and get it. There should be a saw in it. With that, we can cut our way back to the main part of the ship."

He ran back the way they had come, returning with a clanking bag. Fumbling it open, he produced an atomic hand saw with a circular blade field; it crumbled away the molecular structure of a wall before their eyes. With a shrill grinding sound, the instrument bit out a shaky circle in the metal. They ducked through it, working their way almost by instinct to a known part of the deck. As if the ship had come to life while they were in the air lock, a faint hammering filled everywhere like an irregular heartbeat; Scoyt's wreckers were busily at work. The air as they walked grew staler, the dark was hazed with smoke—and a familiar voice was calling for Complain.

In another moment they rounded a bend at a trot, and there were Vyann and Gregg. The girl threw herself into Complain's arms.

Hurriedly, he gave her his news. She told him of the devastation being wrought on the twenties decks. Even as she spoke, the lights about them glowed suddenly to great brilliance, then died, even the pilot lights fading completely out. At the same time, the gravity blew; they sprawled uncomfortably in mid-air.

Welling, it seemed, from the lungs of a whale, a groan rattled down the confines of the ship. For the very first time, they perceived the vessel to give a lurch.

"The ship's doomed!" Fermour shouted. "Those fools are destroying it! You've got nothing to fear from the Giants now—by the time they get here, they'll be a rescue party, picking dessicated bodies out of a wreck."

"You'll never drag Roger Scoyt from the job he's doing," Vyann said grimly.

"Holy smother!" Complain said. "This whole situation is just hopeless!"

"The human predicament apart," Marapper said, "nothing is hopeless. As I see it, we'd be safest in the Control Room. If I can only control my feet, that's where I'm going."

"Good idea, priest," Gregg said. "I've had enough of burning. It would be the safest place for Vyann, too."

"The Control Room!" Fermour said. "Yes, of course. . . ."

Complain said nothing, silently abandoning his plan to take Fermour before the Counsel; the hour was too late. Nor did there seem, in the circumstances, any hope of repelling the Giants.

Clumsily, with agonizing slowness, the party covered the nine decks which lay between them and the blister housing the ruined controls. At last they hauled themselves panting up the spiral stairs and through the hole Vyann and Complain had made earlier.

"That's funny," Marapper said. "Five of us started out from Quarters to reach this place: finally, three of us have done it together!"

"Much good may it do us," Complain said. "I never knew why I followed you, priest."

"Born leaders need give no reasons," Marapper said modestly.

"No, this is where we should be," Fermour said with excitement. He swung a torch around the vast chamber taking in the fused mass of panels. "Behind this wrecked façade, the controls are still sound. Somewhere here is a device for closing off all inter-deck doors; they're made of hull metal, and it would be a long while before they'd burn. If I can find that device . . ."

He waved the atomic saw to finish his meaning, searching already for the board he wanted.

"The ship must be saved!" he said. "and there is a chance we can do it, if we can only separate the decks."

"Damn the ship!" Marapper said. "All we want it to do now is hold together until we can get off it."

"You can't get off it," Fermour said. "You'd better realize the fact. You must none of you reach Earth. The ship is where you belong and stay. This is a non-stop trip: there is no Journey's End."

Complain whirled around on him.

"Why do you say that?" he asked. His voice was so charged with emotion that it sounded flat.

"It's not my doing," Fermour said hastily, scenting trouble. "It's just that this situation is too formidable for any of you. The ship is in orbit around Earth, and there it must stay. That was the edict of the World Government which set up the Little Dog authority to control this ship."

Complain's gesture was angry, but Vyann's was supplicatory.

"Why?" she said. "Why must the ship stay here? It's so cruel. . . . We are Earth people. This terrible double journey to Procyon and back—it's been made, and somehow it now seems we're survived it. Shouldn't—oh, I don't know what happens on Earth, but shouldn't people have been glad to have us back, happy, excited . . . ?"

"When this ship, 'Big Dog'—so christened in jocular allusion to the constellation Little Dog for which it set out—was detected in Earth's telescopes, finally returning from its long journey, everyone on Earth was, as you say—happy, excited, marveling." Fermour paused. This event had taken place before he was born, but the epic had often been retold to him. "Signals were sent out to the ship," he continued; "they were never answered. Yet the ship kept speeding on towards Earth. It seemed inexplicable. We have passed the technological phase of our civilization, but nevertheless factories were speedily built and a fleet of little ships launched towards 'Big Dog'. They had to find out what was happening aboard.

"They matched velocities with this giant vessel, they boarded her. They found—well, they found out about everything; they found that Dark Ages had settled over the whole ship, as the result of an ancient catastrophe."

"The Nine Day Ague!" Vyann breathed.

Fermour nodded, surprised she should know.

"The ship could not be allowed to go on," he said. "It would have sped on forever through the galactic night. These controls were discovered as you now see them: ruined—the work, presumably, of some poor madman generations ago. So the Drive was switched off at source, and the ship dragged into an orbit by the little ships which, using gravity for towlines, acted as tugs."

"But—why leave us aboard?" Complain said. "Why did you not take us down after the ship was in orbit? As Laur says, it was cruel—inhuman!"

Reluctantly, Fermour shook his head.

"The inhumanity was in the ship," he said. "You see, the crew who survived this Ague you seem to know about had undergone a slight physiological modification; the new proteins permeating every living cell in the ship increased their metabolic rate. This increase, undetectable at first, has grown with every generation, so that now you are all living at four times the speed you should be."

He quailed with pity as he told them—but their looks held only disbelief.

"You're lying to scare us," Gregg said, his eyes glittering amid the wrappings of his face.

"I'm not," Fermour said. "Instead of a life expectation for an average human of eighty years, yours is only twenty. The factor does not spread itself evenly over your life: you tend to grow more quickly as children, have a fairly normal adulthood, and then crumble suddenly in old age."

"We'd have noticed if this scoundrel scheme were so!" Marapper howled.

"No," Fermour said. "You wouldn't. Though the signs were all around you, you could not see them, because you have no standards of comparison. For instance, you accepted the fact that one sleep-wake in four was dark. Living at four times the normal rate, naturally four of your days or sleep-wakes only made one ordinary one. When the ship was a going concern—on the voyage out to Procyon—the lights automatically dimmed all over the vessel from midnight to six, partly to give a friendly illusion of night, partly to allow the servicers to work behind scenes, making any necessary repairs. That brief six-hour shift is a whole day to you."

Now the comprehension was growing on them. It seemed, oddly enough, to soak from the inside to the outside, as if, in some mystical way, the truth had been trapped in them all along. The awful pleasure of making them know the worst—they who had tortured him—filled

Fermour. He went on, suddenly keen to make them see how damned they were.

"That's why we proper Earthmen call you 'dizzies': you live so fast, it makes us dizzy. But that isn't all that is wrong with you! Imagine this great ship, still automatically functioning despite the lack of anyone to control it. It supplied everything: except the things which, by its nature, it could not supply, fresh vitamins, fresh air, fresh sunlight. Each of your succeeding generations becomes smaller; Nature survives how she may, and that was her way of doing it, by cutting down on the required materiels. Other factors, such as inbreeding, have changed you until—well, it was decided you were virtually a separate race. In fact, you had adapted so well to your environment, it was doubtful if you would be able to survive if transferred down on Earth!"

Now they had it, knowing it right down to the pits of their stomachs. Fermour turned from their sealed faces, ashamed of himself for feeling triumph. Methodically, he resumed prodding about for the particular panel he wanted. He found it, and they were still all standing in choked silence. Using the saw, he began eagerly to work away the seared casing.

"So we're not human beings at all ..." Complain exclaimed, as if speaking to himself. "That's what you're saying. All that we've suffered, hoped, done, loved ... it's not been real. We're just funny little mechanical things, twitching in a frenzy, dolls activated by chemicals. ... Oh, my God!"

As his voice fell, they all heard the noise. It was the noise they had heard by the personnel lock, the noise of a million rats, flowing irresistibly through the hard honeycomb of the ship.

"They're heading here!" Fermour yelled. "They're coming this way! It's a dead end. They'll swamp us! We'll be torn to pieces!"

Now he had the casing off, tearing it away with his hands, flinging it behind him. Beneath it, severed from their toggles, lay eighty-four double strands of wire. Using the side of his saw, Fermour frantically bashed the pairs together. Sparks flew and—the terrible sound of the rodent army cut off abruptly. Every deck was closed from its neighbor; all the inter-deck doors, on every level, had clicked firmly shut, tombing off further communication.

Gasping, Fermour rocked back against the paneling. He had worked the trick just in time. The thought of the horrible death he had so narrowly avoided overcame him, and he was sick on the floor.

"Look at him, Roy!" Gregg shouted, pointing his sound hand in scorn. "You were wrong about us, Roy! We're as good as he, or better. He's scared green. . . ."

He advanced to Fermour, clenching his one good fist; Marapper followed, dragging out a knife.

"Someone's got to be sacrificed for all this deadly wrong," the priest said, through clenched teeth, "and it's going to be *you*, Fermour—you're going to make the Long Journey on behalf of twenty-three generations of suffering! It would be a *nice* gesture."

Dropping the saw helplessly, Fermour just stood there without defense. He did not move or speak; it was almost as if he saw the priest's point of view. Marapper and Gregg came on. Complain and Vyann stood unmoving behind them.

As Marapper's blade came up, an unexpected clangor filled the dome beneath which they were grouped. Mysteriously, the shutters, closed since the days of Captain Gregory Complain, sprang back to reveal the long windows. Three-quarters of a great sphere all around the five of them was turned in a twinkling into space. Through the hyaline tungsten, the universe breathed in at them; on one side of the ship, the sun burned tall and strong; on the other, Earth and moon were radiant globes.

"How did that happen?" Vyann asked, as the clattering echoes died.

They looked around uneasily. Nothing stirred.

Rather sheepishly, Marapper tucked his knife away. The view was too mighty to be stained with blood. Gregg, too, turned away from Fermour. Sunlight washed over them, seeming to deafen them. Fermour at last managed to speak.

"It'll be all right," he said quietly. "None of us need to be worried. The ship will come up from Little Dog and put the fire out and kill the rats and tidy things up, and then we'll open up the decks again and you'll be able to go on living as before."

"Never!" Vyann said. "Some of us have devoted our lives to getting out of this tomb. We'll die sooner than stay!"

"That's what I was afraid of," Fermour said, almost to himself. "We've always thought this day might come. It's not entirely unprepared for—others before you have found out vital secrets, but we've always managed to silence them in time. Now. . . . Well, you might be all right on Earth: we have taken some of your babies down there, and they've survived, but we've always——"

"We!" Vyann exclaimed. "You keep saying 'we'! But you are an Outsider, an ally of the Giants. What relation are you to true Earthmen?"

Fermour laughed without humor.

"Outsiders and Giants are true Earthmen," he said. "When 'Big Dog' was towed into orbit, we—Earth—fully realized our grave responsibility to you all. Doctors and teachers were your special need. Holy men were required, to counter the vile irreligion of the Teaching— which, vile though it was, undoubtedly assisted your survival in some measure. But there were snags: the doctors and people could not just creep into the air locks and mingle with you, easy though that was, with the inspection way system and the hydroponic tangles to shelter them. They had to be trained at Little Dog Institute to move and speak as quickly as possible, to sleep in catnaps, to—oh, in short, to act like dizzies. And to bear the horrible stench in the ship. And, of course, they had to be abnormally small men, since none of you are above five feet high.

"Some of these men, performing a dangerous mission, you knew and liked. Doctor Lindsey and Meller, the artist, were both Earthmen stationed in Quarters— Outsiders, but your friends.

". . . And you," Complain said. He made a sweeping gesture before his face; a moth circled there, eluding his hand.

"I'm an anthropologist," Fermour said, "although I also tried to help spread the light. There are several of us aboard. This is a unique chance to discover the effects of a

219

closed environment on man; it has taught us more about man and society than we have been able to learn on Earth for centuries.

"Zac Deight was head of everyone on board whom you would call Outsiders. Our usual term of field work aboard is two years—my time is nearly up, but I can't stay here now; I shall go back home and write a thesis on being an Outsider. The field work has its personal rewards: it's arduous, yet not particularly dangerous, unless one runs against efficient people like Scoyt. Zac Deight loved dizzies—loved you. He stayed in the ship long beyond his term, to try and soften conditions and lead Forwards' thought back into more normal channels—in which he was very successful, as you can see if you compare conditions in Forwards with conditions in a Deadways tribe like Quarters.

"He was a wonderful man, Zac Deight, a humanist like Schweitzer in the twentieth or Turnball in the twenty-third century. Perhaps I shall write his biography when I've finished my thesis."

Discomfort rose in Complain at this, to recall how he and Marapper had shot down the old counselor without compunction.

"I suppose, then, that Giants are just big humans?" he said, deflecting the subject of conversation.

"They're just normal-size humans," Fermour said. "Six-footers and up. They did not have to be picked for small stature, since they were never meant to be seen by you, unlike Outsiders; they were the maintenance crew who came aboard when the ship was in orbit and began, secretly, to make the place more suitable and comfortable for you to live in. They sealed off these controls, in case anybody finding them should start wondering about things; for although we always tried to foster in you the knowledge that you are in a ship—in case a day ever came when you might be able to leave it—the maintenance crews were always careful to destroy any direct evidence which might, by inducing you to investigate on your own account, make their job more dangerous.

"Mainly, however, their work was constructive. They repaired water and air ducts—you'll remember, Roy, how you caught Jack Randall and Jock Andrews repairing a flood in the swimming bath. They killed off a lot of rats—but the rats were cunning; they and several other species of creature have changed since leaving Procyon V. Now we've got most of them trapped on Deck 2, we may be able to exterminate them *en masse*.

". "The rings we and what you call the 'Giants' wear are replicas of the same ring-key the original maintenance crews wore when the ship was a going concern. They, and the inspection ways to which they give egress, have made life aboard with you possible. It means we can have—and occasionally slip away to—a secret H.Q. on the ship, with food and baths laid on there. That's where Curtis is probably dying by now, unless closing the deck doors saved him.

"Curtis is not the kind to make a success of his job; he's too nervy. Under him, faults have crept in and discipline lapsed. The poor fellow Gregg speared—who had the welder which has caused so much damage—was working in Deadways alone, instead of being accompanied, as the rules stipulate. That was one of Curtis's mistakes. All the same, I hope he's safe."

"So you were all just taking care of us! You didn't any of you want to scare us, eh?" Gregg asked.

"Of course not," Fermour replied. "Our orders are strictly not to kill a dizzy; none of us ever carry a lethal weapon. The legend that Outsiders were spontaneously generated in the muck of the ponics was purely a dizzy superstition. We did nothing to alarm, everything to help."

Gregg laughed curtly.

"I see," he said. "Just a bunch of wet nurses for us poor dolts, eh? It never occurred to you, you big-hearted bastards, that while you cosseted and studied us we might be going through hell? Look at me! Look at my mate, Hawl! Look at half the poor devils I had under me! And look at the ones so deformed we put 'em out of their misery when we came across them in Deadways! Let's see, seven off twenty-three. . . . Yes, you let sixteen generations live and die here, as near as this to Earth, suffering the tortures we suffered, and you think you deserve a medal for it! Give me that knife, Marapper—I want a peep at the color of this little bloody hero's giblets."

"You've got it wrong!" Fermour shouted. "Complain,

221

you tell him! I've explained about the speed-up of your lives. Your generations are so brief that twenty of them had passed before 'Big Dog' was first boarded and dragged into orbit. They're studying the main problem down in the laboratories of Little Dog all the while, that I swear to you. At any time now, they may find a chemical agent which can be injected into you to break down the alien peptic chains in your cells. Then you'd be free. Even now——"

He broke off suddenly, staring.

They followed his gaze. Even Gregg looked around. Something like smoke, filtering out into the blinding sunshine, rose from a gash in one of the wrecked panels.

"Fire!" Fermour said.

"Rubbish!" Complain said. He pushed himself toward the growing cloud. It was composed of moths, thousands of them. They flew high into the dome, circling towards the unexpected sun. Behind the first phalanx of small ones came larger ones, struggling to get out of the hole in the panel. Their endless squadrons, droning ahead of their rodent allies, had managed to reach the spaces behind the control board before the rats gained this deck. They poured forth in increasing numbers. Marapper pulled out his dazer and downed them as they emerged.

A bemused sensation furred over all their brains, half-sentient ghost thoughts emanating from the mutated swarm. Dazedly, Marapper ceased firing, and the moths poured out again. High voltage crackled behind the panels, where other hordes of moths jammed naked connections, causing short circuits.

"Can they do any real damage?" Vyann asked Complain.

He shook his head uneasily, to show he did not know, fighting away the feeling of having a skull stuffed with muslin.

"Here comes the ship!" Fermour said relievedly, pointing into the gleaming dark. Tiny beside the bulk of the mother planet, a chip of light seemed hardly to move towards them.

Head swimming, Vyann stared out at the bulk of their own ship, 'Big Dog'. Here, in this blister, they had a splendid view over its arching back. On impulse, she kicked herself up to the top of the dome where the outlook was still clearer; Complain swam up alongside, and they clung to one of the narrow tubes into which the shutters had rolled themselves. The moths, it suddenly occurred to her, must accidentally have activated the shutters in their struggle behind the controls. Now the moths whirred about them, uniformly radiating hope.

Vyann stared longingly out. The sight of the planet was like toothache; she had to look away.

"To think they'll come all the way up here from Earth and lock us back away from the sun . . ." she said.

"They won't . . . they can't," Complain said. "Fermour's only a fool: he doesn't know. When these others come, Laur, they'll understand we've earned freedom, a right to try life on Earth. Obviously they're not cruel or they'd never have taken so much trouble over us. They'll see we'd rather die there than live here."

A startling explosion came from below them. Shards of metal paneling blew out into the room, mingling with dead moths and smoke. Vyann and Complain looked down to see Gregg and Fermour floating away to a far corner, away from danger; the priest followed them more slowly—his cloak had been blown over his head. Another explosion sounded, tossing out more dead moths, among which live ones fluttered. Before too long, the control room would be packed with moths. With this second explosion, a rumbling began far away in the middle bowels of the ship, audible even through all the intervening doors, a rumble which, growing, seemed to express all the agony of the years. It grew louder and louder until Complain felt his body tremble with it.

Wordlessly, Vyann pointed to the outside of the ship. Fissures were appearing like stripes all across its hull. After four and a half centuries, 'Big Dog' was breaking up; the rumbling was its death-cry, something at once mighty and pathetic.

"It's the Emergency Stop!" Fermour shouted. His voice seemed far away. "The moths have activated the Ultimate Emergency Stop! The ship's splitting into its component decks!"

They could see it all. The fissures on that noble arch of back were swelling into canyons. Then the canyons were gulfs of space. Then there was no longer a ship: only eighty-four great pennies, becoming smaller, spinning away from one another, falling forever along an invisible pathway. And each penny was a deck, and each deck was now a world of its own, and each deck, with its random burden of men, animals or ponics sailed away serenely round Earth, buoyant as a cork in a fathomless sea.

This was a break there could be no mending.

"Now they'll have no alternative but to take us back to Earth," Vyann said in a tiny voice. She looked at Complain; she tried, woman-like, to guess at all the new interests that awaited them. She tried to guess at the exquisite pressures which would attend the adjustment of every ship-dweller to the sublimities of Earth. It was as if everyone was about to be born, she thought, smiling into Complain's awakened face. He was her sort; neither of them had ever been really sure of what they wanted: so they would be most likely to find it.